T0374358

Sweet Silver
RANCH

VICTORIA STEVENS CHAPMAN

WESTBOW
PRESS
A DIVISION OF THOMAS NELSON
& ZONDERVAN

WestBow Press books may be ordered through booksellers or by contacting:

WestBow Press
A Division of Thomas Nelson & Zondervan
1663 Liberty Drive
Bloomington, IN 47403
www.westbowpress.com
1 (866) 928-1240

Because of the dynamic nature of the Internet, any web addresses or
links contained in this book may have changed since publication and
may no longer be valid. The views expressed in this work are solely those
of the author and do not necessarily reflect the views of the publisher,
and the publisher hereby disclaims any responsibility for them.

Any people depicted in stock imagery provided by Thinkstock are models,
and such images are being used for illustrative purposes only.
Certain stock imagery © Thinkstock.

ISBN: 978-1-4908-4078-9 (sc)
ISBN: 978-1-4908-4080-2 (hc)
ISBN: 978-1-4908-4079-6 (e)

Library of Congress Control Number: 2014910679

Printed in the United States of America.

WestBow Press rev. date: 06/30/2014

To the amazing beautiful women of Bible Study! I am so blessed to have you in my life. You are hands and feet. Love you all!

Chapter 1

Frieda woke up to the usual aches and pains. *Feels like rain, ugh.* Funny thing: as soon as she hit forty-two she had become the most reliable meteorologist, now at seventy-three it seemed comical. Her husband used to ask her if it would rain... funny the things that you remember... "Oh LORD, good morning. I thank you Father for these old knees that keep on going. I thank you for the impending rain and the flowers and animals it will nourish. Father, give me a special measure of your grace today. I don't much like interviews, please guide me and make this old woman an instrument of your unending grace. Or, if it is your will, please let this cup pass. Love you Dad!" After thanking her God, Frieda did what she should; she determined to be a gracious host. Her trademark line: "I am half Jewish, all Southern and a good Christian...I must feed you."

While prettying up the plate with cookies, brownies, and tarts, she adjusted the heat on the kettle and checked the coffee pot, {almost full}. "Good," she said out loud to herself and the cat. Time enough to run the dogs off and cut up some carrots.

By the time the doorbell rang, Frieda had concluded this might be fun. She loved introducing people to the ranch. It was her favorite thing. Even the most emotionally closed people could find something on the Sweet Silver Ranch to make them smile.

Frieda moved to the door where Abbey, the reporter, just smiled. Abbey took note of the plain, peaceful, older woman who was pretty tall and definitely robust. Not fat but definitely a woman that you would want on your side. "Hello, you must be Mrs. Stevens; I think I would have known you anywhere."

Surprised by the pronouncement, Frieda smiled, "So nice to have you visit the Sweet Silver Ranch, hope you didn't have any trouble finding us."

"No, your directions were wonderful, what was your neighbor thinking with that purple house," smiled Abbey.

Frieda gave a wink and a mischievous smile and thought to herself that this young woman was just lovely. *I only hope she brought some shoes suitable for the ranch.* "Where would you like to begin? Can I get you some coffee, tea, maybe bottled water?"

"Oh well. I suppose we could have some coffee and sit somewhere comfortable. My readers are going to love the photos we're bound to get." Abbey kept wishing she worked for a 'real' paper. Maybe then she'd get an actual photographer to go with her. The Christian Times was just barely national, their circulation was one for the old age homes and churches, with an abbreviated on-line version. This was her first and only job since graduating with her BA, stopping briefly to marry, have two children, and ultimately divorce. Not Abbey's ideal start in life.

Frieda had responded, but Abbey had missed it. She followed her into what appeared to be an enormous dining hall. There was a small table set by the window loaded with beautiful foods, pretty little china tea, or were they coffee cups? Abbey never knew the difference. Surely, this wasn't all for her. Wow, she thought, where would this woman find things like that? In Broadway, Georgia??

Frieda pulled a chair out for Abbey and one for herself but was then immediately back on her feet to get the fresh coffee. This reporter wasn't too talkative but seemed sweet and introspective.

Frieda guessed her to be in her mid-twenties. Young by any standards, Frieda just loved young people.

Abbey took a sip of the tea, made a terrible face and looked at Frieda questioningly.

"Oh dear, I forgot to warn you that I habitually serve Southern Sweet Tea," Frieda practically choked with laughter telling Abbey.

Abbey thought to herself, more like syrup. "Oh yes, you are a genuine Southerner, aren't you? We don't have as many true southerners within the Atlanta city limits."

Frieda giggled and started the litany about her love. She began presenting the basics of the ranch and how it worked. She began with the itinerary. "Each day we make a huge breakfast available in the dining hall between 6AM-8: 30AM. We leave coffee and muffins out until 10AM for stragglers. We give our families other staples in their refrigerators in the individual units. Any family can come to the kitchen during the day and acquire things or preorder special needs. Each trailer has a small kitchen, small refrigerator, and table. We do not serve lunch but prepare picnic baskets for the families. That way, they don't have to stop fishing, or hiking, or swimming just because we feel like serving lunch. They take their lunches as they please, but dinner here is a big deal. We want the pastors and their families to feel like they are at a high-end resort for dinner. We try to make our dinners into events. We aim for a variety of atmospheres and dishes. Once again, if the families would rather eat in their units, they are welcome to. The only real variance has been with the priests sometimes. We have served them quietly in the library if they would like a more serene setting."

Abbey absentmindedly drank her tea and was actually feeling a bit perkier for it.

Frieda paused to refresh Abbey's iced tea, warning her, "better pace yourself, you could be in for a terrible sugar coma if you aren't' used to my tea." Frieda grinned like a schoolgirl!

Frieda continued, " We have every available ranch activity you can think of; plenty of animals and lots of trails, and a world class library of Christian scholars and writings. We have a couple of computers; however we frown on too much of that. The children don't have any access. We encourage the families to be families while they are here. It is our aim that the families will play together, and spend time just being a family. There are no phones in the units. Lots of the pastors have cell phones, but the service isn't so good out here. I just love that! I think you will see that our desire is to serve the servers. We want to give these wonderful people a real time away."

Abbey had to ask, "Ms. Stevens, do you have any demands of the pastors that come?"

"Well no, we want to care for them; and Ms. Abbey, please call me Frieda, I am just Frieda. Would you like to meet my babies first?"

Babies, what babies? Abbey was at a loss; she tapped her pen on her knee. She was told this was an amazing Christian worker who had devoted her life to serving the pastors, priests, and workers in the Christian community. Abbey tried to rebound quickly, accepted more tea and stuttered, "Babies? Mrs. Stevens do you have an orphanage here, too?"

Frieda cracked up, "Oh my dear, no, I 'm sorry. I am referring to my field menagerie: horses, goats, pigs, llama, emus, chickens, and ducks. You see, they are my children, some my great grandchildren. I really must insist that you call me Frieda."

Getting a bit sick of the syrup, Abbey switched to the coffee. "Whew, okay, Frieda, I thought I had a completely worthless set of questions." Abbey responded. "This coffee is delicious. You could compete anywhere."

"Oh yes, coffee, tea, and food are staples in my campaign."

Here she goes again, Abbey thought, this is a lot tougher than I expected. "What campaign is that?"

"It's just a silly one really... I think that Martha got a bum wrap!"

"Huh, Martha. Who's Martha?"

"You know, Martha and Mary...I'm really more of a Martha. Mary was doing the better thing sitting at Jesus' feet, but someone had to feed all of those men."

Abbey was pretty sure she remembered the story, vaguely. This woman was going to keep her on her toes. Okay, time to get the thinking cap on. "So about this campaign, are you planning some kind of event or are you just hoping to set up a web site? How does it become a campaign?"

"Oh my, no dear. My campaign's well... my late husband used to call my dedication to things my campaign. I'll never be one of those people who want to rally others; I don't like manipulating people's emotions. I believe that we all have to glorify God in our own way. I do it by taking care of others. I believe that it is what God provided for me to do. He loves me so much. He allows me to take care of HIS people...it is a blessing."

Oh joy, Abbey thought, here we go again, I get to make a 'holy roller' sound sane. Well here goes nothing. "So how did you know that you were called to this particular job?"

"I think my whole life experience provided me for it. God has such blessing for so many. But the best blessing is being able to participate in providing for someone else. I love anonymous gifts. But I also love watching others find blessings."

"Where were you born? Where did you grow up? How did you come to name a Christian ranch for pastors, 'Sweet Silver Ranch'?" Abbey asked.

"Abbey, enjoy your coffee, I am not important. Sweet and Silver were the names of my first two Morgan horses. They were the most beautiful chestnuts you have ever seen. Sweet Pea was a mare and Silver Heels was her brother, a gelding. They were so loving, so sweet, so gentle, and unbelievably patient with a rookie like me. " Frieda glanced down, "do you have some appropriate shoes?"

"Shoes, what's wrong with my shoes?" This old lady probably had no idea what these shoes cost. (They are a few years old; perhaps a little out of date but skinny heels were never out of style).

"Well dear, your shoes are lovely, but they aren't much good for a pasture, for a barn, or for the babies."

"Oh, you want to walk. I heard that you were a big walker. I've got some sneakers in the car, I'll be right back." Abbey realized that the old lady hadn't bothered to answer any of her personal questions. Plenty of time for that, later.

Walking. That young lady is clueless. She's here to write about the Ranch. Was she planning on sitting inside to learn about a recreational ranch? Well, I'll just cover the food and put the coffee in the thermos. Better grab some bottled water. It gets so dry out there.

Father, bless this day and this young lady; give her your wisdom and show her how much you love her. Thank you daddy, Frieda prayed silently.

Chapter 2

Frieda met Abbey outside, and steered her towards the first barn. She thought to herself, *surely, the new fillies; Hope and Grace would get this woman's attention*. Spirit was hollering at Frieda, it cracked her up. Her late husband used to call her Frau Blooka from a silly old movie, <u>Young Frankenstine</u>, that was it. Chuckling, Frieda called for the young horses. The twins raced to Frieda. Abbey was clearly uncomfortable having such large, unwieldy creatures racing towards them. Abbey moved behind Frieda.

"It's okay. Their brakes aren't perfect but they wouldn't hurt you for anything. You see these little ones are twins, which are almost unheard of. Their mom died from the difficulties in the birth. We had to hand feed them, first every two hours, since day one. We actually used goat's milk to feed them, and then they graduated to milk pellets. They are more like large dogs than young horses."

Abbey smiled, "How cool. I wonder what they think of a city girl like me. Do they bite?"

"Well, yes, I supposed they do bite. About being a city girl, well it wasn't so long ago that I was all city! I got over it, and the animals never seemed to notice."

Abbey's jaw fell, and Frieda started laughing like a hyena.

"Yep, that's right, the Southern is from Atlanta! Both my parents were born and bred in New York City! *The* New York City. No country bumpkin here. Nope, I wound up here as a practical joke played by God. Imagine my surprise when Broadway became my home. Only it was Georgia, not New York. Just you wait, young Abbey, your head will spin. This city slicker was more comfortable racing through Atlanta than tripping through a pasture. Things change, as they must, and God pulled a fast one on me. I never knew what hit me. I am still allergic to horses, cats, dogs, and hay. I am a terrible snob in many ways, but I wouldn't live anywhere else in this world, now."

Abbey was flummoxed. Not knowing what to say, she simply turned towards the little fillies. Chestnut in color with huge eyes and ears, they were perfectly adorable. Their skinny legs and knobby knees, and flappy little beaver tails made them look like they were going to fall over. Bounding was the only way to describe them; they danced around Frieda and stuck their huge velvet noses in her face. They clearly loved Frieda. Abbey finally spoke up, "So which one is Hope and which one is Grace?"

Frieda recognized enchantment, and wanted Abbey to enjoy them, she handed Abbey some treats for the horses and showed Abbey how to arch her hand flat so that the horses could nuzzle her palms. Abbey was tickled by the horses and loved the feel of those warm noses.

Frieda led Abbey around the stables, and she shared as many points of interest as she dared. Abbey showed Frieda pictures of her two children. Genevieve, who at age eight was called Geves, and Winston who at six and a half answered to the name of Bug.

Frieda loved listening to Abbey, she was obviously crazy about her kids but seemed worried about the lack of a father figure in their lives. Their Dad decided that he wasn't cut out for "family life" and took off with a local floozy. Frieda wondered if Abbey's explanation didn't harbor some very ill feelings. She spoke of her mother who lived with her, and sounded like a huge help.

"The ranch is dedicated to families, no matter what the unit looks like," Frieda tried to reassure Abbey that she wasn't judging her. They moved on as Frieda began to focus on how Sweet Silver Ranch met the needs of pastors.

Frieda spent an hour out at the barn introducing Abbey to the horses, goats, sheep, pigs, llamas, emus, camels, hens, and some other odd creatures. Frieda had names and stories for each of them. The animals responded to her like she was Mother Earth, and each and every one seemed to know she'd have a treat and it looked to Abbey like none of them really needed a treat. They were all a bit fat. They probably ate better than Abbey's kids. All in all, it was fun, but Abbey realized that it was time to get back to work. Abbey did notice several children and families out enjoying the animals, part of the whole she guessed.

Abbey dug her steno pad out a small backpack, "Frieda this is awesome, and the animals and the buildings are all wonderful, how does the ranch operate?"

Frieda smiled brightly, it appeared as if even her toes were involved, she was obviously delighted to describe the workings of the Ranch. "Well Ms. Abbey, it all started with my Dad. He's around here somewhere. Probably talking to a priest of something."

"My dad was a marketing genius, made his first million dollars and became CEO of a major company by the time he was thirty years old. Dad was not only smart, but he was also a truly honest and trusting man. He told me years ago that the best ideas out there are the ones that meet a real need. Dad honestly never met a stranger. He always believed that every person has intrinsic worth. I can remember him spending time explaining the stock market to a janitor at a mall. The man asked him a question because he saw Dad reading the stock market page in the newspaper. Dad didn't hesitate to stop what he was doing and educate the man. I remembered that.

As a young woman, the one thing that I kept seeing was the need for care within the church. As I aged in the church, I had several friends who were married to pastors and other church workers. You've probably heard all the jokes about p.k.'s…?"

Abbey interrupted, "P.K.'s what is that?"

"Oh, so sorry, a PK is a preacher's kid," Frieda explained.

Abbey tapped her pen on her pad and nodded, "Of course, they were always the wildest kids in the school."

Frieda clucked and went on. "Preacher's kids really lack in so many ways. They are some of the most wonderful kids, but they are forced into this role that they didn't ask for. Expected to be perfect scholars, athletes, Biblical experts and all around humanitarians. Meanwhile, their parents are called on at all hours to take care of everyone but them. The family suffers, but the kids most of all. I watched as so many pastor's families did without."

Abbey said, "Is that why you built the ranch then? For the Pastor's kids?"

"Well, yes in part," Frieda looked pensive. " But also for the wives and the pastors themselves who sincerely wanted to be great Moms and Dads. They long to be superior husbands and sons. But you can only tend to a flock once you've had a good rest. Sweet Silver Ranch is a place where the pastors don't have to be pastors. They can concentrate on being dads, husbands, and sons. We give them plenty of space, we ask nothing of them, and we give them all the tools to spend some real quality time with their own family. They lack only the time and money to do these things. The need is real and I believe that the refreshment makes them better at serving our Lord. Let's walk a little further, so you can see for yourself."

Abbey nodded and followed, trying to take in what Frieda had just told her. She never really thought about what the pastor's needed.

Frieda glanced up the hill and pointed to a spot across the lake. "Over there is Pastor Ted and his son Sammy. They are preparing to fish," Frieda beamed at the sight before her.

Abbey took note that the young boy and his dad were both bent over at the waist and looking thoroughly engrossed in something. Seeing no fishing poles, no nets, or anything, she couldn't figure it out so she asked," What in the world are they doing? How exactly are they preparing to fish?"

Laughing, Frieda explained, "They are hunting worms. You see a small hole in the ground and you pour ground mustard or pepper into it. The worms will jump out and grab hold of your hook themselves. We provide our guests with worms or mustard. It's up to them. There's also a little fishing shed with multiple types of hooks and plastic bait. Not my cup of tea, but it seems to be a right of passage for a Dad to help his son catch his first fish. Honestly, though, I think the little girls catch all the really big fish, makes me laugh."

Chapter 3

"Abbey, let me tell you a story that somewhat captures the essence of this place, okay?" With Abbey's nod, Frieda continued, "Years ago, the most amazing young woman came to our ranch. Her name was Cassie. She was the daughter of one, pastor Charlie Pate of small town in the middle of the country. Cassie was the middle child of three with brothers on either side and a natural athlete. She was born to two parents who spent their whole lives at country-fried church socials, comforting or sitting in between feuding members of their church. Pastor Charlie and his wife Sue were two of the most endearing people. They were passionate about their love for God and their children. But, and there always is a but, Pastor Charlie missed all three of his children's births. He seemed to miss a lot of things. He also didn't see his little girl growing up. In these small country churches, many times the wife has to keep a job just to support the family. The kids suffer a lot."

Frieda noticed Abbey tapping her pen on her thigh and not looking too happy, she wondered what that was about.

Frieda paused to drink some water and offered some to Abbey. While they drank, Abbey waited for Frieda to begin again. They wandered to a bench under a shade tree and enjoyed the peace and their cold water.

Frieda continued, " Well one year the church sent the family to Sweet Silver Ranch for a week. I greeted the family in the main hall, showed them to their cabin and explained all that was available. Pastor Charlie was so kind, and you could see he was tired. His dear Sue, she just needed something. I couldn't put my finger on it at the time. The wonderful thing was that she and Cassie found it on a float."

Frieda seemed to drift for a moment as she finished her water. She began again, "Day two of their stay was a full and wonderful one. The oldest boy, Adam was a natural horseman. He made his way to the paddocks and stayed all night with a pregnant mare. The youngest boy found some baby rabbits with their eyes still shut, caught his first ever catfish and found out that archery was not that easy. Cassie watched, she saw everything; seemingly a part of everything. She helped her baby brother name all the baby rabbits and laughed as the catfish flopped all over the bank. The amazing thing is that Charlie and Sue actually walked and talked for hours. They seemed to really reconnect."

"Seeing her parents, gave Cassie courage. Late in the day Cassie grabbed a whole bunch of rafts and laced them together. She corralled her whole family and they went down to the lake in the silliest looking craft. Their bathing suits were probably about two years too old. They had the palest bodies and huge grins. Pastor Charlie had a bit of a time getting on the raft and the children and Sue couldn't contain their laughter. The giggling got started and they kept falling off the rafts. It was the most amazing laugh fest. These five wonderful people were tied together on rafts in the middle of a lake and laughing to beat the band. Their faces, so relaxed, the joy so clear. It was a sight to see."

"So what did Cassie need courage for?" prompted Abbey.

"Well, much later, Sue and Cassie went for a flower walk, picking and hunting. I wasn't privy to their conversations, but they talked for a very long time. It was later that I saw Charlie and his wife and daughter all crying and hugging. Cassie was a new young woman that day. I learned later that she had been date-raped but too terrified to tell her folks. She found support, grace, and mercy in that time with her parents."

Abbey wasn't really moved; she had expected something more profound. She was actually getting a bit bored with the story and wanted to move on, but Frieda surprised her.

"You know Abbey, as a parent you think you give your kids the time they need or the kind of time they need. What they really require is a lot of time. Time to warm-up, time to feel-out, and time to get their courage up to ask or talk to their parents. Parents need to give their kids as much open time as possible. You remember that with your precious two."

Recognizing that Frieda was absolutely, right, Abby replied, "Yes, Ma'am".

Abbey had to ask, " So how in the world do you pay for all of this, did your dad give you the money?"

"Heavens no. My Dad was so honest, and he just assumed others to be. Hence, he lost all his money. He also had a tendency to give it away at an alarming rate. No big deal, he's a giant in the world of joy and ideas. Dad still advises other people and makes a simple living. He's happy. I bank only on the Lord. It is a day-in, day-out kind of operation. A whole lot of trust on my part, and plenty of surprises on God's."

Abbey had to bite her tongue. She thought to herself, are you kidding? Who banks only on God? There has to be more here than meets the eye. Maybe her husband's death gave her a windfall. There is more here than meets the eye. Either she will tell me the truth or I'll have to dig it out. Somehow, someway, this woman has spent a fortune on this place. I wonder if there's anything illegal. Oh this might be fun.

After a morning of hearing more and more about the families and pastors who had enjoyed the camp, Abbey decided to press the point of the money. It must be coming from somewhere. Time for lunch, I'll pick up more inside, Abbey decided.

Frieda bustled into the kitchen and grabbed a plate of fruit, more water bottles, and some sandwiches. It took another trip to the kitchen for napkins and condiments. Wow, this young lady really wasn't all that interested. Now why does a magazine send a young woman out who doesn't have an interest or a clear conviction? It was time for Frieda to find out what was going on inside Abbey's mind.

Chapter 4

Abbey planned to pursue the money. Track down where that came from and she'd find the truth. They had to get the money to buy the land. Maybe some famous pastor left his inheritance to her. Maybe she'd won the lottery. Maybe she stole it. Maybe, she had a serious life insurance policy on her husband.... Who knows? Maybe they were growing hemp or poppy out here. Abbey decided that between the Internet and other resources she would determine the funding for this 'Ranch'.

Abbey began. "Let's start from the beginning. What gave you the idea for the ranch and when did you get the property?"

"Oh, let's see, ummm... I called myself a 'W.U.S.S' (a woman unable to survive the sticks). I was born for the city, loved being in the middle of it all. So how did I find myself in the twigs, just beyond the sticks? I married a man who had different ideas about how to do life. He bought us a house in the middle of nowhere. I was very alone and very isolated. I had a sick child and had to share a car with my husband. I had no friends or family and no one to talk to. But God met me there. The few times I got out were generally to church. I found a fabulous church, about twenty-five minutes away. It was there that I found great love, passion, learning, and friends. And a couple of fabulous pastors, their wives and kids. I fell in love with the teens first, then the wives, and ultimately the whole family."

"It seemed that God had many ideas for me, one of them was to be forged in obscurity. Yep, I was going to be all-alone with a sick baby in the middle of nowhere. With no one for miles, but a horrible old farmer and a retiree. Ugh. I spend many years studying God's Word, attending and leading bible studies at church. I led youth groups and basically spent all my time at church. My marriage wasn't great, so I clung to my God and my faith. God showed up big time, I just wasn't smart enough to see it at the time. It wasn't until much later that I recognized that among other problems in my marriage, my husband was terribly jealous of my relationship with God and our son. Later, we shared that relationship. Anyway, regarding the land, the long and short of it, we were gifted land. We received some great advice and found out how to do everything. And I mean everything on the cheap. We got twenty of those FEMA trailers, cleaned them up, I can tell you that was an enormous job, yuck! It was quite a while before we could afford to get electricity and water out to them. We took in unwanted animals, loved them like crazy and wound up with quite a brood."

"Remember the crotchety old farmer that I mentioned. Well it took many years, but he became a very dear part of the family. He actually got us established. First, he sold us a small tract of land next to our home, and then He left us a trust of a million dollars and more land to take care of his pets. This is what provided for barns, and paddocks."

"He had two emus, two miniature horses, a goat, some cows, and twelve cats. This was a huge opportunity in light of our dream about the ranch. That dear man didn't care for many people but he loved us and he loved his animals. We even took in his two horrible dogs. They lay by my bed for more than ten years. Oh they were way too healthy and I actually got pretty attached to one of them.

Bits and pieces, and God's sense of humor provided for everything you see."

Abbey wondered what she was missing, it all sounded too coincidental. What did that writing coach tell her, 'follow the money'. With that, Abbey decided to change tactics, "For clarity, what gave you the idea?"

Frieda was quiet for a moment. "You know I think I was always bringing strangers home, always caring for others and loved to throw a party. I think my memories of camp, my love for travel and my desire to run a restaurant all sort of melded together with my husband's desire for a ranch. I think it was a work in progress, and things just fell into place. It wasn't some grand dream that we wrote a business plan about and went to the bank with."

Frieda began to see where she might need to take this young lady, "Let's finish our lunch and go for a walk. I think you should see something." Frieda's idea of finishing lunch was feeding most of hers to the goats and dogs. Abbey ate a small portion of hers and followed suit, now she understood how all the animals seemed sort of rounded.

Abbey nodded in agreement, wondering how this woman stayed such a substantial size with all the walking, my goodness she should be rail thin.

Chapter 5

Abbey and Frieda returned to the kitchen to clean up, both women were cooking up something in their heads. Abbey wondered how to get a handle on the real story here. Frieda prayed fervently for God's leading and the Holy Spirit's empowering.

They each grabbed water bottles and left the kitchen. Heading south and west in the opposite direction of seemingly everything, Frieda led the way, quietly praying to herself. *"Father God, please give me words and wisdom. Help me to see Abbey as you see her. Please Father; open her eyes to see what you have for her. In your precious Son's name Jesus the Christ. Amen and amen."*

Abbey was wracking her brain. It simply didn't make sense that this place was even functioning. There had to be something here. Let the old lady talk. Eventually, she'll spill.

Abbey tentatively asked, "Where are we headed?"

Frieda merely pointed ahead and continued walking. Enjoying the beauty, they came to a large copse of trees where Frieda managed to find a path. As they made their way through they spotted chipmunks, and owl, and a tiny deer. It was truly beautiful. Abbey was starting to enjoy the scenery; she tried to catch as much as she could on film. It was all very pristine.

As they reached a clearing they spotted the biggest horse Abbey had every seen. It was a phenomenal creature. He looked like something you'd see at the circus. All white and gorgeous. All Abbey could say was, "GEE!"

"Abbey, I'd like to introduce you to Moses." Frieda said. She began to explain, but let Moses begin for her. Moses spotted Frieda and ran to her. Naturally, Frieda had a cookie for the horse. Frieda scratched him on his chest and around his bridle path. She had to reach but Moses made sure it wasn't too hard.

Abbey stood to the side in awe. This animal could kill her with a head toss. He was huge and yet he came to Frieda like a tentative puppy. She had to ask, "What's the story with Moses?"

"Moses was bred to be in commercials. His lineage would have made for an amazing trick horse with perfect disposition and confirmation," at Abbey's confused look, Frieda went on to explain, "Confirmation just means he has the perfect frame and look." Abbey nodded so Frieda continued, " Unfortunately, Moses has a condition which makes him unable to feel his front feet. Moses had little of no control and was so tentative that he was perceived to be dangerous. His trainers must have been terrified because he was beaten by them and left in a stall for years. But Moses is a sweetheart. Others would have had him destroyed due to his inabilities, but the thing is, Moses is of great use to us; He has brought us more joy and loves to be around kids. He has even brought two young people together who are now serving around the world. Moses has brought a Priest to tears. Moses is amazing and he is worth his weight in gold to me."

True to his owner's boasting. Moses drew towards Abbey and blew his warm breath across her face. He nuzzled Abbey's ear and just pulled her in. She was jelly in his hooves; what a doll. Abbey found herself petting and stroking the biggest beast she had ever laid eyes on. She found such peace with this horse. He was worth his weight. Forget therapy, Abbey thought, Moses could make you forget your troubles.

Frieda began a tale of two young people.

"About twelve years ago, we had several volunteers come out to the ranch. We had grown quickly and we just didn't have the kind of staff that we really needed. Several of the kids were from the local Fellowship of Christian Athletes group from the college. They came highly recommended. We also had a missionary that happened to be a trained nurse, a young man who was an amazing mechanic and worked for a local landscaping company that had gone bankrupt. We felt like God sent each one these young people. Even so, with seven strangers on the ranch, it was rough going. My husband and I tried to dispense the work but it was really hard to just leave the work to others, I think we were still too attached to everything. The long and short of it was the kids had to make their way, and try to fit in. Many of them found their niches and were pretty happy; they assisted in the fishing, teaching and coordinating of the canoeing and archery. It was great where it worked."

"Our poor Michaela, the missionary nurse, was here on sabbatical and she really couldn't figure out what to do with so few crisis's. Michaela was accustomed to setting up clinics and seeing countless children or victims. Here, she was to rest and be available only for the occasional bee sting, stubbed toe, or splinter. We have only ever had one real emergency and the paramedics were here quickly."

Chapter 6

Frieda continued the tale, " Our darling Mechanic, Christian was a very quiet boy. He was very hard to connect with. He and Michaela met on multiple occasions but they were truly at odds from the beginning. I don't know if Michaela sensed that Christian didn't know Jesus, but she took a strong dislike to him almost immediately. Neither Michaela, nor Christian had enough to do in the beginning. It made them a little too available to find fault with others. Christian came to us a young man with some very rebellious tendencies. He seemed wounded, alone, and rebellious. He did have a gruff charm and the boy could fix anything."

"Christian was quiet and he didn't really connect with any of us, even me. The one who Christian became relaxed with was Moses. Whenever Christian found free time he immediately came here. Moses was very young then but he was so easily frightened that he was often off by himself. Moses used to crash through gates and other fixed pastures. So we decided to let him run the back sixty acres where he would run into the Appalachian Trail or a mountain or a lake if he went too far. We thought it would be safer there for him. Christian loved to find Moses and take him for a stroll. Moses was extremely afraid, I guess I would be too, if I couldn't feel my feet. Horses, in particular rely on their feet."

"Anyway, Christian would demonstrate for Moses that a stream or puddle was safe to cross, and Moses loved him for it. They were so funny together. Christian would make a run to the kitchen after any 'mechanical projects' looking for scraps he could take to feed Moses."

"Moses was an unusual animal, afraid yet ready to love. Very responsive for prolonged periods of time, but not all together settled. Later, it became obvious that Christian was just like our Moses- and they bloomed together."

"Christian was terrific at fixing almost anything mechanical. He seemed to have a sense about the working of any motor. I doubt our trailers would even be here without him. He almost single handedly got each and every one of the trailers working and in order. Christian even wired the entire ranch to run on individual generators. He was just super. We came to depend on him quite a bit. I couldn't have run the place without him."

Chapter 7

"Christian had been with us about six months before he and I really connected, over an incident with my husband. Dan had a stroke, it was a difficult time and Christian was the one who found him in the barn. He got Dan as comfortable as possible, then called Michaela and the paramedics. Christian was just amazing. He found me tending to some kitchen stuff, something unimportant. Christian was so delicate with me; I didn't know a gruff young man could be so tender. He took me by the hands, looked me in the eyes, made sure he had my complete attention, and told me that Dan was in the barn, and too ill to come inside. He told me to grab my phone and purse and to come with him. He helped me all the way, speaking softly and slowly describing all he knew. He assured me that the paramedics were on their way and that Michaela was capably looking after my Dan. Dan's stroke was crippling and terrible. Dan, Christian, and I spent days, weeks, perhaps months in that hospital, but Christian was always available for me. He was more caring than a young man ought to be. I came to understand that Christian had been down this path as a young lad. His mother had been a weak and sad woman who had buried two husbands before she should have to. Her first husband, Christian's father, died when he was only ten, his mother remarried before his twelfth birthday. Her second husband died within two years. Both men died of curious causes, but apparently Christian was the only one ale to comfort her during the mourning periods. He was her only son, her rock and her support. Apparently, his mother lay in bed for months at a time and probably utilized some sort of chemical help. She was despondent for long periods, unable to work or function."

"Finally after graduation high school, he planned to go to college but his mother couldn't handle his departure. So characteristically, Christian stayed and went to a local trade school. He fell in love as a twenty-one year old but wouldn't abandon his mother. He had been utterly devoted to the woman. She had needed him, and it appeared to me that his mother might have been more than weak. I never met her, but I was saddened by her dependence on a young man. Clearly though, it made Christian the most wonderful confidant I could have had."

"As Dan failed to get better, I recognized my need for a ranch foreman. Christian was the one that I trusted. He was still unskilled in dealing with a team of young people, (not at all unlike my husband), but I knew that in time he could be great. I spent a ton of time working with him and got to know him well."

Frieda gestured to Abbey, and they began a slow walk through the trees as Frieda prepared to go on with the story.

Abbey didn't want to break her chain of thought, so she said nothing.

Frieda began again, "Christian began his role a bit awkwardly, never wanting to impose on me or my time. He worked tirelessly at things that he clearly didn't have any interest in. I had several talks with him and tried to outline a reasonable workweek. He was really bright, I was afraid of taking too much from him, but I learned to depend on him for unusual things. Somehow he was always right by my side when bad news arrived, again from the doctors."

Abbey noticed a little farmhouse off in the distance, she assumed they were heading towards it but the paths wound down and around and through the trees. Who knew where they might wind up? The path was cool and covered with pine needles, a Georgia staple. The sun and the leaves created a dappled effect on the path. It was wonderful. She was enjoying the walk as much as the story.

Frieda seemed to be gathering her thoughts, and then began again.

"I did manage to encourage Christian in some things that gave him wonderful confidence. He began attending college on-line and eventually got a farm and ranch management degree from an agricultural school. It was terrific. The even gave him quite a bit of credit for all his experience."

"Christian had a way with all the animals and never was above even the most menial of chores, he would clean out the cat litter box as easily as changing the oil on the tractor. He eventually managed to communicate with many of the other young people on the ranch, and he could get the best work from all of them. Christian became the ranch manager that I had prayed for. He was so completely capable, and his farm & ranch management classes gave him fantastic tools. God sent me Christian; he held me up and made the ranch great. What a joy that young man was and remains."

"What Christian became in short order was an expert on travel itineraries, numbers and schedules. He also began overseeing care of all the animals and added quite a few. He managed our hay schedules, and created stock ponds that would make a fishery proud. Christian established our canoeing and got together with a local rafting group to arrange outings for our guests. By the time I got my head out of the clouds, Christian had turned our little farm into a well-functioning, clean and beautiful ranch. He also hired some hands to assist him and trained them well."

"Christian really came out of his shell, he was truly the leader of the ranch and all who watched for any period of time came to trust him and really respect him."

Chapter 8

"During the time while Dan was sick, and Christian was coming into his own on the ranch, the players shifted a lot. Our FCA kids would rotate and change; we always seemed to have a couple of kids. Christian would often find young people while he took his online classes. Several missionaries came through and Michaela was in an out depending on her mission board. She worked for a group that would attempt to send her to orphanages around the world after a disaster, so it was very sporadic. We always welcomed her back, though. She had to have noticed the change in Christian over time but she made it clear that she was disinterested. She always checked on Dan and me."

"For sixteen months I watched as Christian grew, and Dan faded. I was terribly concerned about Dan's suffering. I prayed like crazy and was terribly torn between my guests at the ranch and my husband. He was in and out of the hospital, mostly in and he suffered horribly. God had a plan in all of it, and He reminded me that I really wasn't necessary. I really thought I was important to the ranch, but in the end, God made it clear that it was a privilege to serve but in the end I am not needed. What a gift to simply enjoy the service and not struggle under the responsibility."

Abbey interrupted, "Oh Frieda, of course you were necessary. It was your dream, your purpose, and your gifts that were used to build this place. That's your legacy."

Frieda recognized immediately that she must choose her words carefully, "Abbey God is in charge. He has always done what He has always done. This ranch was such a surprise. Yes, I dreamed about it, but I must tell you…I didn't' do any of it. Each piece, each little insignificant part, as well as the significant parts all happened. I couldn't have done any of it. I had no capital of my own, no knowledge, no license, no nothing. God designed this all and planned it all for the benefit of his servants. I tell you, I can only imagine all the ways that I have gotten in God's way. Yes, He gave me a heart for it. Yes, He gave me a passion, but Abbey, girl, I am simply the recipient for now. I praise Him! Please don't credit me."

"Okay, I suppose," Abbey really hadn't understood. She continued, " I understand that you won't take credit. Surely, though you know that there just aren't very many people who would take on such a monumental task?"

They had finally made it to the small A-frame house and walked in to a pretty little chapel. There were comfy sofas, and fresh smelling coffees. As they sat down, Frieda offered, "Abbey, it is always God's people who are destined to take on the monumental tasks."

Chapter 9

Abbey made a mental note to remember to ask again about Christian and Michaela. Being a writer, she hated when a book or a tale ended abruptly, and without any closure. Frieda seemed to have either a very nimble brain or Attention Deficit Disorder.

Frieda started anew, "Years ago, I had this silly idea. I remembered my own prom and it was horrible. I had a perfectly miserable time. So, I wondered what it would be like to host a Christian Prom. We invited all the youth groups within a seventy-five mile radius and sold tickets for five dollars each. We hired a Christian DJ and invited our church youth group to be the host. Our youth were amazing. They really got the vision and had such a ball planning. They picked colors, themes, designs, foods, etc... and they took ownership by doing the decorating themselves. We ordered nine hundred balloons and created spiraling arches over the main room. We had almost four hundred kids coming based on ticket sales. The local community college had a culinary department and we bought huge blocks of ice, which they carved for free. We worked like crazy to set up fabulous tables with floating candles in great big fish bowls on mirrors. We purchased mementos for each youth; glass hurricanes with inscriptions about the night and the theme."

"The room was incredible, the food was ready, and the DJ was set up. The photographers were in place, only one problem, the local meteorologists were anticipating an ice storm, the like of which we don't usually see. We just don't do winter well in Georgia."

Abbey grinned remembering the last 'snow jam', if it looked like snow, most of the city would just shut down.

At Abbey's smile, Frieda continued, " Now Abbey, imagine getting four hundred teens anywhere, now imagine an ice storm heading our way. No matter what I did, I didn't have the power to make the kids come or to stop an ice storm. I was so disappointed that the prom wouldn't happen but I was crazy with worry about how much money I had spent preparing for the event. If I had to return the ticket holders' money, we would have been at a terrible deficit."

Abbey was transfixed; she remembered her own prom not being so great. She was imagining the evening. She wished she could have seen it, but she must hear the rest. "Well, what happened, did the kids come, did the ice storm hit?"

"Clearly God wanted the prom. Not only did he stop the ice storm, but He also brought five hundred and seventy-two teenagers. The evening was a grand success, something we have continued for seventeen years. It is one of our most popular events. It even pays for itself, now. ..So can you understand that no matter how much effort, no matter how popular, I could not have made it all work without God, He held off the ice storm, kept our power on and brought those wonderful kids."

Abbey got it, "Okay enough said, I think I get it, but what about Michaela and Christian?"

Chapter 10

"Michaela was such a lovely young woman. Of course, she didn't know it. Or maybe she, like most young women, couldn't accept it. I don't know. Abbey, do you recognize how lovely you are?"

At the shocked look on Abbey's face, Frieda had her answer. Frieda continued, "Dear you are beautiful! I once was lovely, not model material but pretty enough. I didn't see it either. It's funny when we're young we don't see ourselves or the gifts we were given. Yet, we are entirely self-absorbed. You can see it in your daughter, can't you? She's lovely isn't she? You get to be old like me, and you know how great you had it. Healthy bodies, shiny hair, no beard, oh never mind, you don't want to hear all of that. Michaela was a woman who saw herself being wasted in her surroundings and waiting to get started again."

Abbey chimed in, "Didn't you say that she was a missionary nurse or something?"

"That's right, precisely; she was sent home to rest and garner more resources. Missionaries have to constantly raise funds, they have to be salespeople and marketers and go home to various churches to raise money to keep on with their work."

"Well that hardly seems fair, why would a capable nurse need to sell herself?" Abbey questioned.

Frieda considered for a moment, "When our people go out to minister in foreign countries, they find it difficult to make a living. They are often in places where they cannot work or they are in areas where the people are simply too poor to pay for any services. Churches and people who believe in what they are doing must financially sponsor them. Michaela was involved with some volunteer medical groups. She was a competent nurse and was fantastic with little ones. God placed her here, I believe to get her heart ready for working with doctors and tribal people."

"Was it an attitude problem?"

"Perhaps, but I saw it as more of a perception problem. Michaela believed that the children deserved, but had a hard time with the parents; who appeared to have given up and an even harder time with the doctors who were there for only short periods of time. Michaela had been 'in country' for four years and had learned a great deal. She spent the entire four years learning the culture, enduring the living conditions, and watching the people. She had gotten a little bit of pride going and she was wrestling with it as she came back to the states."

Abbey identified with Michaela and responded, "Well I can imagine how she felt with doctors, and I would have felt the same way. You know most doctors have the 'God Complex'. They all think they know everything. And I'll just bet they probably hated the bugs, or beds or both."

"I'm sure you are right, but the doctors all had practices and careers going in the states and India and Europe. They, too, were giving their time and talents but didn't' have the exact same 'call on their lives.' At any rate, Michaela had a little bit of a chip on her shoulder. Christian had a way of knocking it off."

"I pity Christian then," Abbey smiled.

"Yes, well to know Michaela is a gift. It is worth the time to get to know her. She is like all of us, a work in progress and we all have a lot of growing to do. God can take us in, the small lump of clay that looks like trash, and turn us into beautiful works of art. We must slow down, listen, pray, and learn as much as we can about our Father in Heaven. He has the plan. He will work it out, we must listen and learn."

Abbey wondered about her own lump.

Frieda continues to explain how Christian's growing role at the ranch and Michaela's lack of work ran into each other. Michaela suffered for her pride, Frieda went on to explain that the romance happened with some grudging realities. First Christian respected how Michaela handled Dan and the paramedics and finally when Moses needed some medical help. Michaela became Moses's nursemaid.

"It was a simple thing really, Moses pricked the soft part of his foot, called the frog, with something. Either he stepped on something or maybe he kicked at a fence, perhaps it was a thorn, who knows. Anyway, he wound up with an abscess, which is a bit like an infected blister. The problem is that horses cannot just put their feet up for any length of time or keep them clean. They are on them almost constantly. When Christian discovered the abscess, he grudgingly approached Michaela for help."

"Now everyone knew Moses, and as you have seen, to know Moses is to love Moses. Michaela became an almost constant companion and a respect grew between Michaela and Christian. They became friends and helpmates as they tended to Moses. He required some very basic treatments, but with an animal that size, even the most basic procedure required a bit of finesse. Soaking his foot in Epsom salts was quite a job. They actually had the poor horse in some bizarre boot, with iodine stains. They were very good to our guy. And our Moses brought those two young people; two very raw lumps of pride and need; together through working which eventually led to love."

Oswald Chambers said something wonderful, " Salvation is not merely deliverance from sin, it is deliverance out of self entirely into union with Him."

Frieda paused and smiled in a peculiar way, " You are never totally free until you are free to be with Him. Loving God and serving Him. For Michaela and Christian, Moses, God's amazing creature, gave them a chance to just serve together. They tended to a 'useless' animal with love and great tenderness. Through that they both found joy."

Abbey questioned inwardly? Deliverance from self? Clay lumps? This was all weird. She actually would have liked more details on Christian and Michaela, but maybe Frieda didn't know. Abbey wondered if the pride issue was what she was dealing with. Frieda seemed so happy, and she certainly exhibited humility. Abbey prided herself on being a good reporter, but she wasn't sure she had gotten a lot out of the old woman. Frieda could have suffered with delusions. Abbey was slightly confused but she was getting the gist of what Frieda wanted her to know, she thought.

Chapter 11

Frieda lead Abbey back to the main hall. Out of nowhere, there seemed to be around thirty people all headed the same way; also a three-legged dog of unknown origin, another mutt, and a cat. Abbey wondered what was happening and then Frieda announced, "Now you'll see how dinner's served on the ranch!"

Abbey hadn't realized how late it had gotten, but she was starving.

As they moseyed up to the lodge, the smells became intense. There was a band setting up, a large roasted pig, tables, chairs, a dance floor and the most beautiful display of fruit. Huge baskets carved out of watermelons, filled to the brim with cut fruits. "Yum," Abbey wasn't sure if she'd said out loud.

Frieda explained, "Tonight is country night, although I suppose it's always some version of country night. We will enjoy southern barbeque, fried chicken, fruits, veggies, and all things pie tonight. Do you square dance Abbey?"

"Huh? No ma'am, I don't dance at all, at least not in public. I only dance with my kids in my kitchen. How did you get all this done, while we were out?"

"Oh honey, I have these things lined up, down to the tiniest detail by now. Remember we've been here a while. The folks who work here, my dearest friends in the world, are amazing and they are better at doing my job than I could ever be. I count on them.

Sometimes, it is more important to tend to the people here, than the work of the ranch. Don't get me wrong I am definitely more of a Martha than a Mary, but you are worth it."

Mary and Martha again, Abbey thought, still don't really get that reference. "I appreciate your time for this article but it's really all about the publicity that you will get isn't it?" Abbey chided.

"Actually, no it isn't about the publicity. I doubt your readers will read the article. They'll see the pictures and skim your article and we'll have a copy somewhere. But we aren't the kind of place that draws folks out of a magazine. Our little ranch is a place for healing. People only come here by divine appointment. I learned that a long time ago. I have no reason to recruit or market, God will bring those who need to be here. You are here, that is enough for me. After all, we cannot be sure of our tomorrows, only today, For now, dear Abbey, you are the only thing that I am certain God has sent with regards to your article," Frieda responded.

Abbey thought she may have offended the woman, but Frieda didn't seem to notice the slight. Okay, well at least the food will be good.

Frieda led Abbey to an area to get cleaned up and they both met back up to join the diners. Food was served buffet style and a cowboy who had a banjo led the prayer. Interesting. The food was amazing and as Abbey looked around she was people of many different ethnic backgrounds and many ages. There was a beautiful African American family, picture perfect and Abbey wondered to herself if they weren't staged for her photos. Well, she'd take them anyway. Two other families; one with five young children that were getting food all over themselves, and another with a really young baby. Abbey thought she would hate to deal with the larger brood but had to smile when she remembered her own babies. There was a priest in long black garb, man he must have been miserable. There were several cowboys and men huddled together laughing and smacking their lips over the fried chicken. What an eclectic group, Abbey almost had to laugh. It was hard to tell who was serving, and who the guests were. But it seemed that several of the younger cowboys and a couple of gals kept checking the buffet. They would sit down from time to time and eat. It seemed like a very strange set up. All in all, though Abbey hated to admit it, the whole thing seemed very comfortable and well run.

Frieda introduced Abbey to a woman named Sharon, who gave Abbey the play by play on how everything was accomplished, and who did what. Sharon explained the options for the evening where the children could go, or what activities would be available to them. Sharon obviously loved the ranch but it seemed that she loved Frieda more.

Abbey thought that Sharon was probably one of the most beautiful women that she had ever seen. She wasn't a model or anything; she just seemed to radiate love. She had a sort of brilliance of character. Abbey made a mental note; she could use that as a title for an article.

Meanwhile, Frieda moved from table to table speaking with most everyone, she physically touched each and every person and you could hear her laugh over and over. She was quite a skilled hostess. Abbey got lost watching her and was lulled into the role of a peaceful spectator and occasional photographer.

Everyone was eating and seemed to be quite comfortable when a whole table got up and went into the band area. They plugged in and got set up and the music began. Kids started dancing, some with each other some with their parents. Folks were strolling under the stars. Some of the ranch hands were demonstrating for the teens and a few courageous parents how to do some country line dances.

All in all, it was actually a lot of fun. The evening wound down around nine and people made their way to their individual trailers. Tiki torches had been lit to guide the families' home. The kids had those crazy lights on their heads, they all looked like they were heading out like the dwarfs from Snow White. Abbey thought about how much her kiddos would love this. She decided to call it a night so that she could make a quick call to her darlings. She bid goodnight to Frieda and made her way up to the lodge.

When Abbey's editor had arranged this job for her, he had made sure she had a place to stay. Frieda had seen to her bags and placed her up in the Lodge in the 'family quarters'. Abbey called her children and promised them some special treats upon her return. Her Mom was doing fine with them.

Abbey was checking through her digital images, thinking she should have gotten a few more pictures, but pleased with the overall effect. She heard the rain begin and decided she was ready for bed.

Chapter 12

Abbey bolted upright in her bed, forgetting where she was for a moment, she panicked. "Roosters, are you kidding me????" After a night of almost no sleep, due to all the noise, Abbey had to drag her pillow across her face. It was impossible to sleep with all the 'country racket'. There must have been six thousand crickets and frogs all performing below her window. It was like the plague. The clock said five, as in AM. What a ridiculous hour to be awakened. AGAIN! What a noisy place, Peaceful country, hah! May as well get up, clearly she wasn't going to be able to rest. No doubt Frieda was up and ready for action. Abbey stretched and her muscles complained.

Abbey looked out her window, her room overlooked the wrap around porch in the main house, and she looked towards a mountain way off in the distance. It was a bit foggy but she saw him standing there. Moses was looking her way; what a fantastic beast. Abbey made a promise to herself that she would visit Moses with carrots or something, but first there had to be coffee.

She dressed comfortably, and headed toward what she hoped would be a large pot of caffeine with her name on it. She spotted Frieda, that sly dog, sucking down the world's largest cup of coffee, ever. Well, it had to be good.

"Oh Abbey, you look exhausted, you have circles under you eyes. Didn't you sleep?"

"Well, to be honest, it was kind of noisy last night. I think there were some crickets in my room with me."

Frieda tried to suppress a chuckle, unsuccessfully. "Oh dear, you must forgive me, you sound like me. I have always said that at least the sounds in the city are clear. A Siren is a siren. A horn is a horn, etc... Out here you're just hearing the most amazing assortments. And trust me, just when you think you've heard it all, you'll discover what a 'screaming rabbit' sounds like," Frieda responded conspiratorially.

"A screaming rabbit, are you serious?" Abbey was immediately sorry she asked. Frieda just laughed and mumbled something about Monty Python. Abbey was sure she must have heard wrong.

"Let's get you fed, and then I have someone you must meet," Frieda dragged Abbey to the kitchen and offered her a banquet. Abbey wasn't used to eating this much or this often, she was mostly interested in coffee.

Once they were armed with lots of caffeine and had freshened up, they were off to one of the ponds on the property. An enormous lake of a pond, but a pond nonetheless.

Frieda introduced Abbey to Matthew and asked Matt to tell Abbey about the hatchery and to show her the options for visitors to the ranch. He responded to Frieda and Abbey detected his accent. Matt was clearly thrilled to help Frieda in any way that he could.

Abbey hadn't expected to be pawned off, even for a little while but thought she'd use the time to get some perspective from one of Frieda's employees. She really looked at Matt, and realized that he was quite handsome in a rugged and slight way. He was very masculine without being a monster or hulk of a guy. His first words to her were bizarre until she realized that he was probably from Ireland or something. "My lady."

He took her elbow and guided her through barns, sign-up areas, boat-filled docks and baby birds, baby fish, even baby peacocks.

His accent was beautiful. Now she was wondering if maybe he was Welsh. Abbey hadn't been around enough to recognize the singsong sound. She was honestly curious. "Well Matt where do you hale from?"

"Actually, I am from Australia but spent a lot of my youth in Scotland. Did you know that the children in Scotland still learn Gaelic? My accent throws a lot of people."

"In Melbourne, we tend to sound like the English with just a bit of the New York twinge. It's fun here in Georgia; you all think I have an accent. Oh my. You southerners are hilarious. And the expressions... 'Hotter than a blue tick hound bumping into a frog." Matt attempted the southern drawl...very funny.

Abbey was charmed and caught completely off guard by his attempt. That ridiculous, albeit accurate depiction of southern colloquialisms was just too hilarious. "Are you in charge of the entertainment here?"

Matt thought a moment, and then with sudden realization, " Oh Miss Abbey, I don't work here. Well at least not regularly, I am more like one of the family. Frieda is such a mom that she takes us single pastors and turns us into her kiddos. We all show up from time to time and pitch in where we can. Sort of touch base with Frieda and then earn our keep. I think that she saw my fascination with the animals, and thought I'd be perfect to show it to a newbie."

"And a newbie is...." Probed Abbey.

"Someone new to our family here at the ranch. I've been coming here for the past nineteen years. It started when I came with my parents. They were missionaries in New Zealand and Scotland. We came twice, then I came to the states to attend seminary. I grew up in boarding schools and saw my folks from time to time. While I was in seminary, I was mostly broke and couldn't fly to see my folks, so I came here. Frieda and Sweet Silver Ranch were the only constant in my life. Now, I pastor a small church in Alabama, just across the border. I come here as much as I can."

"Wow, you could probably be an enormous help to me. Can you tell me about your stays as a family? How has it changed? How it is now coming back as an adult? How did you come to feel that this was home? What made it click for you?" abbey was thrilled to get this man's perspective, and his voice wasn't hard to listen to.

Matt shrugged his shoulders, "Well it's kind of a long, boring story. It is even a bit sad. Are you certain you want to hear it?"

"Oh yes! Oh and did Frieda tell you why I am here? About my article for the magazine and my desire to really understand this place?"

"Yes, Frieda told me that whatever I say could wind up in print, but I'm not that interesting of a fellow. Let's see, my parents were missionaries. Europe had gotten so anti-Christian and we were not well received. Each day was a battle to be faithful to the work of evangelism and not becoming frustrated with the government. We moved a lot. Living there was tedious. We worked really hard to earn our way. Dad taught literature by day, Mom was a nursing assistant. I was in an American school at the local military base. It was tough. We would come back to the states in between moves throughout Europe and we would report in to the mission board. We worked in Spain, and Germany, Scotland and Ireland, mostly. We came here two of the times when Mom and Dad were seeking support from churches in Atlanta. They would leave me here with Frieda. It was so great to be here. I just loved the comforts, the freedom, and well, Frieda." Matt got quiet for a moment, they began to walk towards some porch swings in the shade and he gestured for Abbey to sit.

Matt continued, "Then Dad got really tired and it became so hard. The support churches couldn't see a lot of fruit from the work, maybe they were just bored, but Dad got less and less financial support. He would work harder but it just began to consume him with anger. I believe that my Dad got into missions work because he really believed in it. He just didn't have any obvious success to enjoy, and never saw any definite potential. Eventually, it took its toll on my parent's relationship. Dad became very harsh with my Mother, but she always wanted to help. Mother never understood. I think it was my Mother who had the real drive to do missions, but Dad was the one with the title. Anyway, he started drinking, and eventually abused my Mother. First it was verbal, but then became physical. He ultimately beat her up. Appalled by what he had done he begged forgiveness. He went to the board of missions and asked for help. Mom asked to come here to the ranch. She and I came home to the ranch and Frieda where we spent a lot of time healing. It was great being here. My schoolwork was a breeze cause I didn't have to deal with all the 'military brats' and I became the man of the house. Oh how I loved that role. I was so happy here, until my Dad joined us. He came here looking for forgiveness and grace. Having gotten counseling and redirection in his life he no longer drank and was really very considerate. Mom forgave him instantly. But it just wasn't enough for me."

Matt appeared to be lost for a moment. Abbey thought about prompting him, but decided he'd continue in his own good time.

Eventually, Matt found his voice, "Frieda talked to me about my own life, my own sin, my anger. We talked about how not forgiving my Dad was unbiblical and could only hurt me. It was a lot to take in at sixteen. But after a lot of talk with Frieda, more with God, and some time with some fantastic priests and pastors that were here, I realized that I loved my Dad. I needed to give to him a small portion of what God had already given me."

Matt smiled softly, "You know with hindsight, it was fantastic. Mom was so happy, she and Dad wound up back on the mission field wound in the Philippines. They found a group of people that they just love, who love them back. Every time they come back it is with hundreds of requests for Bibles. It's awesome. They have been there for seven years now and are just elated. They are flourishing. We found healing here, because we could hear God. I really believe that when you are placed in a field of love, you can finally sense God's enormous capacity for us. I am a product of this place. A priest here, Father John actually convinced me to go to seminary."

"That's quite a story. So are you Catholic?" asked Abbey.

"No, I am a protestant pastor. Although I still love the Catholic Mass. I don't' think I could give up the whole marriage and children thing. I look forward to having a family when God decides to bless me. I just have to be careful of all those sweet old ladies at church, who believe it is their job to get me married off. What a challenge they are! The only good thing is that they are afraid to get me "hitched" to one of their people. They are afraid I'll run off with my bride to Australia or the Philippines. I think both places seem like the other end of the sky to some."

Abbey thought to herself, this guy must be the most eligible bachelor in all of Alabama. He is a cutie. The last thing that I need though is a love interest. Especially, an accented one in the middle of the Deep South. Nope, not gonna go there. Instead of allowing her mind to continue, she asked Matt, "So do you miss the travel and the other countries?"

Matt beamed, "Nope! Not even a little bit. I love being settled. I would love to one day take my own family on trips overseas, but this is home. Besides, on a pastor's salary I doubt I'll be going 'round the world any time soon." Matt continued grinning not at all embarrassed or disappointed with his statement.

Abbey thought it was strange to see a man so content with so little, interesting.

Chapter 13

"So that is more than enough about me. What brings a smile to Abbey's face?" asked Matt.

"My two children." Oh that was abrupt. But he's still smiling. Abbey tried to cover, "I was married very young to an abusive man who decided that he didn't much like the whole marriage and kids thing. So, he is no longer in the picture. I have the most normal but wonderful kids in the world. Genevieve is eight and her brother Winston is six and a half."

"Now those are two names to grow into," Matt responded.

"Well to tell you the truth, Geves and Bug are what they go by most of the time. Winston couldn't get out his sister's name and he just looked like a bug when he was born," Abbey shrugged and smiled.

"It'd be a pleasure to meet Geves and Bug someday. Would I have to wait and use their proper names?"

"Oh, you'd have to with your delicious accent." Oh no, Abbey recoiled, did I just say delicious to a pastor, uggghhhh! Abbey wanted to crawl under a rock. Fortunately, Matt was still smiling.

"I'll do my best to give Geves and Bug the full treatment. Make my own mama proud" Matt declared with a terrible southern drawl.

Thank goodness he was a good sport. Probably had more attention from women than a guy could stand. But wow! That accent, he really needed to give up the southern drawl though it was the pits. Why do accents and uniforms work so well for a girl? Abbey merely smiled at Matt and refused to put her other foot in her mouth.

Mat got up from the bench and offered Abbey his arm. He was ready to go again. Too bad Abbey was enjoying the simple flirting. Although, maybe not so much when she remembered he was a pastor. No way, not my type. Too everything and poverty wasn't that much fun. Time to get back to work.

"So Pastor Matt what would you say is the most spiritual thing about Sweet Silver Ranch, and how does Ms. Frieda pay for all of this?" inquired Abbey.

"I'll attempt to answer your last question first. Ms. Frieda does everything on a shoestring, and has been given gifts by practically anyone and everyone you can imagine. I have personally never known her to ask for money, but it seems to come in none–the less. I know that her husband left some insurance money, but she is by no means well to do. Funny, I don't think I've really thought all that much about the money issues. You should ask her. Regarding the most spiritual thing, well that depends on your relationship with Jesus Christ. Abbey, do you know Jesus?"

Abbey looked down and then away, she had almost forgotten that Matt was a pastor; she was really enjoying their talk until now. She tapped her pen a few times on her thigh and tried to answer, "I don't know. I know about him. I just don't really understand your question."

Matt was taken aback; he assumed that Abbey working for a Christian magazine would surely have a relationship with Jesus Christ. Well, that took her down several notches in Matt's book. He had to speak carefully, "Abbey, you and your children, do you know what God demands of His people?"

" Do you mean the ten commandments?"

"Exactly, the ten commandments, but do you know that even thinking about murder, or considering a theft, is the same as breaking the commandments?" stated Matt.

"That hardly seems fair. God expects us to be perfect. That cannot be right. I thought he knew everything."

"Once again, you are precisely right. God knew that we were going to feel envy that we would want things that didn't belong to us. So He gave us a way out. God sent His Son to be the perfect sacrifice for our sins." Matt paused, hoping that Abbey was receiving this input. He prayed that the Holy Spirit would enable her to understand it. Matt looked at Abbey and saw a beautiful and thoughtful woman; he really hoped she could grasp God's truth.

Abbey chose a different route; she rushed right into her article to defray this line of thinking. "Well, anyway, I've got to get back to the article, if I'm going to make my deadline. Do you know how pastors afford to come here? Are there any corrupt pastors here?"

Shoot! Matt thought he must have blown it. Well it was up to the Holy Spirit. Thank goodness, not up to him. He might only be one in the long line of witnesses to her. He needed to pray like mad for this woman and her children. And what was it with 'reporters' always looking for the ugly. Corrupt pastors, seriously.

Before Matt could address her questions, little Sammy Watson came bounding up, all red faced and clearly distraught. "Pastor Matt you gotta come quick. They need help! Please come fast." And, he was off like a shot with Matt running right behind him.

Abbey rushed to catch up. They were rounding the bend towards one of the larger ponds. Abbey tried to imagine what it could be. Maybe a drowning or she hoped maybe something simple like an overturned canoe or maybe it was a large fish.

Abbey could see Matt and Sammy but couldn't hear them; she was trying to catch up.

Matt was on his knees and Sammy was pointing out into the middle of the pond. Whatever he was saying, he was clearly worried. Sammy was crying and making huge horrible gestures with his hands and pointing to the middle of the pond. Feathers were flying. It appeared to be a couple of ducks that may have been fighting. Matt had a funny look on his face and as Abbey finally got close enough to hear, she slowed to listen.

Matt spoke gently and consolingly, "Sammy, the duck is okay. They are duck wrestling so that they can decide whether or not they want some baby ducks." Matt was just sure this was some kind of terrible joke on him. Here, he had to explain, in the most generic terms, about the birds and bees to a little guy who wasn't' even his own. Ugh, and Abbey was listening. Great way to make an impression, she'd probably make fun of him in her article.

Abbey, upon hearing, and then seeing the conundrum had to turn away. She was afraid that she was going to lose it. Laughter was bubbling up in a painful way. Matt was pretty tender with this little boy. How would she have explained it to Bug? She walked quickly back so that her giggles didn't escape and hurt the little boy. If there was one thing she knew for sure, no matter what their age, males hate to be laughed at. She absolutely knew that she was going to lose it, so she tried to move quickly.

After calming Sammy down and returning him to his parents, (and a shared snicker with his dad, Brother Sam), he went back in search of Abbey.

Sheepishly approaching Abbey, Matt tried to think of something clever to say. Abbey spared him…She was leaking, her nose was running and tears were streaming down her face. She was even shaking. At first Matt thought he should console her. But as soon as she calmed a bit, she guffawed and said, "Matt that was just great, duck wrestling to decide whether or not to have babies! What a hoot. I cannot believe you kept a straight face. You are truly a great shepherd."

Matt wasn't sure if she was having fun at his expense. "I wasn't quite sure what he was ready for. But he was certain that duck was trying to kill the other duck. I didn't want him to worry. I must admit, it did appear to be an attempted drowning." Matt finally saw the humor and lost it, he let out a huge deep laugh and joined Abbey in a fit of laughing.

Abbey was brought down to the ground. They both laughed so hard their faces hurt. It was exhausting and wonderful. Abbey snorted at one point and that got them both started all over again.

After patting their faces dry with everything they could find, shirtsleeves and one small tissue Abbey produced from a pocket, they made their way back to the lodge to see about Frieda.

Frieda was thrilled to see Abbey and Matt come in together. She listened as they explained their demeanor and their run-in with the ducks and little Sammy. Frieda laughed a great big honking laugh that brought Abbey up short. Frieda's laugh seemed so out of character. It was the one 'no class' thing that Abbey had seen in Frieda. Frieda laughed again and asked her if she should get a waiver in the future for 'birds and bees' proximity. They all laughed at that.

Matt excused himself to do something, somewhere, but smiled warmly at Abbey and gave Frieda big smooch on the cheek.

Chapter 14

It was the evening of the Italian feast and the smells emanating from the kitchen were just too much. Abbey had to get in and see what was happening. "Frieda, is it alright if I watch the preparations for tonight's meal?"

"Oh absolutely, it is almost impossible to keep me out of the dining room or kitchen. Come with me, we'll get you an apron and you can do whatever makes you happy," Frieda chimed.

Suddenly, as they passed into the main dining room it had become an Italian Café. Small round red globes with candles, wine bottles, (all appeared to be non-alcoholic), were placed on every table. Giant overstuffed booths were scattered throughout the room. Il Divo (the amazing gorgeous group of males singers) was blasting over the speakers. There were dangling grape vines, Italian maps and pictures on every wall, gazebo looking shelters. Over some tables, what appeared to be stars in the sky, (actually small twinkling lights over the booths).

Abbey questioned, "Now how in the world did you do all of this?"

"We've been doing this for some time. We've collected lots of stuff over the years, and we simply move things around for our theme nights. Tonight will be lasagna, fettuccini, linguini, and pizza pie for the kiddos. We have tiramisu and even our own gelato. It is fun, isn't it?" Frieda responded.

Abbey asked about gelato, Frieda explained that it was a very special Italian ice cream. Really the only way to eat it was in Italy, but they made a pretty good replica of it for Georgia. Abbey began her article questions again. "Why so much effort? Surely a good meal, and a nice place to stay are sufficient?"

Frieda looked as thought the thought had never occurred to her. Finally she said, "Abbey, God gives us gifts. Mine are hospitality, encouragement, and serving. When God gifts us, He does not do so for our pleasure only. He does it for HIS glory. These people who lead our churches, literally, give of themselves constantly. They give with very little thanks less rewards and at the greatest possible expense. Now, if God is going to let me serve them for a week or two, then I must do it to the best of my abilities. It is how I praise My GOD with everything I have in the way that He designed me to. Sometimes it can be exhausting, sometimes it can be costly, but it is the only way that I have to be who God made me to be. It will be my greatest day when I know that I have caused God to smile. It is amazing Abbey, the God of the universe smiles because of us. Isn't that fantastic? This dinner, these people are so important to God. He made sure that I could have all the things needed to serve it. He brought the people here to eat it and enjoy it. It is for Him and by Him. Beyond that, it just doesn't matter."

Abbey grew pensive for a moment. She was thinking, trying to figure out where to go with her questions and trying to understand who she was interviewing. Frieda lights up when she talks about Her God. She had to be one of very few people who fit the Holy Roller profile and really believe it. It could be why her questions weren't netting any results. Abbey decided to roll with it "Frieda you've mentioned 'serve the server' before. How do you see that really, how is that provided for?"

"Well, pastors, priests, other church workers and their families tend to take care of people. In Acts, when the church was established, they clearly identified jobs and roles in the church. Throughout God's Word, even going back to the Levites, it clearly says that we are to offer up tithes and grains and other giftings to our teachers and workers. Nowadays, you call the church for every major life event and most of life's problems; churches are always called upon in crisis or stress. The difference going back and looking at it today is that the family and the pastor himself were generally members of the privileged class. It is really only in the last two hundred years that people have begun looking down on the work of the clergy. Do you know how few people are entering this vocation? I am not a numbers person but I know the seminaries are struggling for students. Abbey, we are fortunate to have men like Matt who will take the time to care for the Sammys of this world. There are fewer and fewer like him. In the church today, a congregant believes himself to be the boss of the pastor. Can you imagine? Thank goodness Jesus was our example and not our modern day 'civil servants.' Oh Abbey, I am sorry, did I answer your question?"

Abbey realized that the dissertation was over. She had learned a lot abut Frieda. Including that she was no push over. Hard to dispute anything she said, but it was curious that what gain was it really to Frieda? She answered and figured she would try to probe a little as they worked, " Yes Frieda, you are very clear on those things that you care about. Thank you."

Abbey continued, "What can I do here?"

Frieda handed her long matches to light candles on the tables, and then beckoned her to join her in the kitchen.

Abbey enjoyed the work, and thought a lot about what Frieda had said. She tasted everything in the kitchen and wound up being too full to eat. She worked all night with the kitchen, ran food to tables, and bussed tables. Each table held someone interesting. Abbey spoke with almost everyone at some point and enjoyed the private jokes she was included on, and the ability to give people something special. She took great delight in bringing out the beautiful deserts. It was actually a great deal of fun. When everything was put away and the kitchen cleaned, she was so exhausted that she decided to go straight to bed.

Frieda was in her element and truly enjoyed the evening, too. Running around the dining room felt great. The meal was huge success, and everyone enjoyed the operatic group at the end of the evening. Abbey was a joy to watch. It was such a great thing watching her. Abbey grinned from ear to ear as she placed gelato with all manner of toppings in front of little kids and grown-ups. She clearly loved seeing everyone enjoy themselves. She had a bit of a spring in her step as she spoke with the guests and refilled water glasses. It was wonderful to see someone enjoy serving others. It was true what all the psychoanalysts were just now figuring out; doing for others is the best medicine! Frieda cleaned up the last of the decorations, readying them for next month and prayed out loud. "Father, my wonderful, Abba, thank you for sending Abbey. I praise you for the joy of young people, for the questions and the opportunities. I pray Father that you would rain down the Holy Spirit on her. Fill to overflowing and open the floodgates of blessings on her life. I pray for her children, Lord, that they would belong wholly to you. I love you Father. I praise you, you are amazing. Thanks Dad." With her final thanks Frieda turned down the lights and went to bed, exhausted and hopeful, three dogs at her heels.

Chapter 15

Abbey awakened after the best night's sleep ever. She couldn't believe how refreshed she felt. Wow, she thought I cannot believe that I slept through those crickets and frogs. She stretched and got up ready to go. She found Frieda in the dining hall speaking with a young woman about picnic specifications.

Abbey chimed, "Good Morning, what are we working o this morning?"

Frieda was delighted to see a very well rested Abbey in such a good mood. "Are you hungry, can I get you anything? We're working on the menus for today's picnics. We had a change in our order that was unexpected."

Abbey poured herself a cup of coffee and said that she wasn't hungry but wanted to understand the problem with the picnics.

"Oh well our food supplier delivered no deli style meats for today. So, we're taking last night's meatballs in marinara sauce and making meatball heros for the picnics. Great thing about them is they are terrific cold." Frieda continued, "Abbey you look super this morning, you rested well, I assume?"

"Well as a matter of fact, I think I rather like working the dining room. I fell into bed last night. But it was a great nights sleep. The best I've had in years. Must be all the outdoor living, honest work, and great food, et al. I must tell you Frieda, I think I am getting a sense of the joy you experience in your service to others. It isn't like being a parent. Not exactly, but it has a quality like that."

"You do understand. This is a total labor of love." Frieda chuckled and clapped her hands, "I am just delighted with you Abbey! Waitressing is such great fun, at least if you aren't trying to support your family on it. Well and, having such grateful, joyful customers."

"I'm not sure if it was the waitressing part so much, it seemed more like, oh I don't know, purpose or something."

"Well Abbey, you know God designed us each to do something. We have our own unique purpose." Frieda noticed Abbey's confused expression and began again. " Oh I can see you haven't heard this before, have you ever heard of Tabitha or Dorcas in the Bible?"

Abbey couldn't remember if she had or not but simply shook her head.

Frieda grabbed a Bible and paged through. "Here it is, Acts nine, I'll tell you my version and then let you read it for yourself. Dorcas or Tabitha is the only named woman in the Bible that was raised from the dead and it was because of her individual talent and desire to serve."

"Dorcas was a seamstress who always helped the poor and she could be counted on to make clothing for the orphans and widows, then she died. Men in her village ran to find Peter who was in a nearby town and begged him to help with Dorcas. The people held vigil and Peter came and raised her from the dead. It's really that simple. God used Dorcas to help the people with her simple ability to sew. She was a blessing to all who knew her. When she died, Peter raised her in Jesus Christ's name and many people believed. Our gifts are the most important tool for reaching others."

Abbey read it for herself and was surprised. As she digested it all, Frieda sat nearby fussing with tables and the buffet set up. Well, it was obvious that Frieda had a gift. It seemed to Abbey that God gifted some with spectacular gifts. It didn't seem to include her. She supposed that when it was her turn, God was fresh out of great gifts.

Frieda wondered if Abbey was seeing herself in Dorcas. She recognized that Abbey was really thinking, but worried about the pensive look on her face. She approached, "Abbey do you see yourself in that story?"

Abbey shook her head, 'no'.

Exasperated, Frieda piped up, "Young lady, your words and photos reach people. There are not many who can communicate with the written word. I cannot imagine the gift you've been given. Me, I can't take a picture to save my life. I have no patience for it." Frieda softened her tone, "Abbey, you are precious. I wish you could know the lavishness of God's love. He has clearly poured it out on you. Can you return next weekend?"

"Um, what, why would I come back next weekend?" Abbey answered.

"Well, dear, it's time you bring your kids and come back here after some thought. I will send you home with one of our minivans, so that you don't have to put mileage on your car. I want you back here with your children." Frieda was smiling, " I need you to see the camp with your kids and through their eyes. You need this, Abbey, and I need you to be here. I will call your editor and demand it," Frieda winked.

Abbey thought about it. Really it would be amazing to bring Geves and Bug here. What a wonderful vacation for us. I don't know. Oh what the heck! "Okay," it'd be nice to get home early. "I don't really need to take one of the vans, though."

"I am delighted, and you will take one of the minivans. I want this to be a different week for you; you and your children will be special guests. I wish I had thought of this before. Sometimes, I am such a dope. Anyway, the vans all come with gas cards. I will take no arguments and I will meet your children, when?"

Abbey thought for a second, "the kids have a break coming up so we can be here early Friday. Is that okay?"

"Naturally!" Frieda was very excited.

The spent the next 30 minutes getting Abbey packed and shuffled car seats into the van. Frieda was smarter than she looked. The van was the key to getting Abbey back here. She couldn't very well back out when she began her internal argument about the 'wasted time'. Frieda sent Abbey off with food, or course, and so many prayers.

Chapter 16

Matt came in that evening and enjoyed the Mexican Fiesta, replete with piñatas and a Mariachi band. He was looking around the whole evening and when Frieda settled in next to him, he finally asked, "So where's Abbey?"

Frieda's suspicions confirmed. "Well honey, Miss Abbey will be back next weekend with her children," She answered. "Are you planning to grace us with your presence?"

Matt quickly caught on that Frieda thought she'd glimpsed something in him. "Well surprise of all surprises. You very well know that I plan to be bringing the youth on Saturday for games, my lovely stateside mom."

Frieda chuckled, she couldn't help wanting to see Matt happy and dealing with someone from outside of his church. He was a wonderful, dedicated pastor but the small size of his rural church was bound to be limiting for a world-traveled young man. Abbey could certainly use some time with a believer like Matt. Frieda patted Matt's hand and smiled as she headed out to the kitchen.

After checking on the prep for breakfast and assuring that all the sombreros were put up properly, Frieda let her dogs out of her room and headed outside for a nice walk before bed. Shasta her beloved border collie stuck by her side. While walking she enjoyed conversing with God. Thanking Him, imploring Him, and praising Him for all that He provided so consistently. She said special prayer as she returned and readied for bed, one for Matt and one for Abbey. God would have to work there; it would be too easy for an old nosey woman to get in trouble. Finally, she climbed into bed and turned off the light.

The week flew by, and it was Thursday before Frieda realized that Abbey was due back soon. She hadn't heard from her. Frieda assumed that everything was on, as planned. She promised herself she wouldn't worry it to death. God was in control. It was all up to him. It would be fine. Frieda readied three of the rooms in the main lodge. She wanted to have the children nearby so that Abbey could have freedom with them, and perhaps from them if need be.

Friday morning came and Abbey was so sorry that she had said yes. Packing and getting the kids to bed had been a nightmare. The kids had about a million questions. Geves may become a reporter after all; the way that her mind twisted and turned was awe-inspiring. There was always the fear that she'd be a lawyer that or perhaps wind up in prison for white-collar crimes. They had both fallen asleep to Beauty and the Beast on the long drive. The van had been a real treat. Both kids were going to hate getting their car back.

Abbey's old Honda smelled kind of funny. At some points squirrels or something had built a nest inside the engine. They must have kept all sorts of things. Whenever the heater or defroster ran it smelled just like maple syrup. Whenever Abbey had to run the heat for any length of time the kids would start requesting pancakes or waffles. Abbey almost missed the smell. It always cracked her up when a new passenger would first smell the syrup.

She was half way into the long drive, and realized that she couldn't wait to show the kids all the animals, the ponds, the baby horses, and well everything. She also wondered if Matt might be there. As Abbey got closer to the ranch, she peeked in the mirror; just to see if she should add lipstick or something. Abbey thought she was being ridiculous, this is a job, not a date.

Chapter 17

Frieda couldn't help checking the windows. The day was a bit gray and Frieda was pretty certain that her arthritic knee was announcing rain. Ugh. Nothing worse than taking city kids, bringing them to a ranch where they had to be inside. Oh well, no sense in being down, we'll make lemonade. Tonight is French Riviera night. It will be amazing. The kids will love the frozen drink machines, the messy food, the singing, and the neckerchiefs.

Abbey felt a new appreciation pulling through the Sweet Silver Ranch entrance, this was a place that she felt comfortable and knew. So different from her first entrance.

"Geves and Bug, time to wake up. Geves, honey look at the horses. Bug, Bug, Winston! Wake up!"

"Win, we're here, we're really here. Oh I wish granny could see this. Suzanna will be so jealous!" squealed Genevieve.

Bug was slow to awaken, but he quickly caught up with his sister, "Oh man….Mom, can I go fishing?"

"Sure honey, I think so, although it looks like rain. But I know you'll get to fish at some point." Answered Abbey.

"Oh mom!" always with attitude.

Abbey calmly pulled up to the lodge, smiled as she noted Frieda and her grin coming through the front door.

"Welcome back Abbey! Well you must be the amazing Genevieve, and the awesome Winston. Welcome to Sweet Silver Ranch, my name is Frieda and I am so glad that you are here. Your Mom just wasn't happy here without the two of you."

Frieda had bewitched the two children and had them on either side of her while entering the lodge. Abbey followed after getting some things from the van. That certainly didn't take too long. Maybe all the preparation, oh who knows, maybe the kids are just comfortable with her. It was amazing.

Frieda showed the kids and Abbey to their rooms. They were delighted with the lodge, and the giant soft beds. But Frieda was pretty certain the kids would wind up in bed with their mama. Abbey's kids were really cute and obviously delighted with their mom. She must have worked herself to death to give those kids so much of herself. Frieda couldn't imagine being a single mother. She was really impressed with Abbey and she felt a love for her that could only come from God.

"Genevieve, darling are you ready to meet some critters? Get your brother and let's go."

Frieda suddenly had all the energy in the world. "Abbey, honey, why don't you grab some water and some treats from the kitchen, you know I think we should take the kiddos to meet the same favorites today."

Abbey gladly complied, then looked out the window, "Miss Frieda, it looks like rain."

"That's fine, we'll be headed towards the barn. It'll be great." Frieda responded.

As the kids raced out the front door, Abbey grabbed a bucket with carrots, celery and some water bottles. She was thrilled to see her kids here. They practically skipped to the barn with Frieda leading the way.

Frieda introduced the kids to the fillies, Grace and Hope, the llamas, the emus, the ostrich, and the hens. In between Geves fell in love with some kittens and Bug found mud! The kids ran from creature and barn to pond and hay bales. The kids had a great time and ran with abandon. Abbey barely kept up, she laughed and found the myriad of benches dotting the property. Funny how you don't notice nice quiet spaces until you are in the company of your children. She watched her children closely and noticed a peacefulness. For the first time it occurred to her, they weren't bickering. Wow! They were having such a great time together. Maybe this is what brought people to this camp and brought families out of it. Interesting concept. She needed her notebook. Suddenly, the sky opened up and rain pellets started hitting all of them. The kids squealed and Frieda danced. Abbey sprang up, ready to run, but stopped when she saw Frieda and realized that it felt cleansing. The half-ran and half played all the way back to the lodge.

Giggling like a pack of hyenas, they all practically fell in the door of the lodge. Frieda announced. "We need to start providing shampoo outdoors!" And then, "Off to your rooms, rest young ones and then get your outfits on, tonight we dine on the French Riviera.

Abbey found Frieda in the kitchen later, "How did you know my kids' sizes, Miss Frieda?"

Startled, Frieda spun around, "Oh honey, I thought you'd be resting. Well, I guessed. You showed me your precious pictures that first day and you told me they were eight and six and a half so I guessed. It hasn't been that long, and remember there have been hundreds of kids here over the years. Our pastors are a prolific breed, pardon my play on words," Frieda giggled.

The kids looked picture perfect. Abbey looked pretty cute, too. The French berets, striped shirts and neckerchiefs. Very French, very Fun! They entered the hall and couldn't believe the tables, the settings, and all the small touches that made it feel like the room was completely different. There was a waterless waterway complete with bridge and large fake white swans. Okay, so maybe Abbey had never been to the French Riviera, but for tonight she would pretend. The kids were flying around the room looking at and touching almost everything. They were ducking under a 15-20 foot cardboard Eifel tower, knocking it just a bit. Poor Winston couldn't help himself; it was just too much flutter and glitter. Too much excitement. It was a bit like a grown up playground, too. There was this long curvy buffet with the most amazing display in the center: a beautiful lit vase made of ice filled with flowers, (it appeared they were from the property). Flowing down from the ice was what looked like an explosion of fruits. Whole fruits, cut fruits, bowls of blueberries, strawberries, kiwis, pineapples, mangoes all cascading down to silver chafing dishes with hot fondues in white chocolate, dark chocolate, and milk chocolate. There were crystal bowls with coconut powdered and brown sugars placed in between and, upon closer inspection, several creatures shaped out of fruit. There was a fuzzy kiwi mouse with a lemon curl tail and raisin eyes. There were frogs made out of limes, melon swans and rabbits out of papaya.

It was a glorious fruit fantasy. There was a machine at the end that was churning out some concoction and a station set up with what appeared to be a flamethrower, (Abbey was really excited to find out what that was for). Chefs were running back and forth. Chafing dishes were steaming and being filled with amazing smelling concoctions. In between the artichoke dishes, and the veal limonene were kids style foods: French Toast and fried Brie with raspberry sauce, Chicken nuggets, (thank goodness, Abbey knew Bug would eat that), and French fries. This was remarkable. The colors, smells and textures could have kept Abbey writing all day. It was beautiful.

A large chime sounded outside announcing the dinner to folks still out on the ground. There were several more campers there this week. Over one hundred men, women, and children streamed in, all wore neckerchiefs and looked famished. The music was going and Abbey could see the excitement on their faces as they entered the hall. Abbey paused to listen to one of the wives as she described the scene to her husband. She was terribly excited and gushed about the cut glass look of the ice, the blues and reds, the waterless waterway with chasing white lights. She did a breathtaking job of explaining all of it to her blind husband. It was wonderful. Abbey knew then that this was exactly how she would write her article. For the blind, someone who couldn't see it for themselves. The couple obviously enjoyed all of it. For the husband, Abbey guessed, he got to see more because of his wife than he could have on his own. This convinced Abbey of the way to go. Abbey subconsciously looked around for Matt. She didn't even know she was looking until she caught his eye. Matt had come in through the kitchen, naturally and he had donned an apron. Frieda must be short staffed.

Matt approached, "Abbey welcome back. What am I saying, Frieda will fire me," he paused, and swept his arm back, "Mademoiselle welcome to the Riviera."

It was without a doubt, the worst French accent Abbey had ever heard. A laugh bubbled up and Abbey choked, "Pepe-le-pew, I presume?"

"Mademoiselle, Fife La Fume?"

"Don't even go there, I do not know enough of this stuff. I was just comparing your accent. It is pretty terrible. Didn't you acquire the gift with the years overseas?"

"Nah, I was little and unfortunately I just never could do the accents. I have no gift with languages. But Frieda likes anyone working to put on for the fun of it. Many of the pastors and their families are on such tight budgets that they could never afford to go on their own. This is Frieda's way of being Auntie Mame."

"Wow, now that is a throwback. I loved Auntie Mame, it was one of my mom's favorite movies. Wasn't that Rosalind Russell? I loved how she changed her apartment every so often. It was fantastic. You know Frieda is a bit of that character." Abbey was just getting too much here for just an article. Maybe her editor would be interested in a prolonged piece. She would have to get writing and see what happened. It sure would be hard to stop.

Suddenly in a blur of red, blue, white and blonde, Abbey's kids landed near them.

"Pastor Matt, I would like you to meet my flying squadron, Genevieve and Winston."

Matt turned on the charm and the bad French accent, kissing Winston on each cheek and Genevieve's hands, " A pleasure to make your acquaintance." After Winston's grimace over his kisses, they both cracked up. Matt made Geves promise him a dance after dinner. She gladly accepted. Matt bowed and the kids just beamed.

The music died out and Matt stepped to the middle of the room. He was all seriousness as he asked everyone to bow their heads and prayed: "Father God, we are gathered together to praise your wonderful name. You are our very help and our source of all that is god. We thank you Father for the amazing provision for this special place and the love that goes into all that we enjoy. Father your creation is outstanding your creativity matchless, please help us to enjoy the family that you have created and the body of people that you have assembled. Bless this meal, may it refresh and nourish our bodies. Go with us Lord, be with us and help us to cause you to smile. We love you, our Father. Amen."

"Amens" were heard all around. Abbey and the kids complied. Winston was a bit too loud. All were invited to eat and enjoy and the music began anew.

Frieda made certain that Abbey, the children, and Matt were seated at her table, although she rarely sat. Frieda and Matt bounced in and out of the kitchen helping the staff. Abbey wished the kids weren't with her, so that she could help. But it was great watching them pay attention to all that went on. They sampled a lot of the foods and the kids spent a lot of time with the fruit and chocolate. The kids begged for the flaming cherries jubilee, Abbey doubted they would actually eat it, but relented and ordered one to share. The flame was exciting, and the cherries were fantastic. At least the blowtorch was explained. The food, singing, and dancing all seemed to be a big part of the ranch. Although that confused Abbey because she thought religious people were opposed to all of that. She would have to ask some more questions.

Matt returned for his dance with Geves, Abbey begged Winston to join her on the floor, but he refused. Abbey let it go, he's still a little boy, she thought. I used to hold him in my arms and dance all over the place. He used to giggle when she would dip him. While it would be nice to go back in time it was amazing watching him grow up. Winston is still really noisy but he is also very contemplative. He loves fiercely and hurts equally. He is so passionate about justice that he often only sees his truth. It was a struggle but it was amazing to know this boy. Abbey loved him so much!

After the big meal and the dance, the kids were reminded that they were planning to help Frieda put the chickens to bed. So they ran off with her. Abbey helped Matt with putting away France, and started peppering Matt with questions.

Matt tried to be diplomatic, "Abbey slow down. I'll be here tomorrow for several hours, and then again in the afternoon on Sunday. I am happy to answer your questions, but some take a bit longer than others."

"Okay, fair enough, but can you just explain the dancing, drinking and music. Aren't there an awful lot of you that don't believe in all of that?"

"Sure there are groups of church divisions that shun dancing and certain types of music and drinking. Frieda tries to give the broadest of experiences for her guests without crossing her personal beliefs. She works her best to organize her groups to be of similar thinking. Frieda does not have a liquor license and serves no alcohol. Some of the people who really want wine or something bring it themselves to their trailers or cabins but it has to be kept there. Frieda is pretty tight about that rule, 'never cause a brother to stumble,' music is a little bit more complicated because everyone seems to have a different opinion and some is simple taste. Frieda does her best. She always prepares an itinerary in advance. Guests have many options and are never forced to participate. I can think of only one instance where it was a problem."

"Do tell!"

"Let me just tell you what Frieda said at the time, I've never forgotten it: 'We can never condemn someone for not doing something that they believe to be wrong. Whether or not we agree, we do not criticize. We will support and do our best not to thwart their efforts.' I think that taught me all I ever needed to know about the diversity within our faith," stated Matt.

"So what does that mean?" asked Abbey

"I won't find fault with you for not dancing, or not drinking, or not listening to Christian pop or rock I will respect your decisions and choices and I will not attempt to get you to do any of these things. If you believe that it is God honoring to avoid these things, then by all means, avoid them."

"Okay, that makes sense." Abbey grew pensive; she tapped a spoon against her leg absentmindedly. She wanted to ask more, "I grew up with a grandma that was the queen of the don'ts...don't do this or that. My mom went a little nuts the other direction with follow your heart. God allows us to be human. It is hard to know where to draw the line. I think with raising my own children, I am beginning to understand the confusion. When do I allow my precious daughter to date, or what music to listen to? It is hard to know how much room to give, when you know the dangers inherent. Some things are so culturally acceptable, that they make you seem strange."

All at once, a crash and no lights. Abbey screamed without realizing it. Matt rushed to her side, and assured her that the generator would kick up in a second. Abbey felt like a fool and wanted to get to her kids and mostly away from Matt. As soon as the lights came back up, Abbey excused herself to check on her children.

Matt finished up in the dining room and got ready to leave for the night. He checked with Frieda and found her talking to Jonathan, the latest handyman on the ranch. Jonathan was a great gift to the ranch and managed to keep everything up and running, and in tip top order. He was another one of God's great provisions for Frieda. Jonathan worked at the ranch for insurance benefits only. He was a fan of Frieda's and probably had a crush on her, but she didn't ever seem to notice. She responded like she was everyone's mother and not a lovely lady.

Matt guessed that Jonathan was around seventy but it was hard to figure. Frieda and Jonathan were discussing the power outage when it kicked back on. The generator had carried them through once again. In retrospect, it was nothing but they tried to stay on top of any problems at the ranch. All the animals and barns had checked out, no fences were down in the immediate pastures, but someone would need to check the back pastures and Moses, of course, in the morning.

Matt said goodnight to them and made the forty-five minute drive home. He hated to leave without praying with Abbey, but he planned to make his drive time all about her. He prayed as he headed out for Frieda, as always.

Meanwhile, Frieda made her way up to bed. She could hear some soft little snores coming from Winston's room. It reminded her of her own boys. Boys were so different. Frieda had three sons, no girls. The biggest difference was the noise level. They just can't do anything quietly, including sleep. Now, that of course is unless they are being sneaks. Her own boys spent hours hunting. Frieda cracked up imagining her boys sneaking up on some poor unsuspecting animal. It was no wonder they rarely came home with anything. Usually, just took their guns for a walk.

Chapter 18

After an uneventful night of rain, the morning looked promising. The place looked and smelled so clean. Abbey looked out her window to see the fog lifting over the pastures, it was way too early. Both kids had come into bunk with her by four o'clock in the morning and she had to give up her bed. Bug snored and Geves kicked.

Abbey found fresh coffee in the kitchen, for which she was grateful. She made her way out to the wraparound porch and walked towards the back. The hills of Georgia were just gorgeous. It was a little cool and even kind of eerie, but pretty too. Abbey heard a cracking sound, but couldn't see anything. It made her nervous at first, but then the curious reporter came out... she wandered to the edge of the porch and saw Moses, coming towards her from the mist. Ethereal, like a part of the mist, there he was. She said hi to Moses and ran inside to grab some treats. She went back out, carrots in hand and reintroduced herself to the giant white horse. Moses reached down and blew in Abbey's face and smelled deeply of her scent. He then wrapped his head around her shoulder and leaned his head on her back. It felt like the best hug! She was so delighted, what a great way to wake up. She half-wished the kids could see this. But then again, it was a nice private moment with an incredible creature. She wondered about Moses' understanding. In many ways he seemed such a perfect Hercules of a horse, and yet just knowing his weakness, he became approachable. People were made up of faults, Abbey wondered to herself if that was why God was so unapproachable for her.

Frieda's soft footsteps came around the bend, "well, well Moses. We must have a fence down. It is good to see my friends together this morning."

"Good morning Miss Frieda, how are you?' asked Abbey.

"Well, I slept beautifully. Have you ever read Suzanne Sommers? She is just the best writer. She wrote about life after forty, and she explained that she takes twenty-five milligrams of melatonin for a good night's sleep. So, I listened to her and have been taking fifteen milligrams and sleeping like a baby. That, and the thrill and exhaustion of running around with your kiddos. How about you? I saw that the children migrated during the night," Frieda responded.

This lady was always saying something unexpected. Her mind was always working. When in the world did she have time to read?

"Oh, I was fine until Geves started her kicking routine. That little girl can pack a wallop. I think she swims in her sleep, that or she has some latent ninja tendencies."

"Abbey, have you ever seen an active dog or young puppy sleep? They do appear to be swimming. It cracks me up, unless they are large and in my bed." Frieda laughed, "I remember my youngest was the worst. My parents were staying in a hotel one time and they invited Caleb to spend the night. They returned looking so haggard, apparently my little tiny boy managed to cover the king-size bed the entire night."

"Well my Geves could take the challenge."

"This is why we have children, Abbey, to learn how to love, serve, and suffer. It is truly a labor of love, and it is one we do gladly, most of the time. God uses a mother's love to teach us so much. He even compares his love to that of a mother's love. The fierceness of it, the sureness of it. He speaks in the Psalms of gathering his chicks to him and covering them in his wings. You should be here when the chicks are hatching. It shouldn't be too much longer, but you'd see it first hand. It is awesome. All the chicks pretty much look alike but a hen will grab hers, all of hers, and protect them, no matter what. You know I remember seeing a story about a hen in the middle of a huge fire. She had used her body to shield her babies, and they survived. The pictures were disturbing. Those darling, perfect, little, yellow, fuzz balls coming out of the charred remains left an indelible image in my head. The truth is we will protect our children, even to our own detriment."

Abbey remembered some articles that she had written about just this thing.

"You know you are right, I couldn't understand it until I had my own. There is something all consuming about being a mom. Did God really compare himself to a mom?"

"Let's see, I believe it is in Luke and Matthew. Jesus is quoted mourning over Jerusalem's sin." Frieda grabbed a bible and returned to Abbey's side. " I am just so bad with addresses. Here it is… 'O Jerusalem, Jerusalem, you who kill the prophets and stone those sent to you, how often have I longed to gather your children together, as a hen gathers her chicks under her wings, but you were not willing.' My notes say that Jesus was so saddened because Jerusalem was the city of God and the largest in the nation of Israel. God had sent many prophets to her over the years, and they were all rejected. I know your children are young yet. But, have you ever wanted to teach your children by telling them something, only to have them ignore it and get hurt?"

"Well sure, Bug has to touch everything and it is always a challenge to treat his burns or pinches, due to his not listening. God must get really frustrated with us, huh?"

"Yes, I often wonder how God can stand us. I know what you mean about your Bug, my own sons were just terrible. I have quite a memory of frustrations over times they did not listen. However, I only have to remember that I, too, frustrate God. I don't learn, even from the same mistakes over and over again. So, let's see about your lovelies and get them fed. I imagine they will have a big day today."

"Okay, sounds good. Do you think I can convince them to let their mother nap?"

Abbey said this half-jokingly. It was nice to share time with Frieda. She seemed to mother everyone. Abbey wondered what the story was with Frieda's children. She would ask over the course of the day.

After getting the kids some breakfast and speaking with one of the young men at the ranch, they had their day somewhat planned. Fishing, horseback riding, a picnic, and a ride around to meet Moses. Frieda had arranged to get him escorted back to his pasture, and ready for visitors.

Genevieve, Winston, and Abbey dressed for a day outdoors, loaded up on sunscreen, bug control, and chapstick. The kids were bouncing off of each other and every time Abbey tried to put sunscreen on Bug, it was like bathing a cat. He refused to be still. Philip, their guide for the day, was a nice and energetic young man. Somewhere around twenty years old, he was right in between the kids and their mom. Cool by the kids' standards and old enough to make Abbey feel safe. They immediately went to the pond up the hill, which was huge and had a dock, a grill, and several small paddleboats. Philip set the kids up to fish from shore. He mentioned to Abbey that the kids seemed too wound up to get in the small boat.

The fish were biting in no time. After the first thousand pictures and giggles, Abbey took a good look around. It was really beautiful; weeping willows with yellow buds were dipping into the pond. The still water was cold, every time the fish was pulled from the water, Genevieve would shriek and shout "cold mama". The rocks and grasses growing along the bank were colorful and warm. With the water from all the rain the previous day and the trees and hills in the distance, it felt lush and rich. Abbey longed for a hammock and a good book. She could well imagine that anyone could find rest here; even the most tortured soul would have to relax.

After a short ride on some very slow ponies, the kids were hungry. Philip produced a picnic lunch and took them to some great picnic tables in what seemed like a whole new area of the ranch. This place seemed enormous. Must be all the hills, thought Abbey. Abbey realized that she hadn't thought enough about her article, may as well pump Philip for some insights.

"So Philip, how long have you worked here at the ranch?" asked Abbey.

" Well it's been summers since I was twelve, and now I work during my spring break and sometimes, Miss Frieda will call me over Christmas break. She makes it easy for me. I love being here. I love the outdoors and I get paid to show others, it just doesn't get much better." Responded Philip.

"That sounds pretty good, where are you going to school, and what is your major?"

"I am actually attending Mercer College and my major is in accounting, with a minor in agricultural studies. I hope to help my family and other farming families with their books. Farmers aren't known for keeping good books, so I hope to be a resource. It may not seem really exciting but my plan is to be my own boss and work for clients that I will respect. I figure I'll be working a lot of nights, weekends, and off season times so that the farmers can do their work and meet with me when they cannot be productive on their farms."

"Now that is a great plan. Although, I guess I thought, there wasn't much farming anymore. I was under the impression that more and more of the farming in this country were becoming the mega farms. Is that right?" asked Abbey.

"Yes and no. While it is true that the mega farms are taking over large tracts, they aren't the bulk of the produce in the U.S. Actually; there are thousands of small farms across this country. We are a dying breed, for sure, but those who love it, love it. I think there will always be a lot of us, even the hobby farmers. Did you know that many of the wineries in the U.S. are a result of people wanting to get back to the farm, but too pretentious to do it." Philip paused for a moment, "You know Miss Abbey, I think if more people like you would get out of the city and take their kids, they'd see the draw. It is a peaceful existence. There is so much less fighting, less arguing, less frustration. The work is physically grueling but we're too tired to fuss when the day is over. We also get plenty of vitamin D and very little smog. I'll quit preaching. " Philip laughed out loud. "There is more than enough of that here!!!!"

Abbey laughed too and helped Philip clean up the picnic. They walked towards an outbuilding, where Philip said he was getting the mule, whatever that was. Suddenly there was a roar and Philip came out of the building n a funky looking golf cart. With 'MULE' printed on it's side.

Abbey and the kids piled on board, and headed towards the back pasture, and abbey hoped, Moses.

As they rode, Philip pointed out a variety of small animals and large birds. The kids were amazed to see a petrel fishing in the stream. It was grey and blue and looked prehistoric, it stood perfectly still on one leg until it would spot food and then it would grab the small fish so quickly you could miss the whole thing in the process of blinking. They saw a whole herd of deer, spotted babies, bright shiny as copper Does, all grazing in the tall green grass. Philip drove along the fence line where a herd of bison were sunning and drinking from a muddy pond. Philip would pause along the way showing them the ripe gooseberries, which, while edible tasted terrible. Genevieve reminded Abbey that Snow White made gooseberry pies for the seven dwarfs. They passed through a hedgerow into an open field; Winston popped up and pointed screaming at a golden eagle carrying something. Abbey was startled but got Philip to stop 'the Mule' and they watched the eagle swoop up to a huge nest in the top of an old cottonwood tree. The kids were enthralled. Abbey thought that the day couldn't be any better. A few minutes later, they passed through a gate, and there in the shade was Moses. The 'Mule' stopped and Philip helped the kids out while grabbing a bag with a bunch of carrots and what appeared to be cookies.

The horse saw them and headed towards them. He wasn't moving quickly but he was purposeful. He definitely wanted them to visit. Abbey told the children about Moses and they seemed excited to be around him, although she could sense they were a bit nervous due to his sheer size.

Moses slowly approached and put his head down, level with Winston and Genevieve. They were slow to respond until he blew air out his nose at them. Genevieve's hair moved and she giggled. Winston thought it was funny the way the horse was sniffing him, he claimed that Moses was trying to tickle him. Abbey and Philip wound up feeding Moses all the carrots and horse cookies while Bug rubbed his velvety soft nose. Abbey hugged Moses and reminded him that she thought he was awesome. The kids got bored quickly and were ready to go do something else. It was past time to get the kids in to rest and clean up before dinner. Where had the day gone…? Abbey hated to leave Moses but she couldn't wait to see what dinner would be tonight.

After returning to the lodge, Frieda assured Abbey that she needed to rest with her kids and just get ready for dinner, which she promised with a twinkle in her eyes, would be fun. The kids eventually fell asleep and Abbey, while not able to sleep, rested a bit.

A little before supper, Frieda popped in with some 'outfits' for them. Abbey's was a spectacular oriental Kimono style dress in blue silk . Geves had a similar style dress in pink and for Bug there was a cool Samurai looking outfit. They each had hats and for Abbey, earrings. Abbey couldn't wait to wake the kids. Frieda said she would be back for Winston, as she had a special job for him.

Winston and Frieda had been gone for two minutes when Abbey heard a loud gong!

Oh! I hope he was supposed to ring that, Abbey thought. They wound their way down to the dining hall and took in the lanterns, oriental rugs, screens, and all the beautifully fringed table linens. *Welcome to the Orient* read the sign at the door.

The smell was a combination of ginger, cinnamon, and soy, it was intoxicating. The food was served at small intimate tables with pretty little teacups. Guests were able to pick entrees, which were delivered by oriental princesses. Abbey was used to drive through Chinese, so she imagined this to be like a very posh restaurant. Abbey and the kids loved the bright linens. The egg rolls were enormous and filled whole plates, stuffed with shrimp, pork, cabbage, and a ton of veggies that even Winston didn't seem to notice. He soaked his in duck sauce and devoured almost half of it.

It was announced that the famous Sword and Samaria team would perform, followed by Geisha Dancers. The Sword team reminded Abbey of the color guard or the elite military presentations that she had seen the presentation of the swords and the movements were so precise and beautiful. The waving swords caught the lights and kept everyone enraptured. Winston couldn't take his eyes off of the swords. The Geisha dancers made everyone want to get up and move. It was very modest and fluid, the ladies used fans and umbrellas to spin and twirl. Genevieve pointed out that it looked like a whole lot of butterflies. Leave it to a little girl to call it right.

The kids were drawn up to dance with the ladies and Winston joined as soon as he saw a slew of other boys getting up. Abbey laughed and danced in her seat watching her children turn into butterflies.

With the festivities over, the kids exhausted, Abbey took them up to bed. Frieda was nearby, so Abbey changed and went back to help with clean up.

As she headed towards the dining hall, she realized that she felt really good. She looked forward to pitching in and found that she enjoyed both the comaraderie and the self-satisfaction of contributing.

As soon as she hit the dining hall, she ran into Matt. He was dragging tables and stacking chairs.

"Hi Matt, I didn't realize that you were here. Have you been here all night?"

"Hey Abbey. The youth group and I had some talking to do, and then they started on the outdoor games, I figured I was of better use in here. How are Geves and Bug enjoying themselves, did they love the swords?"

"Absolutely, they are having the time of their lives. I am, too. I have to say it is a really different experience coming here with my kids. They are showing me a whole ranch that I missed the last time. It is a gift to see the world through your kids' eyes."

"I'm delighted for you all. I have never had the pleasure of seeing it through my own kid's eyes, but I have had a little taste with some of the big brother kids. It is like a whole new world for them. I think especially for someone like me who grew up coming here, I take it for granted. I miss the basics that are so obvious to anyone who hasn't been here before. I love this place but it is more like home, we miss the particulars when we become too familiar."

"So what is your youth group here for? Don't you have to preach in the morning," asked Abbey?

"The youth group is having one of their work/lock-ins. Frieda lets them earn their keep here. They can clean up around the camp, work in the kitchen, organize or fix some props, and then they get to have a lock-in and party in the barn house. Frieda always does so much for the kids, but mostly it's the time together that builds the relationships. The kids also get to run chapel in the morning. We have four parents who will stay to keep the peace. I'll be driving back tonight, and yes, preach in the morning. Then I'll return in the afternoon with the church bus, I am, unfortunately, the only one with a license to drive the bus."

Abbey laughed, "I can only imagine, you have to drive the bus, of course! Is there anything that you don't do?"

"Hey, I'll have you know that I am the proud pastor of a church of sixty-seven people, and still we have our own bus. I'm pretty proud of that fact. Our youth group is exploding but the kids have yet to get their parents to come and join the church. In due time. Did I tell you that I failed the first bus-driving test? I backed over a bunch of those orange cones on my first attempt, but by the third try, I nailed it."

They shared a laugh.

She watched Matt's face, seeking a twitch or wink or anything that might indicate dishonesty; none that she noted. It was so unusual for her to know a pastor like him- all those in her past had been such arrogant men, but she found herself wishing he was for real. She hoped that his humbleness wasn't just an act.

Tomorrow, Abbey decided, she was going to try to strike up conversations with some of the other pastors visiting the ranch. Maybe it was just at this place. Frieda had told her that this place was about letting the pastors be. Perhaps that was the difference.

Matt noticed that Abbey had already left their conversation, so he thought it best to go. " I'll need to head back now. You have a wonderful evening and hopefully I'll see you tomorrow. If not, please know that it has been my great pleasure to meet you and your children. Frieda really likes you, and she has excellent taste. I hope to read your article and perhaps we will meet again," he turned to go, "Good night Abbey."

She heard 'goodnight' and responded "Goodnight Matt, drive safely." Definitely time for bed, *I am zoning.* To bed.

Abbey peeked in on the kids. They were both snoring, all the fresh air was really knocking them out, and they were eating well, too. She wished she could afford to provide this kind of life for her kids, but it was impossible. On her salary she was lucky to have a working car. Forget land, amazing food, and animals. IT did all seem to suit the kids though. As she readied for bed, she wondered if Frieda's own children had been raised here, it seemed like Frieda was part of the land. Abbey would press her tomorrow. She stifled a yawn and was asleep in no time.

Chapter 19

Sunday morning saw the chimes going in the little chapel. Abbey dragged the kids from their beds and they made their way to the dining hall. The kids ate quickly and decided to take in the whole ranch experience. They walked towards the chapel, into which dozens of people streamed.

A group of teenagers were in front of the church singing a simple tune about God reigning. They were also teaching everyone the simple sign language that went with the songs. Geves saw Philip and ran up to him. Both kids wound up joining the teens with the hand motions. She hadn't seen them do that before, but maybe they had seen it at school or on television or something. After three similar songs the kids returned to sit with her. The teens were apparently leading the service.

Abbey listened while watching her kids, really focusing on what the teens were saying. They read from the book of Romans about living a life of prayer, hope, and patience. Each had a small portion and read other Scriptures that Abbey hadn't heard before. All tying into the theme, <u>Joyful in hope, Patient in Affliction, and Faithful in Prayer.</u> Somehow it rang true, but Abbey wondered how you could do all those things. Afflictions came at the most inopportune times, and she had yet to find any joy in it. It seemed a little over her head. However, Genevieve seemed to really get into it. Of course, what would an eight year old have to be worried about? Geves never had to wonder how she was going to raise two kids with no dad. Easier to just be the kid. Abbey wanted that so much for them both. She knew that Winston worried more. He seemed to need more security, hording his money and toys. He would always stop before making a decision to look at his options. Safety seemed to be his pension. Abbey wished she could take away his need to be the 'man of the house,' he was only six and half.

The music had stopped, the prayers ended and Abbey was ready to take her kids back out to being kids. She was stopped by Philip and one of the teens.

"Excuse us Miss Abbey, this is Jana Kay and she is here for a serve day, we wondered if we could take Winston and Genevieve on a scavenger hunt. We have teams that are dividing up the kids in the camp to go hunting." Philip handed Abbey the list of items while Jana Kay smiled and talked to the kids.

The list was wonderful; twigs shaped like the kids initials, arrowheads, animal bones, feathers, numbers of trees along fences, and ponds shaped like dinosaurs. Abbey thought it was a terrific idea and realized she had probably better get some more info for her article. "Okay, we'll meet back here later. Oh, what about lunch?"

Jana Kay and Philip said "noon" at the same time and then cracked up. Apparently, this was a regular thing for the kids and Philip. Abbey nodded and headed towards the lodge. She walked past the dry lot where Gracie and Hope were and couldn't help watching them for a while. They were the most awkward looking things, she got the giggles just watching them run and play with each other. It reminded her of Bambi on ice, all legs and no coordination.

In no particular hurry and relishing the time, Abbey made her way up to the lodge. She found Frieda sitting by herself with her eyes closed. While Abbey was figuring out whether or not to interrupt, Frieda opened her eyes and smiled.

"Good Morning, Abbey, did you take the children to Chapel?"

"Yes, it was very well done. I was especially impressed by the teens. Are they all from Matt's church?"

Frieda nodded, "Yes, aren't they a wonderful group? Many of them come here to get away from their homes. Most have just learned the joy of serving. They really encourage me. I think they put together the most ingenious games, they genuinely like to help."

"They showed me their scavenger hunt list," she shook her head smiling, "ponds shaped like dinosaurs? I may ask for a copy for my article."

"Oh they'd be happy to give it to you. I think they'd be delighted to be included in the article. I have a deal with them, they get to come here and have lock-ins once a month, but only if they help me by working around here. Most don't have a lot of money and I think it makes them feel pretty grown up to be working. Mostly they do stuff with the campers, and help me with clean up after our suppers. They also get to lead Chapel, if they like. We leave that up to Matt. He has to feel confident that they will lead well. They must present to him what they want to do, and then he approves or disapproves. I used to try to get in the middle of it, but that boy feels deeply responsible for their spiritual development and so he ahs taken it on himself. It's a wonderful thing to watch."

"Miss Frieda, if you've got some time now, I'd love to ask you some questions- find out a bit more about you."

"Abbey, I have plenty of time for you, let me just check on tonight's dinner and we'll go for a walk. Okay?"

Chapter 20

Abbey nodded and ran to get her shoes, pens, and small notepads.

By the time Frieda reappeared, Abbey was ready to go. They walked straight out towards the barns- it seemed that Frieda was happiest out among the trees and animals.

Abbey began, "You told me about your prompting for <u>Sweet Silver Ranch</u>, but what made you think that you could do something like this?"

"Well now, that's a loaded question. Let's see… I went to college in Atlanta. It was a small wonderful school, but I had always preferred working to school. So, while I was in college, I worked for a major hotel, first in room service, then in the restaurant, and finally by my senior year, I was a catering director. I was in a convention town, and I felt like a professional party planner. I'd always been kind of a party girl, so it was fun-I got to wear great suits, and let my creative mind go a little nuts. I worked with amazing chefs who could take a chainsaw and turn ice into a flying eagle, and banquet captains who could fit all manner of people into a particular space. I had a lot of fun, and even managed to graduate from college, not with any great grades, mind you. I spent years in the food and beverage end of it and got to participate in some wild events. One of my greatest successes was the 'Taste of Buckhead" all the best restaurants and our hotel were lined up outdoors to show off what we could do. When I found out that we were stuck between two of the best I panicked and decided to do something off of the wall. At the time, everyone in Atlanta was competing for the Sunday Brunch crowd and we had instituted a children's buffet as part of ours, so that's what I brought. We created low tables; decorated with Disney sheets and served corn dogs, chicken nuggets, chocolate candies, bananas dipped in chocolate, and peanut butter and jelly sandwiches sans the crust. We also created these beanie style hats that had propellers. The event was black tie and evening gown, by the time the General Manager arrived; you could see a sea of our beanies all throughout the event. We actually had to take a list of names and addresses because we ran out. Half the tuxedoed men were carrying corn dogs. Many were excited by the fact that there was food that they could pronounce! It was a hoot. Anyway, it was a great success and the fun of it was intoxicating."

Frieda waved towards a bench under a tree, sat down, and continued, "All that definitely got into my blood and came in handy when I ran a youth group at my church, and when I was involved in women's ministries. The funny thing was that I always thought big-it was so hard for me to temper or scale back, I guess I always wanted another 'sea of beanies with propellers'. I got quite a reputation at church and people were never quite sure what to do with me. Some thought I was showing off, others just thought I was out of touch. Our associate pastor was the one who always let me go and do things my way, but there was always this terrific tension. We get caught up in the churches about what appears to be right and wrong. Between doing something well and appearing to spend or do too much. Unfortunately there are always the inevitable toes to be stepped on. I never set out to step on anyone's toes, but well they just seemed to wind up under my big feet. Eventually, I got tired of having to do back flips to avoid conflict...politics are not my nature."

"So were you asked to leave the church," asked Abbey?

"Oh my no. People were always gracious and wonderful on the outside; I just gradually had to pull back. That was really hard for me. I kept pulling back until I didn't quite know what to do. It was rough. I was raising my boys, and wound up home schooling them. That had to take precedence in my life, and so that's where I poured my efforts. My boys were my sole focus for years. I did have a Bible study in my home and tried to serve the ladies in my immediate community. It was fun cooking for them, but I still had this heart for pastors. I was also very committed to my neighbor. He was desperately old and lonely. When I first met Tom, he had no use for me. We had very little money, one car, and my son was sick a lot. My first born son had died as an infant, so I was desperate to keep my second son healthy."

Frieda stood up and stretched but kept talking, "my boy and I spent a lot of time outside visiting with our neighbor who became like a Grandpa. He had Black Angus cattle, and he would walk or ride a four-wheeler back to the edge of our yard everyday. He would just sit out there until we came outside to say hello. Over the years, we grew to love him. He was tough, but quite a sucker for my boys. When my third boy came along, we'd practically been adopted. Tom is the one who left us the land, and the money for the barns. He had animals that he wanted us to care for, so he left us enough to take care of them well. This is what started the ranch."

Frieda began walking and tried to point and describe how the land had originally been divided up. She gestured towards fences and pointed saying east, west- but abbey didn't really get all of it. The fact was that the old man had given them over two hundred acres, apparently Frieda and her husband had purchased another one hundred and fifty. The acreage came very cheap because it was all land-locked, (with no access to a street). Acres weren't something that Abbey could really grasp but she did know that the land was vaster than she had originally though.

Frieda went on to explain the trailers, the electrical, the wells, and the barns. The animals were another story. "Most of the animals were either unwanted or just good fortune. God has provided us with enough horses for riders, and plenty of variety to keep things interesting. Even the bison were a gift from another farmer. He gave us over five hundred head and they keep on reproducing. We've really enjoyed them. They are a bit intimidating, but they provide some wonderful food and a bit of income for the ranch. We've even been able to donate some meat to a homeless shelter in Atlanta."

Abbey still hadn't found exactly the right answer so she suggested. "How do you afford to keep the ranch operations? How do you provide such fancy foods, and all the help?"

"A lot of the help is from people who are on sabbatical, either missionaries on leave, or seminary students & professors in between assignments or on break. We have a paid staff of sixteen to eighteen people at any given time. Matt and others are here because it feels like home to them. I don't currently have a foreman, but I have the Agricultural or Ag students from Mercer University who deal with the bison and help with the chickens and the goats. I also have a retirement program for 4H students, kids who have become too attached to their projects and don't want them sold for food. They can bring their 4H animal out here and leave them for free. They have to visit for at least two weekends a year and help with their animal's home. It seems to work well. My dad is here all the time and he helps the pastors with any business questions. We do have classes here three times per year which gives the pastors an opportunity to learn business, legal, human resource, and financial matters. We try to run them in tandem to weeks with their families. Oh, and there's Jonathan, he's priceless – works here for simple insurance. He retired from the railroad after being a machinist- he has been a lifesaver, and just loves the pastors. You met Philip; he and several of the students over at Mercer love to work here during breaks, I'm still trying to convince the school to give them credits for their work here."

Before Abbey could ask again about the food, Frieda snapped her fingers, "a lot of the food is grown here, and we cook it all ourselves. I am quite an efficient shopper with Amish families in Mableton; Leah, Sharon, Lori, and I do pretty much all of the cooking. Celia is around sometimes to help. Well except for oriental food, I just cannot make it taste like our Lori. She doesn't let me pay her at all. She is a wealthy woman who just loves the life here and the service. She lives here in a pretty bungalow and I think her grandkids just love coming to visit. But Sharon, is a dear friend whose kids and grandkids live in Atlanta. She is also a fantastic fundraiser for the ranch. Our pastors pay little to nothing to come here, but their churches will provide the funds for a week's stay, it's usually a gift from the congregation. Otherwise, we have scholarships set up by my late husband, my dad, and some wonderful, successful pastors. Most everyone who invests here has a connection with the ranch. You will find that many have come through our gates and many have been changed. All who come here are special to me, even though some haven't recognized it. I pray like crazy for every person here. It is my heart's desire that they will know that we love them, and that we so much want them to feel cared for. I do my level best. It may not ever be good enough, but God fills in all my cracks and crevices. Since this is God's ranch, He provides."

Abbey felt like she was finally getting a handle on the financial side of the ranch, time for more personal aspects. "So how did you know that God wanted you to start this camp?"

"I'm not sure that I ever knew it, Abbey. I am one of those people who has to hear the beeping, you know?" At Abbey's confused expression, Frieda continued. "Have you ever heard of people who get an e-mail and just know that God has spoken to them?" Abbey nodded so Frieda went on, "Well I'm not that quick. I am one of those people who gets hit by the truck, then hears the beeping as the truck backs over them for the third time before I get it."

Abbey chuckled, "I think I'm also someone in that beeping category."

"I'm so sorry for you dear, I wish I was a bit quicker. Anyway, God gifted us with the land, he gifted us with the money and the barns, he sent animals, and he even sent the pastors before I realized what was happening. I think that the ranch was running long before I got wind of it. It just kept happening. I love to serve, love to feed, and it just began. I think that is why I've never known how to charge or even what to charge. I think if anyone ever did a cost analysis, we'd be in trouble. Letting go and letting God do his thing is the only way this place works. I promise you Abbey; this was no more my idea than landing on the moon. I would imagine you've seen that in your own life." At Abbey's quiet look, Frieda went on, "Have you ever felt like you were sent by God to do a story?"

"Oh, I suppose. I haven't had one that has been a 'wow'. But I sort of see your point. Working for a Christian magazine has given me a lot of freedom to be with my kids. It has been very safe, and for that I am grateful."

"Who knows where you've been led, I haven't even figured everything out for myself, and I'm an old woman. Once, I had a foster daughter, I loved her, although it was not easy. I lost her two weeks before our final adoption was to go through. It was crushing and I never figured out why. Some things you just don't understand, they happen for a reason and perhaps it has nothing to do with me. Maybe it was for her; maybe it was for someone that she would meet later. I have often wondered if my sons will have use for that time later in their lives. God will use it, of that I am certain. I may never know why, at least in this world."

"Why would God do that? Why would he do something so painful to you and then not explain it?" abbey continued, "What's the point anyway?"

"Abbey, that's one of the difficult questions. It is why we must have faith. We do not have the mind of God. We cannot see all or know all especially from his vantage point. Have you ever done needlepoint, hooked a rug, or tapestry?"

"Oh sure, as a young girls, didn't everyone?"

"Well from underneath, it doesn't make any sense. You know all the knots and starts and stops, you cannot tell what it is until you flip it over. It's like that with God. He knows what will be; He knows things that we cannot imagine. He has a purpose and a plan. Abbey, what is hurting you that you are struggling against?"

"Honestly, Miss Frieda, it seems like everything. Why my divorce? Why are Genevieve and Winston being raised in near poverty without a father? Why did my dad die? Why so many things. I don't know. It's a hard life. I'm not blaming anyone. It just seems that if God is really in control, that things would be so much different."

"One thing you must never confuse is God's sovereignty and our ability to make mistakes. God allows us to blow it. He just works out the areas where we blow it. He takes even our bad stuff and works it into his plan. Great theologians who are a whole lot smarter than I am have struggled to explain this. Kirk Cameron made a wonderful movie about it; I am trying to get permission to show it down here. Anyway, I can tell you that there are consequences for our mistakes and missteps. God will give us options and he will respond to us, even pull us out of our pits. But never make the mistake that God causes us to fail or choose badly. Nope, God lets us choose."

"That's the thing I will never get, why does he let us do bad things, why does he let us choose a bad husband or a terrible career path? Why Frieda, what's the point? What does God gain by allowing us to screw up?"

"Hon, it isn't what God gains but what we gain. We learn, we grow, and we come to rely more fully on God when we have fallen. It is when you recognize your own failings that you can run to God. Okay let's take the puppet analogy-can you make Genevieve or Winston love something that they don't love? Would you want them to?"

"No, they are definitely not puppets. I wish I could make them like what is good for them. But you're talking more about feelings. I guess I sort of wish I could. I would love for them to appreciate me and love each other all the time…"

"Abbey, if you could make them appreciate you, what satisfaction would that bring? What if they were to jump for joy every time you came in the door and thank you for working and taking care of them? What if you trained them to do so? It might feel good for a week or a month but eventually, it wouldn't be very satisfying. After all, you trained them to do that, they don't genuinely feel it. It wouldn't be special; it would not even be desirable. God doesn't dictate our feelings or our actions to us or for us. God want us, but he wants us to want Him. We must choose that relationship, as well. It is critical that we love him. God has angelic beings who love him and see him. He didn't create us or our creation out of a need for company. He wanted to display his incredible creativity and he wanted something to have a relationship with where there is choice. I believe, and here some scholars will disagree with my verbiage but I believe that God calls us out to be his. He falls in love with each of us as he designed us. We discussed purpose before- He created us with gifts and talents and abilities, He pricks our hearts toward him. We have to take that leap towards him. We must say YES! 'Yes', I am a sinner'. 'Yes to Jesus', 'Yes to his death for our sins', 'Yes to his resurrection' and 'Yes to an eternity because of Jesus'. An eternity with God in the Holy of Holies. 'Yes to a relationship', living day to day with God as our Lord and love. Abbey, God wants to be everything you feel you are missing. He will be your husband, the father to your kids, your dad, and your provider! HE loves you. He really does."

Frieda swept Abbey up in a hug and just held on. Abbey was fidgety and not prone to hugging. It felt odd. She was trying to get her head around Frieda's input; her heart would take more time.

Abbey eased herself from Frieda's embrace, "I will think about all you've said. I know that you really believe what you say and I appreciate your sharing it with me. Do you mind if we take a break for a bit, I'm supposed to meet Philip and Jana Kay with the kids for Lunch, okay?!"

"Certainly dear, do you know which way to go?"

Abbey nodded and hurried off.

Chapter 21

Watching as Abbey headed off, Frieda began to pray quietly, "Father, please let this young lady find her way to you. Overcome my poor word choices and my stumbling. I pray Father that the Holy Spirit would so infuse her and her kids that she would be unable to pull herself away from you. Bless this family, help me Lord with discernment. Thank you Father for everything. I love you."

As Abbey made her way to the barn she thought of her grandmother, a Holy Roller and Bible thumper. All she ever said was no and you should not. Frieda sounded like her sometimes, but she had a bit of a sweeter twist. Grandma was not a lovable woman, but maybe Abbey had heard things in a peculiar way. Who knew? Her mom certainly didn't turn out to be the warmest person, Abbey always blamed in on Grandma. Oh whatever.

Outside the barn Abbey heard music, singing and shouting-sounded like a wild party. Abbey opened the door expecting total chaos, she smelled pizza. All the fancy food at the ranch was great, but pizza was her favorite! Geves and bug were in two separate groups and they both appeared to be having a good time. Bug was making faces with some other boys and Geves was stringing flowers for a necklace. Abbey figured they'd both be sneezing before too long. Oh well, it's a right of passage for a little girl. Abbey waved to Geves, Bug, however, didn't notice her. Geves held up her necklace and with Abbey's grin and nod, Geves held up a second necklace of clover that appeared to be for Abbey. Hay fever, or no hay fever, the kids were having a great time.

After a huge lunch of pizza; the teens separated themselves and broke up the party. The kids were disappointed that their time with the big kids was over and they reluctantly joined their parents. Abbey's own kids were quizzing, "what's next?"

Abbey knew she should get back to the article but put that thought on hold. She grabbed the kids, a few bottles of water, put her clover necklace on and set out towards the hatchery. She wanted to see how close the chicks and ducklings were to making an entrance.

Abbey opened the door to the hatchery and saw a young girl working with the lights over some eggs.

When the young lady turned, she offered a big smile, "Hi, I'm Jess, are you Abbey, the writer?"

"Yes, how did you guess?"

"Well, I've heard all about you and your kids, I am an agriculture or 'ag' student at Mercer and I heard about the article. It's kind of important to some of us around here. Frieda is trying to get the school to give us some credits for working here, and your article is something that I hope to use for proof of the actual work."

"Oh," Abbey said, "I don't know if it'll be any kind of help that way, but we'll see. I will definitely be discussing some of the work you guys do here. I, frankly, don't see how this ranch would function without you all."

"Perfect, so, Jess turned to the kids, we had some little ones hatch this morning, do ya wanna see some baby chickens?"

With a clear and resounding, "YES!" they went towards the back incubator.

Jess showed them fluffy white and yellow chicks all amazingly cuddly and soft. As they watched others were busting through their shells. Sharp little beaks, stiff little legs all topped in a wet slimy pile of feathers. They were much cuter after they dried out a bit. Jess told the kids all the facts and showed them the incubators. The kids were enamored with the fuzzy little things but equally enthralled with the ones still in the process of hatching. Abbey found herself wanting to help them get out of their shells faster. It seemed like such a lot of work for them to peck and claw their way out.

Geves, as if reading her mother's mind asked, "Why don't you help them get out, it's so hard?"

Jess smiled, "IT's actually really good for them to fight their way out- it builds up their little muscles and gets them hungry enough to eat when they are finally out. It is the way God designed it, he never makes mistakes."

Winston and Genevieve were satisfied with this answer and stooped to see if more chicks were hatching. Abbey was just tired of the whole God thing.

Winston asked Jess about the Chicken and Duck moms.

Jess tired to put it delicately but it was just a tough reality. "Unfortunately, when we let the hens keep their eggs out in the wild, very few survive. We were seeing too few births. One duck kept putting her nest at the top of a bank, and the eggs inevitable rolled down the hill and busted on a rock or something. We also have no small amount of raccoons, snakes, foxes, and other critters that love scrambled eggs. It was just not good for babies. We brought the incubators and now we rescue as many eggs as we can. Sometimes we have tricked the duck hens with fake eggs, so that once these hatch we can replace the fakes with the babes, but it is quite an effort. We want the hens to be moms, but nature can be kind of tough."

Jess took them all outside and pointed up into the trees where there were dozens of raccoons sleeping, they were curled up into forked branches at the tops of trees. Jess showed them how to spot them nestled in mini hammocks. It was funny to realize that they had been there the whole time. Abbey and the kids hadn't ever know to look for them. It made Abbey kind of nervous, would any of the raccoons fall or suddenly drop down on them? With a slight shiver, abbey tried to listen to Jess and ignore her concerns. After all, she hadn't even known the 'coons had been there before.

Jess pointed out some nesting geese and told them where they could go see a pair of swans. Apparently, the waterfowl didn't enjoy each other and weren't in the habit of sharing a pond. Abbey could well understand this. She preferred her own space, too. They walked around the hen house, with Winston always available to announce the obvious, "P. U. it stinks!"

With a giggle and some yawns, Abbey decided it was time to rest before dinner. Abbey was always excited to see what dinner would be. She didn't ask, because she didn't want to try to imagine what would be. She preferred to be awed by the surprise of it. The kids contested laying down, so Abbey turned on a video for them, naturally, she had brought Free Willy, kind of a dumb choice, no where near the ocean. She should have brought Bambi or even Fantasia.

With the kids settled, Abbey took a long hot shower and thought more about the Purpose vs. Puppets concept. Someday she would write an article about that. Abbey wondered what theologians would argue with Frieda and what they would say. She'd have to do a rough draft, who knows maybe the article could turn into something, maybe an essay or a paper, was there a book in it? Who knows? The pay couldn't' be any worse and ultimately, she knew that she was a good writer. She dried off and decided to lie down and rest her eyes.

Chapter 22

"Knock, knock, Abbey honey, are you awake?" It was Frieda.

"Oh no, what time is it? I must have fallen asleep, Are the kids okay? I am so sorry."

"Honey, it's okay, everything is fine. They're dressed for dinner and are helping me. We're just terrific. I wanted to give you plenty of time to rest and now I want you to try this on for tonight. Take your time, there's still forty-five minutes before dinner," Frieda cooed.

"Okay, what is it? What's tonight's theme?"

"It's a surprise, just try on the outfit, it won't make sense until you come down. See you in about forty-five minutes, the kids will be with me."

As Frieda left, Abbey rushed to open the wardrobe bag…it looked like a princess dress. What the heck kind of theme requires Cinderella at the Ball? Abbey laughed to herself. Okay, well, it is bound to be different. She looked in the mirror and realized that the bad part about falling asleep with her hair wet, is that she looked like Cinderella cleaning the house, not going to meet the prince. She had work to do before she'd put on the organza and taffeta dress. After a creative job with a curling iron, she swished her way into the dress. It was long and although white, it had that organza quality that made it shimmer with every hue. Abbey loved the blues, pinks, golds that appeared as the light hit the material. It was lovely. Abbey saw the pretty little ballet slippers and immediately hoped that her daughter was dressed like it. Oh, Geves would love it! Maybe she could get that illusive family photo tonight. That'd be fun.

Abbey made her way down to the dining hall where Geves and Bug were waiting, when they saw her they raced to her. Geves looked so pretty, her gown was similar but it was lilac in color. Bug had on what appeared to be a little tuxedo shirt in blue. She grabbed the first person she saw and asked them to take a picture of the her family.

Geves couldn't contain herself, "Oh Mama, you won't believe it, it is awesome. Oh Mama you are beautiful, I am beautiful, I am Beauty and you can be Cinderella - You won't believe it!"

True to form, when Abbey walked through the dining hall doors, it was transformed into a wonderful ball. The tables each had gingerbread stagecoaches with horses for centerpieces. They were painted in icings that matched all the organza streamers. There was tulle wrapped around each table with little white Christmas lights underneath that made it appear magical. The ceiling was lowered with more tulle and lights hanging down over the middle of the room. A fairy tale ending to their wonderful weekend. She couldn't help smiling; only Frieda could envision "Dinner at the Castle."

Abbey kept thinking that this place could make a ton of money, if they would make it less about Christianese and more of a private inn. Maybe that was part of the story, too.

Frieda sat Abbey at a table with another woman and her three children. Apparently, the kids had met earlier with the teens at the barn. Geves and the little girl, Tabby, were giggling and whispering and couldn't stop gushing about the decorations and the lights. Bug was sitting up really straight and trying so hard, if one of the boys was chewing on a straw, so was Bug. Marilyn and Abbey introduced themselves and Abbey asked Marilyn how she came to be at the ranch.

Marilyn was obviously tired, but seemed happy to be in a beautiful gown at this ball. She smiled, "my husband and I are missionaries to the Philippines and we are back in the States for our three-year sabbatical. We have to raise our own funds, so my husband is traveling to some of our sponsor churches."

Abbey responded, "That must be tough. So you are here with the kids for the whole three years?" –that didn't sound right to Abbey.

"Oh goodness no, Frieda opens this place up to all of us, but none of us want to take advantage. We are here while my husband visits some sponsor churches that don't have accommodations for us. We will stay with our families and in a sponsored apartment near our Mission home base. This is just a lovely break. Isn't it spectacular, the décor, the clothes, and the presentations? What brings you and your children here?"

Before Abbey could answer, foods were rushed out to the buffet, all in bite size pieces and served on silver platters, and glass cake stands. With all the tiers, glass, silver, mirrors, and lights it was like a fairyland. There were the requisite kid foods with pigs in a blanket, but there were small quiches, cucumber sandwiches, Brie and raspberries wrapped in filo dough. Everything was so delicate and pretty and there was a ton of food. Maybe the small sizes made it look like more, but the tiered cake stands were lovely. All of the drinks, mostly flavored lemonades were served in champagne flutes with small pieces of fruit in the bottoms. The kids popped up for food, they just couldn't wait.

Marilyn and Abbey quickly followed. Marilyn asked, "Can you believe all of this? Isn't it a bit overwhelming?"

Abbey was pensive, "You know, it is. To answer your earlier question, I am a writer with *Christianity Today* and I am here to write an article about the ranch. I came about a week ago to speak with Frieda and she wanted me to come back with the kids and see it through their eyes."

Abbey looked around for Matt, she really thought he was supposed to be here, wasn't he picking up the youth group today? Oh, it occurred to her maybe Marilyn knew Matt or his parents, Matt had been in the Philippines, too and Abbey recalled that this folks were serving there, too. She asked, "Marilyn, do you know Pastor Matt or his family? I met him when I was here last time and his family have been permanent missionaries to the Philippines."

Marilyn really couldn't respond, she suggested that her husband knew a lot more people and that she didn't meet very many Americans. Abbey also didn't have much detail; it was tough to know for sure. She suggested that Abbey could introduce her to Matt if she saw him.

After loading their plates and agreeing on some favorites, "Marilyn and Abbey sat down and really talked.

Marilyn began. "You know I am thrilled that my kids are having this experience, but I am really glad we don't stay here for very long." She paused, when she saw Abbey's blank expression, "We have been living in a difficult area and we have had our home raided by guerillas so often that I travel with a change of underwear, a pot, a kettle, and my Bible in my purse. It has been really bad the past year, so dressing, as a princess is quite a blast. I only hope that Tabby doesn't get used to the idea. I have tried to acclimate the kids, but there are two totally different worlds." She half giggled half choked took a sip of her lemonade and continued, "Have you ever seen *Lifestyles of the Rich and Famous*? It was an old television show...I think I just fell in to an episode!"

Abbey grinned and did her best impersonation of Robin Leech and his famous line: "<u>Champagne Wishes and Caviar Dreams</u>." And after they both guffawed, "I know what you mean. I am not sure how I'm gonna get my daughter out of that dress. I am a single mom and we live about as far from this kind of life as you can get in the

U.S. of A. We don't suffer the conditions that you do, but we don't eat out often and usually only when there is a 'kid's eat free night'- so this is quite a departure. I do think that is Frieda's intention. She loves to 'WOW' us and give us a great experience. I gathered from her comments that she wants to create a memory for the families that come here. She just doesn't realize what an impossible bar she creates. I mean, how do you plan the next kid's birthday party?????"

"You're right, Frieda wants to give us something that we never even dream about. Her heart is really all about the fun and joy of it. I don't think she recognizes how amazing it all is —and, while I worry that my kids might get too used to things, I am so grateful when things are horrible and I can sit down with one or more of my kids and remind them of a night like this. There have been nights were Tabby has awakened with a nightmare. She has seen a lot in her short life, the raids are constant and I have to admit they scare me, too. When I go to her, we sit and talk and I know the next time, I am going to talk about princess dresses, stagecoaches made of candy, and balls. I am so thankful for that."

Abbey was awed by the simple wisdom of Marilyn. When you are at your lowest, you can dig out; with a beautiful memory... Abbey may use that on herself.

After stuffing themselves with all the tiny foods, the kids laughed and played at the table. A string quartet began playing some waltz style music and while the girls squealed the boys balked. Several teens showed up, the girls were brought to the dance floor and taught to do a simple box step. The young men escorted the boys outside to collect fireflies; they had a stack of clear plastic cups, plastic caps, and rubber bands. Abbey thought they were creating nightlights. As long as it kept Bug from breaking things, she thought it was a good idea. The girls danced with each other and then with their mothers. The boys returned and the firefly lights were used to light the dance floor. Eventually, the boys consented to dancing with their moms, too. It was so sweet.

After the ball, Abbey and Marilyn exchanged addresses and promised to keep in touch. The boys took the fireflies back outside and released them. The kids were very reluctant to split up but exhaustion won out.

Abbey still wondered about Matt but didn't want to ask. She really enjoyed Matt and had hoped to at least say goodbye. It had been a relief to meet an attractive man who wasn't a jerk. Not Abbey's type, no she leaned more towards the jerks.

Abbey didn't see Frieda as she was taking the kids to bed, and she realized that while they had been dancing, all the buffet had been broken down and the lights and tulle were gone, even from the ceiling. So the fireflies enabled them to clean up, too. Very ingenious.

Once in her room, Abbey put the beautiful dresses in the hanging bags and reluctantly added her own slippers. She would need to remember this for all the reasons Marilyn suggested, but also ---maybe, she could recreate a little of it. Thrift stores around home always had wedding/bridesmaids/prom dresses cheap. She could find something for herself and Geves. Abbey would serve Stouffers and use her champagne glasses. The gingerbread coach and horses might be a bit much but they could improvise. She packed as she thought more about Marilyn. She realized that she would be the one to keep the memories alive for her children. She also thought more about Marilyn's story. Her life sounded so difficult. Abbey would have to look into other articles written about missionaries. It might be a neat story and a tandem to the ranch.

By ten, she was exhausted and ready for sleep. She'd have to get out early. Frieda was always up by six, but just in case, Abbey decided to leave her a note. Digging out a pen and her ever-present legal pad, she began crafting a 'thank you'...

Dearest Frieda,

What a pleasure it has been to visit with you twice. It hardly seems possible that our wonderful weekend is over and you have certainly earned your reputation as a consummate hostess and party giver. I don't think the kids and I have ever had more fun, and I know that I will remember these hours and days forever. I will think about all that you have said, and I will be honored to write about your ranch. My editor will send you the approved piece, but I will send you and advance copy to be certain that you are happy with it. Please know that I admire and respect you... you have given me the best possible gift; that is your time and your friendship. I hope it is okay with you that I have come to consider you a friend. I certainly would understand if you have too many already, but I plan to stay in contact with you and wish you the greatest success.

Thanks so much for everything!

Your friend,
Abbey

It took about three sheets of paper and two revisions, but Abbey thought is sounded okay. She was used to someone chopping her work up. She was also used to typing! Abbey planned to knock Frieda's socks off with her article and she'd have a lot more energy and a lot more time to craft that.

With Monday fast approaching, Abbey clicked off the light and went to sleep. She dreamed of mists, a certain guy, and Moses.

Chapter 23

Monday morning came way too quick, and with pleasant dreams and a comfy bed, (without the kids); it was really hard for Abbey to get out of bed. The frilly curtains and the giant bed had been a fun and welcome change. Just being on a 'working vacation' had been a great change of pace. She dressed quickly and helped the kids. They were so crabby that she almost punished Bug; but then decided that it would be better to finish the vacation on a positive note.

Abbey, Geves, and Bug grabbed a quick breakfast after placing their things in the car. She was amazed at all the stuff the kids were leaving with, Abbey recognized the sticks shaped like their initials, 'arrowheads', feathers, and some other items. She was a little concerned with the eggshells, which might be a problem, later. There were an unusual number of rocks, hence the weight. Perhaps the rocks would remedy the eggshells. {Mom outsmarts kid!!!}

They ran into Frieda in the dining hall.

"Good Morning Miss Frieda," the kids sang, it was the nicest they had sounded all morning. Abbey was relieved.

"Good Morning Genevieve and Winston- how did you sleep? Any dreams of castles and parties?" Frieda asked.

The kids laughed and Geves nodded. Abbey decided to nod too. Frieda just chuckled, while Bug made a curious face. He shook his head, noting the women around him and looked disgusted. Even at his young age, he didn't understand women. Frieda and Abbey recognized the look and winked at each other.

Abbey began, "Miss Frieda, we cannot thank you enough, this has been spectacular. The kids and I have had a fantastic time. I will never in my lifetime regret the time spent here. It has truly been a gift, and a generous one at that."

"Abbey darling, may I tell you that it is a gift to me, to take care of the three of you. I cannot imagine my life without the grace of meeting you all. I appreciate all your help and the article that you will eventually write. I only hope that you will remember how much God wants to lavish you with his love."

Abbey, started to say something, but Frieda chimed in, 'OH I almost forgot, here this is for you."

Abbey looked at the folded paper, (she panicked for a split second thinking it might be a bill or something), umm, "what is this?

Recognizing Abbey's look, Frieda quickly explained.

"Don't look so startled dear. Matt got here yesterday while you were probably in the egg house. He looked for you but was in such a hurry that he decided to leave you a note. There was some crisis with one of his parishioners, and he had to arrange for rides for the youth group. He took back the ones who had no other way of getting back and left the rest here for our <u>Dinner at the Castle</u> night."

Abbey was relieved first, then thrilled. Instead she said, "That's nice, certainly not necessary."

"Our Matt is a proper young man. He did tell you that he would be here to say good bye, didn't he?"

"Well, yes, he did but he doesn't owe me anything."

Frieda knew this to be a bold faced lie, but who was Abbey lying to, herself or Frieda. No matter. Frieda just wanted to be careful not to say the wrong thing. She had a habit of doing that…..

"Okay kiddos, into the chariot." Abbey announced and smiled at Frieda. Frieda hugged them all and Abbey twice. They went through the gate and onto the highway before Abbey realized that there were tears running down her face.

She looked in her rearview mirror and saw the kids and the hills behind them. She was usually not so emotional but it had been a wonderful weekend. The kids had been different; they were very excited but very relaxed at the same time. Abbey recognized that she, too, had been very relaxed. That must be it; it is hard to leave a sense of peace. There was also the fact that Frieda had hugged her more in their short relationship than her own mother ever had. Well, surely it was the combination. Abbey looked forward to revisiting all her feelings as she wrote out her article.

As they got closer to Atlanta, and home, Abbey reluctantly started making to-do- lists for herself. Laundry, dinner, shopping, and an oil change. Too much. First to get the kids fed, they slept most of the way, which was preferable to the usual bickering. It sure would be tough to ever top this vacation that was for sure. She wondered how much she would tell her mom about it and looked forward to reading Matt's note in private.

Once the kids were inside and done greeting their hamsters, the fish, and their grandmother, in that order, they were off to put up their favorite items from the trip and ran to the kitchen for juice boxes.

Abbey's mother was quiet and almost seemed sad that they were home. She detected something in her mother, but didn't dare criticize. They walked a tight emotional wire around one another. Her mother was cordial, even a huge help, but not a warm woman. Abbey feared that they would get into another argument over her job and the unneeded influence of 'heavy religion' on the kids. Her mother had been brow beat as a child by her parents and taken to every kind of revival meeting know n to man. Grandma had been a huge Jesus fan never let anyone forget it. Religion had become the biggest line of rebellion for Abbey's mom, probably her only way to cope. She was a moral woman with a huge feminist streak. It was one more bone of contention between them. While Abbey believed in equality, she would have much preferred to stay home and be a wife and mom. She would have given anything to be the *Kool Aid* mom serving all of the kids in her yard, while creating water slides out of trash bags. She loved the picket fence and porch swings, she planned out a cottage garden to bring ladybugs, butterflies, and humming birds to her yard. She wanted family dinners, and a spouse who brought his boss home for dinner. Her mother never understood that. She wanted a partner who looked to her for advice. Instead, she had married a bum, someone who wanted to be one of the children, with Abbey running rough shod over him. Oh well, water under the bridge. Maybe Abbey's mom was right all along; it sure hadn't worked out for Abbey and her plan.

After a hectic day and many preparations for the week: laundry started, frozen fish sticks eaten, groceries purchased, and baths done. Abbey found a few moments for herself. She took a long hot shower, put on some eucalyptus spearmint body lotion, a flannel nightie, and settled in with Matt's letter.

Hastily written, it still had Matt's charm:

"Dear Abbey,

I am so sorry that I missed you today, but I have thought much about our conversation and wonder if I didn't botch it totally.

I would be grateful if you are willing to correspond by e-mail. I haven't yet mastered the bloody thing, but I am trying. Forgive my clumsiness.

Yours sincerely, Matt"

He'd enclosed his e-mail address and his regular address. Abbey thought it was sweet. She wasn't sure if she wanted to correspond with him, but she didn't not want to. Maybe a friendship would be a good thing. She had a lot of friends; it was just tough keeping up because she had the two kids. It seemed like most of her friends that had kids were married or sharing custody. And the rest were always dating and traveling on exciting business trips. The grass is always greener. Yep, another friend seems just what the doctor ordered. It would be different having a pastor for a friend.

Don't dare let mother know what he does!

Chapter 24

Abbey spent the rest of the week working on her article. She struggled a lot with the notes and impressions from her first visit out to the ranch.

Initially, she wanted to write it as if she were describing to a blind man. Much like the woman at the ranch. She wanted to lay out the vision of the ranch in its entirety but as she wrote it just didn't work. Perhaps there were many ways to approach it, as the analytical reporter or maybe simply as an elated mom. She edited, rewrote, and crafted two completely different pieces. She still had some holes to fill –she needed more research. After doing some internet searches on the ranch, and some financial reporting, she opted to check her other source, Matt.

Speaking with Matt by e-mail was going to be different. It had been almost a week; at least she wouldn't appear desperate.

Hi Matt, It's me, Abbey, Got your note, greatly appreciated. Sorry we missed each other. I am presently working on my article. Can you advise me on the actual costs of housing people at the ranch? I couldn't find it in any of my notes. If not, that's okay; It'll be great communicating online. I am not much for snail mail, though.

All the best, Abbey

Ps-Geves and Bug say hello and they loved your Youth Group

It was almost a full day before Matt got back to her. She was miffed when she kept checking her e-mal and nothing. She double-checked his e-mail address and, was frustrated. Finally on Sunday evening a response came.

> *Abbey,*
>
> *Ciao, great to see you online. I am delighted to talk. Tell Geves and Bug that they were very popular with the youth. Lovely to hear that kids behaved themselves, actually, I'd be totally shocked, if they hadn't.*
>
> *Sorry I had to bolt, one of my people had a newborn baby with severe defect, and I needed to be at the hospital with the parents. The babe was delightful and just so perfect, only lived for four days, and the funeral was yesterday. I've never seen such a small casket. Heartbreaking and poignant at the same time. I will think on this for some time.*
>
> *I was honored to be with the family, but it is a time when pastors really don't have good words.*
>
> *Anyway, I have no idea of actual costs for the ranch, but I kind of doubt that Frieda knows herself. You should ask Sharon or Lori: They have a better handle on the math regarding the food. Then ask ole Haney about electric bills. The ranch itself is paid for, so just some taxes and minimum amount of salaries otherwise. The local college Agricultural provides a lot of tools, but I don't know otherwise. Sorry I'm not more help.*
>
> *Please know that you can ask Frieda anything, she loves to gush about the ranch. It is hers to tell.*
>
> *YBIC,*
> *Matt*

Abbey was saddened by what she read about the baby. Gentle but terrible words. Burying one of her children would have killed her. After blowing her nose, and wiping her eyes, she tried to think of the right words to respond to such a horror.

> *Matt,*
> *No need to apologize. That must have been awful. I cannot imagine soothing like that. How is the family? Do they have other children? What is YBIC?*
> *-Abbey*

Not knowing how long it would be before she received a response, Abbey went to the kitchen and made herself some cinnamon tea. She had quit drinking so much coffee while she was at the ranch. It was nice having teatime. Frieda was having an influence.

By the time Abbey got back to the computer with tea and a pair of socks, Matt had responded.

> *Abbey,*
> *The family and no other children, this was their first little boy. The parents are strong Christians, so they will be fine. It is tough but they are secure in the Word of God and know that their little one is with God. Julie, the mom, said that her little baby Christian was just too good for our world. That God blessed them with their short time together and that God wanted him back. She is so sad but she is completely secure. I admire her strength. I don't' know if I could be so strong. It is good to see how God's people are surrounding them, though. Those people have more food at their house than Miss Frieda does. It is*

astounding; someone sent Julie a pajama gram. Their small group is taking turns going by to check on them, and one lady in or church that lost a baby twenty-seven years ago delivers Julie's favorite coffee every afternoon. I am so crazy proud of our church body. The youth group is planting a small garden outside for the baby so that Julie will see it each Sunday. They have planned it so that there are evergreens and flowers year round. There's a small placard made with one of those kits, you know cement and marbles or something. The body of Christ in action. What a huge blessing for this family and their pastor to see.

Anyway, sorry for the ramblings. Did you contact Miss Frieda?

YBIC<>< Matt
(Your Brother In Christ)

Well that explains that. Naturally, everyone would want to do something for such a tragedy but she had to wonder how they help people in normal circumstances or just through the hard day to day. Maybe another article in the making- like 'where is the Christian community day by day'... Best get to work. Better send Matt a note to tell him.

Hey Matt,
Thanks for clarification on YBIC, I get it. I must stop emailing if I am ever gonna get my article done. See you later, online.

Your friend,
Abbey

She spent the next few hours compiling notes on costs for retreat centers and secular camps and came up with a ball park cost, after some guesswork and taking her averages, she came up with a number. For a family of four to stay in a separate facility, (i.e. the trailers), dine, enjoy live music, fishing et al, it would average out to approx. five thousand dollars per week. Since the trailers and land were paid for, the ranch had it's own energy source, a good percentage of its own food supply, Abbey took the number down to two thousand seven hundred and ninety per week. Of course, it was impossible to figure in the volunteers, but still it seemed like a lot for a pastor. It was probably a cheap vacation all things considered, less than Disney and most cruises for a week, but pastor salaries in the United States average about fifty thousand dollars. Churches made contributions so that their clergy could go, but where did the extra money come from? Abbey would have to call Frieda tomorrow.

Her article was really starting to flesh out and Abbey was pretty close to considering it finished. It had all the excitement of a travel brochure, but Abbey was concerned about her inability to get a hard fix on what Frieda's books looked like. For the article, it might not matter all that much but it was a question that Abbey assumed readers would want. They would, at the very least, want to know what it cost to send their own pastor or their family.

Abbey was confident that she had shared her own joy and love of the ranch and she hoped that it would make Frieda very happy.

Chapter 25

Sleep finally found Abbey later that night. After far too little sleep, she woke to the alarm and realized that it was back to the grind for the kids and it was Monday. Ugh. School after spring break was always tough. She might be in for a battle this morning.

Abbey was correct, it was a battle to the finish, neither child looked their best on their way to school but after tears, the inevitable battles, and a lousy breakfast because she burned the eggs-which wasn't shocking. She hated putting the kids on the bus like that. What did the bus driver think? Oh who cares, so she wasn't going to be made mother of the year. Nothing-new there.

When she went back inside she settled in to call Frieda, Sharon, Lori or whomever else she could reach. The phone was ringing and Abbey imagined the scene at the ranch. She thought about Moses and wondered if he was close to the lodge. The sixth ring, and Frieda picked up, "Sweet Silver Ranch, this is Frieda, how can we bless you?"

"Good Morning Ms. Frieda, this is Abbey."

"Moses and I were just talking about you this morning dear. How are you? How are the children?"

"Funny, I was just thinking about Moses, too. Did he break through another fence?"

"Naturally, while it might not be the most exciting place in the world, it is nice to have some regularity with old Moses," Frieda laughed. Abbey could hear Frieda walking around outside on the porch and she thought she heard one of 'the Mules'

puttering past. Frieda said good morning to someone there, and then asked Abbey, "How is your article coming along?"

"Well that is what I am calling about actually, although, I wish you'd give Moses a carrot for me."

"Already did!"

"Wow, service with a smile." Abbey was sitting on the end of her chair, she realized she was smiling. She tried to shift her mind back..."Okay, well I need to know how you are able to afford to keep the place running. I know you trust the Lord for your provision, but exactly how does it work? If someone called you and asked how much they needed to collect to send their pastor and his family, what would you say? How much, on average, do you get from the churches and how much do you have to supplement? How do you supplement?"

"I am not that good with numbers Miss abbey. Basically, we have the churches that want to send their pastors take up a free will offering. That varies from church to church and from time to time. The people know what it is for and they are usually pretty generous. Of course, there are really small churches, and really large ones but I would say that we get anywhere from eight to fifteen hundred dollars for each family- I think Dan's old estimate for cost was about twice that."

Frieda was pacing the porch and trying to give Abbey as much detail as possible. Lori and Jess passed by and waved and Lori blew kisses, which Frieda returned... she continued, " We make a lot of our own energy with solar, and some wind which we then turn around and sell back to the power company. Our buffalo meat is used for barter and sold outright at market each year. That brings in quite a bit of income; we actually had a contract for several years with the big NFL team in Atlanta for the meat. There are two cell towers on the property at the farthest ends on the east and west sides, we get a good rental stream from that. We also have master gardeners who plan and plant our gardens for us. One of them is an area pastor's wife and she is amazing. Her tomatoes are the best! We are fairly self-contained that way. As you know, we have more volunteers than paid staff. It wasn't always that way, but that in and of itself is proof that God is making this place run."

Frieda paused, she sad down on the swing and tried to think what else…. "Oh, and the Amish community is where we get so many things. There are some wonderful women who create the most fantastic jams, jellies, nuts, breads, candies, and oh the honey. It's all-amazing. I get some meat from them as well. They are the fairest prices for such fantastic quality. So all in all we are pretty self-sustaining. Our biggest expenses are for machine parts, and feed. I wish we made more money, because I'd love to support more missionaries, but we do what we can."

Abbey wrote as fast as she could and hoped she'd be able to read her chicken scratch later. She taped her pen on the page and tried to gather her thoughts, what did Frieda say???? She doubled back over her tablet and tried to find the word or phrase she was looking for…oh that's it "Frieda thank you, I have a question did you say that you barter?"

"Oh yes, we raise our own hay, we've got about thirty seven acres that is strictly for hay and has been greatly productive. We share with the Amish folks and very often they will share other things. It is actually a lovely relationship. My favorite is Mr. Miller, he is a dear- his wife makes the best cakes. The Millers have the best hogs this side of the Mississippi too all our bacon is from Mr. Miller and he takes a buffalo each year for himself. The buffalo require pretty strong fencing, so it s better for him to let us raise them, and then trade with us each year."

Abbey really cared for Frieda and wanted to please her, she would never have offered to anyone else, but for Frieda she had to, "I am going to finish the article up and then I will send it to you electronically, will that work?"

"Certainly dear. I doubt I have enough ink in my printer but I will read it with excitement. How did your photos turn out?"

"The pictures are spectacular. I will include those in a separate email. You may want them for your next brochure."

"I will look forward to it Abbey. You are a special young woman, your children are precious- please know that you are always welcome here. I have come to care for you all and would really like to feel that we are friends. Please feel free to call or write anytime. I must go deal with Moses. Blessings dear. Good bye," and with that Frieda was gone.

Abbey hung up the phone and smiled. Frieda sure was a sweet lady and so busy, even if she was a bit of a holy roller. Not that that's such a bad thing. Abbey would finish the article and send it to Frieda as soon as possible.

Abbey decided to focus on the version of the article that she had centered on her family. She finished the article and sent it to Frieda. She received a sweet return email, saying that Frieda was pleased and knew that Abbey had found the heard of Sweet Silver Ranch. Abbey forwarded the approved piece to her editor, Ed. He responded in an equally positive way.

The rest of the week flew by, with too much to do and more assignments for phone-type interviews and a book review. Abbey heard from Matt once during the week and he seemed pleased with Frieda's response to the article. He asked if he could have a copy for the article, only he wanted her to autograph it. Silly man.

Chapter 26

Abbey worked diligently, and tried to get through her book review assignment. It was an anonymous short story, and well written. She enjoyed it although it felt a bit like a sermon. Abbey was feeling devoid of the real world, and decided to rent a movie. Something current, something even a bit racy.

She sat in her room, after the kids had gone to bed and watched the screen. She loved the funny scenes but each one ended up with the characters hoping in and out of bed with one another. It was kind of gross, and it was disappointing when every other scene had a naked body part and more sex. She wondered it all of her time with Frieda and the article about the ranch was turning her into a prude. Was she starting to think like them? I guess it wasn't the worst thing. It just made the movie a terrible disappointment. Oh well, she was a mom, and maybe it was nature's way of protecting the children.

Finally, Saturday morning, the kids were up watching cartoons and Abbey's mom was off to the store. It was tough trying to think of something to do with the kids that would engage them as much as the previous weekend at the ranch but she thought it would be fun to take them to the Chattahoochee River, and walk the decks. It would be crowded, but the kudzu vines would be blooming. That smell, just like grape soda, it tickled Abbey's nose, (most likely due to allergies), but it reminded her of that Nehi grape, when you drank from a full can the bubbles would pop up into your nose. Abbey tested the waters with the kids, asking them about walking and they jumped from their seats. So it was a plan. She wrote her mom a note and they headed out.

Geves and Bug ran from one spot to the next claiming to be spotting frogs, fish, or ladybugs. By the time one or the other would reach the location, the other would claim that they just missed it. Abbey was smiling at the elaborate way that they made the sighting sound. Perhaps, a couple of writers in the making, dramatic writers... There were hundreds of dogs and the animals were running and leaping for Frisbees, or just straining on the leash. If it was possible, the dogs seemed to be smiling, too. The kids stopped to pet every dog that they could. It didn't seem to matter how large or small the dog, Geves had to touch it, and if Geves did it, so did Bug. Pete and Re-peat! After a little too much sun, Abbey offered McDonalds, and they were off again.

Abbey's vice had always been their French fries. Best ever. After lunch they headed home and seemed tired enough to sit down and play a game of Blokus, it was perfect for both kids because it was space and shape, the ages were irrelevant. Abbey threw all the makings for chicken noodle soup in the crock-pot for dinner and got the game out of the closet. The kids would eat chicken noodle soup for lunch and dinner, although Abbey's mom wouldn't be impressed. At least dinner would be made. The key to Abbey and her mother's living arrangement was as little conflict as possible, which for Abbey meant tiptoe and don't complain. She only wished her mother would follow her lead.

By the time the kids were down for bed and Abbey had snapped her computer shut, it was too late to call her friend Cindy. She'd been thinking she should call her old buddy, but time got away from her.

After a lazy Sunday and very little accomplishment, the week began anew and then one ran into another and another. Routine ruled Abbey's home in general; it was almost time for school to let out for summer. Abbey couldn't believe it. Five weeks had gone by since they had been to Sweet Silver Ranch. It was funny how it sort of got under your skin. Abbey wondered if it was because she spent such a concentrated time there and then had to write, rewrite, and refine her article.

It still struck Abbey that she thought about the ranch, Frieda, or Moses at least once every day. How could four days have impacted her so? It didn't make any sense. Abbey's article had been published, and she'd received several notes on how well written it was. The editor had even gotten several positive reponses from former visitors to the ranch. Many people were grateful for the article because it reminded them of their time there. It was fulfilling to do a good job, and to get the kudos for it. Raising kids sure didn't give you a lot of that. And abbey's mother was not one to waste her time giving compliments.

Abbey realized that the article, and the ranch had been a lovely thing in her life. A gift to open up and revisit at least in her head.

Chapter 27

After a particularly exasperating first week of summer with the kids, her mother tired, and work in short supply, Abbey found an invitation in the mail. It was from Frieda:

My Dearest Abbey,

It is really busy this month at Sweet Silver Ranch, we have so many lovely families here and it is just booming with babies. We had two more colts born and a filly. We also had our largest number of buffalo babies ever. It is fantastic. I find myself in need of asking for some help. Please don't feel obligated, but I could really use a hand at running some of the evening events here. I thought that you had enjoyed that particular aspect of the ranch. Your whole family, please include your mother, would be welcome to stay as my guests. Abbey your help would be huge and I would consider it a big favor. Thanks so much for even considering this old woman's request. You are such a delight. I could really use help any time in the next six weeks that you are available. Love to you and my special friends Genevieve and Winston. Love, Frieda Abbey was delighted with the idea. First she would contact Ed and see if she could work out another article. There had been so much interest from the last one. She could easily do book reviews and phone calls from the ranch. IT would be great to go back and what a summer for Geves and Bug. Oh, she just had to make this work. She had to convince Ed that there was more to do at the ranch. Abbey hoped to spend more time in the kitchen this time; maybe she'd learn something. Even filling the buffet had been fun. People smiled as she placed huge platters of fresh food in front of them. Talking to people as she showed them to tables, and decorating was all a blast. IT would also save her a fortune on day care. It might even do her mom some good to getaway. And if she could tone Miss Frieda down a bit it might be a good thing for mom, too.

After several calls to her editor, she got the green light. He didn't particularly care where she wrote. He figured she could get another article out of the ranch, even interviewing some of the guests. Missionary stories were a regular feature. He was also interested in the agricultural students or the Four H maybe bringing a different group to the magazine.

Abbey had to be more careful with her mother. She found her getting coffee, "Mom, remember the ranch that Geves, Bug, and I went to? Well they have invited us back, because the owner needs some help. She has asked us all and we would stay in beautiful rooms. I think you'd enjoy it. There is no work for you to do, but you may really like it there."

"Is this for some article or something?" Her mother asked.

"No this is actually to work for the ranch, although I will work on another article. It's because Miss Frieda needs some extra hands."

"Oh."

"Does oh, mean yes or no?"

"Well it seems that you have already made up your mind," her mother quipped.

"Well yes, Mom, the kids and I would love to go," she hesitated, "I am asking if you would like to join us." Abbey's mother, the gifted Geraldine Lewis, was very critical and hesitant. She was mostly a sad woman and very disappointed in her daughter and her life.

Geraldine considered Abbey for a moment and then asked, "for how long?"

"I haven't committed to anything at this point, I wanted to go and play it by ear. I can always bring you back here if you don't like it. It sounds like Frieda mostly needs me at night for the evening functions. They have a packed house. I am hoping that it is because of my article: maybe it has pumped up their guest count."

Geraldine didn't agree or disagree just said fine, after a few moments She was never an optimist but her negativity always affected Abbey. Even packing became a chore. As soon as Abbey suggested what her mom might bring, her mother reacted. All Abbey had said was that she might want a pair of dressier shoes for dinner. But Geraldine looked aghast and laughed at Abbey, as if Abbey didn't get it.

Abbey could not remember the last time that Geraldine had been agreeable.

Abbey called Frieda and told her that they would come, they discussed when and what Abbey would need to do. Frieda was delighted with the plans and seemed genuinely enthused that Geraldine was coming. Abbey thought, that's until you meet her.

When the day came for the trip, Abbey tried really hard to please her mother and the kids. It was a daunting task. She grabbed videos for the kids and hoped that her mother might consider napping. She actually found herself praying as she walked around the car. It was just a really long trip. Four fun filled hours of not so much bliss.

Abbey had the kids watching Fantasia, she hoped the music would be adult friendy and subject her to somewhat less criticism. Geraldine naturally thought they should be reading. Geraldine didn't like the driving games and wanted to, instead, discuss what they were seeing as they drove. Bug quoted from a movie called Dr. Doolittle where the dog speaks as they are driving and says, "line,

line, line" for the lines in the road. Bug took it too far, but Abbey started laughing so hard, she had a little trouble driving. Naturally, Geraldine wasn't thrilled.

By the time Abbey pulled through the front gate, she had determined to ditch her mother as soon as possible. She found herself wondering what if she had grown up with a mom like Frieda instead of Geraldine.

She parked the car; surprised that no one came out of the lodge right away. The kids were eager to get out and see what animals were moving about. She told them to stay close by and made her way into the lodge – her mother grumbling behind. She walked straight in and shouted to no avail. She showed her mom to one of the rooms at the lodge and told her she would see what was going on. Then, relieved to be rid of her mother), she wandered around to the kitchen where Lori and Sharon were working hard. They had pots boiling, and the oven ablaze. They didn't even hear Abbey, over the sounds until she was right next to them. "Hi," she said.

Lori and Sharon grabbed Abbey and hugged her, Lori kissing her ear. Both gals were shorter than Abbey, so she was hunched over. Sharon stood Abbey back up and they were both talking at the same time to Abbey and made it clear that they were thrilled to see her. The women were so youthful even though they were probably her mom's age. Sharon had a pixie quality to her bouncing from pot to pot. She had an apron and all manner of wooden spoons sticking out of her pockets. She had even coiled her hair into a bun with a wooden spoon tucked through it. She was tiny but strong. Lori was sturdier and seemed like she could do it all. She was no nonsense but so kind. She was short but just seemed so strong. Even her hands were strong, probably from all the gardening. Come to think of it, Abbey had seen her pushing wheelbarrows loaded up with soil last time she was at the ranch. No wonder she seemed so strong, she was!

Abbey attempted to jump in, but wanted to check on the kids first, make sure that they were behaving. "I will come back and help, but I need to make sure and get the kids channeled some where first. Where's Frieda?"

Lori responded first, "Our Frieda is laying in bed. Get your kids squared away, and then go on up and see her. She'll be thrilled to see you."

"Laying in bed. What in the world is going on?"

Sharon and Lori shared a look before Lori answered, "Doctor says it's a mystery. He's pretty sure it's something to do with her age plus all the work she does. Of course, Frieda claims that she's fine, just really tired. We're trying to keep her in rest mode. As you can imagine, it isn't easy."

"Does the Doctor think that she needs surgery, or drugs, or something?" Abbey asked feeling slightly alarmed.

Lori answered, "Talk about that with Frieda. She doesn't take too well to being the patient but we've gotten about as much information out of her as we can."

"Okay, well, I'll go up." She turned slightly, " Do you think she's sleeping? Oh, never mind; I'll just go on up, it'll be fine. Thanks so much. I'll be back soon to help you two."

Lori and Sharon smiled and returned to the food. They knew that Frieda believed that God's hand was all over this. They said a quick prayer for Frieda.

Abbey found the kids and got them to their room, she checked on her mom. The kids planned to show their Grandma the new baby horses. But Grandma wanted them to settle their things in first. The horses would wait. So, knowing they were all together, Abbey sought out Frieda.

Shasta the mutt bounced up to abbey and licked her as she entered the room. Abbey giggled and noticed that Frieda was watching them. With her signature smile, Frieda said, "Abbey, I'm so delighted to see you. Give me a moment and I'll come down to greet your family properly."

She rushed over the the old lady and all but pushed her back into the bed. "First of all, Miss Frieda. You tell me what's going on with you," she demanded.

Frieda was not used to taking orders and a little surprised at Abbey's tenacity. "Oh honey, I'm just an old woman. Didn't they tell you about that? Old ladies get tired, and have to become old ladies. I'm not mentally equipped to be an old lady. So I have been behaving foolishly. I'm fine, really! I did several dumb things in a row. I stayed out in the barn for several nights while the mares were foaling. I just love seeing those new babies. Sometimes, I feel like the mares are my own daughters. If I can comfort them at all, I like to. Then, once the foals were born, I couldn't stand not being with them out in the barn for hours on end. I think my poor old bones just couldn't take it. The aches and pains make it hard to sleep. So, I get tired. I just have to learn, my body won't have it any other way."

"Surely there's more to it than that. What does the doctor say?"

"Not too much. He gets a bit fussy from time to time, but really I need to pay a bit more attention to what my body tells me. I've been trying, to stop pushing so hard. There are plenty of people more capable than me. I suppose I just watched my dad for all these years. Here he is over ninety years old, running rings around me. I told him, he's healthier than I am only because he never had to give birth or be married to a man!" Frieda laughed at her own joke.

Shocked, abbey wasn't sure whether to laugh or scold. "Well, is that why you invited us here to help? Are you truly sick? Is this just precautionary? Should I worry?"

Frieda chuckled, "Slow down Abbey, it's fine. Yes, I need your help, but I also believe that God has his own purpose in this. I don't know how serious it is- I don't seem to be healing like I used to. I know that God is in charge. Whatever he says, goes. You are a wonderful dose of medicine. I am thrilled to see you. Rest is what the doctor has prescribed and the Great Physician has brought you here to help me get it."

With this, Frieda eased out of bed, her face grimacing in pain and slipped her shoes on, but once up, she waltzed past Abbey, turning slightly as she passed, "It's just the getting up and down that hurts, let's go welcome your mom."

It was hard to watch anyone in pain; Abbey could never be a nurse. She suffered from too much empathy. "Um, okay," Abbey walked behind.

When they reached the rooms designated for Abbey's family, Frieda smiled her big smile and hugged Geves and Bug as best she could. She gushed about how happy she was to see them both. She then tapped on the door to Abbey's mother's room.

Abbey's mother opened the door tentatively, "Yes?"

"Welcome to Sweet Silver Ranch. I'm delighted to meet you. You are truly a gift to your beautiful grandchildren, and your gifted daughter."

Abbey stepped in before her mother could say something cold. "Mom, this is Frieda Stevens and Frieda, this is my mom, Geraldine Lewis."

Geraldine sized up Frieda as just what she expected, she was polite, "It's a pleasure to meet you. I thank you for this beautiful room and your attentions to detail."

"It is I who cannot thank you enough for bringing Abbey. She is such a help and I know that she would be handicapped without you here, too. Those grandkids of yours are everything that they should be and that makes them a handful. When I realized I needed some help, I spoke with the staff and Abbey's name came up over and over again. We are so grateful that you are all available. Thank you so much."

Amazingly, Geraldine became a few inches taller as Abbey watched. Abbey was blown away. Maybe just maybe her mom could enjoy this time. *Oh Please God*. Abbey thought.

Frieda asked Abbey to meet her in the kitchen. She sent the kids to the hatchery to help Jess, the student they had met last time, and she squired Geraldine into a small sitting room.

Abbey made her way down to the kitchen. She walked in to find Lori doubled over and Sharon holding a towel over her face. They were shaking with laughter. Abbey couldn't help but laugh, but wanted to know why she was laughing, "what's so funny?"

Lori could barely talk; she was holding her stomach and pointed to Sharon to speak. Sharon turned to Abbey, dropped the dishtowel, and straightened up, "Hi Abbey, we were just being silly. We were talking about all the ways that we could change the dinners in Frieda's absence. It isn't even that funny, I think we are over tired or something. You know, we will go with all paper products and serve fast food and beanie weanies and spam, that kind of thing…" With that Lori started up again. They were both a wreck with laughter. Abbey thought it was humorous but they were losing it.

"Okay, guess I needed to be here for the entire conversation." Abbey really wanted to laugh with them, and it was funny but, well…"Well how can I help? Frieda said that she would meet me here."

Lori again, "Frieda will be here any minute. That's why this is making us giggle. We are doing southern fried tonight, so we were talking about making a run to KFC. Hook up with the Colonel and get us a bucket… it will never happen, but we thought it was rather a comical idea. Actually, the food is well in hand. The smoker is outside and has been going since early this morning. How about you get started on décor. Do you remember?"

"Oh sure, it's down the hall in the back room, it's all marked right?" I think I even remember the set up. I may come back if I have any questions."

Sharon looked up, "You've got it! No wonder Frieda wanted you here. She was just sure that you were the one and only person who could help. We praise God that you are here Abbey."

Chapter 28

Abbey smiled and headed through the hall to the storeroom. She heard some noises and someone digging around in the storeroom. She looked in. "Hello, is someone in there?"

Matt popped his head out, "Hello Abbey! Welcome back and thanks for coming to my rescue." With that he handed her a box filled with Checkered tablecloths and cowboy hats.

She was delighted to see him. "Ciao, Matt how are you?" Thank goodness she had the huge box in her hands. She wasn't sure if a hug was appropriate or a handshake? SO awkward. Maybe Matt felt the same way; which is why he handed me the box.

Matt grabbed another two boxes, and they walked out through the hall to the outdoor dining area, cheerfully chatting as they put the tables together for the dinner. A band arrived during one of their many trips to the storeroom, and began warming up. They worked well together, and with just a few questions here and there, they got the whole area looking great. The buffet tables were ready to go and the torches were set in place to light the way back to the cabins. He let Abbey know that it was too soon to light the sternos or the torches. So they headed into the kitchen o see what the cooks were up to.

Both had the kitchen well in hand. All the food smelled and looked amazing with intoxicating smells. Abbey asked Matt if they could talk.

"Of course Abbey, what's on your mind?"

"Frieda. How is she really?"

"Honestly, I don't know. She keeps reassuring me that she is fine. I spoke with her dad and he's concerned. But he says that she doesn't know when to say when- he believes she has to be forced to be still."

"So there isn't a diagnosis, a plan, any special consideration or directions?" She raised her hands and raked them through her hair.

Matt watched her not knowing if she was angry or not, "Abbey, there isn't much we could do regardless. Frieda is a special woman with a special role in life. She will do what she thinks is best, even if it isn't best for her. She is something of a fatalist. I don't know what we could or rather should do. We will gather around her, and help her as much as she lets us. Otherwise we should pray and trust God. Would you like to pray with me now?"

Abbey hesitated. What would be expected of her? She considered Matt's words, and realized that he was probably right. Funny how the gender roles shifted: here she wanted to solve problems and he understood the relational role. She realized that she should probably go rescue her mom from Frieda, instead. "Actually Matt I better go get my mom away from Frieda, she is not the easiest woman. I'll see you in a bit. Thanks Matt."

And with that she was gone. He wasn't surprised, but a bit disappointed that she had skipped the opportunity to pray with him.

For her part, Abbey wandered up through the lodge and stood just outside the sitting room where her mom and Frieda were still chatting. (She was shocked, were they actually laughing together, her mother was laughing????). She couldn't hear everything but she could hear them snickering and it sounded like they were relating to one another. WOW! Mom sounded happy. Abbey couldn't help herself; she had to see this for herself.

"Well hello, I seem to be interrupting you ladies." At her announcement, thy burst into laughter. They actually seemed to be sharing a private joke. Seemed to be going around the Lodge.

Frieda gathered herself together. "Abbey, your mom has been precisely what the doctor ordered. We are two peas in a pod. I am so glad you brought her. What fun. Is everything set up outside?"

Abbey stuttered, two peas in a pod, Frieda and Geraldine. Either Geraldine was putting on an incredible act or Abbey had severely misjudged Frieda. Huh, this was not familiar territory. "Yes, everything is ready," Abbey felt blindsided but continued, " Lori and Sharon have the food well under control. Matt and I got all the tables set up, the band is here and warmed up, the only thing left to do is light the torches and sternos, and he is on it."

Frieda spoke, "Oh, I am glad you found Matt. He was so pleased when he learned that you were coming in to help. He's very taken with you. I think you've found yourself a good friend in Matt." Turning to Geraldine, she continued, "Geraldine why don't we take a minute to freshen up. Won't you please join me at my table tonight for dinner? I hope we'll have tons of time together. I am so pleased that you are here."

Geraldine nodded and then bent down and hugged Frieda, then left the room.

Abbey tried to help Frieda, but she waved her off. She shooed Abbey to the kitchen.

Abbey ran out to the barns to check on the kids and Jess. She spotted Geves running through one of the entrances, obviously having a tough time keeping up with her brother. But it was so great that they had this kind of time together. Abbey was imagining what it would be like to live here with her family. She'd put a huge bell right by the kitchen and ring it every time she wanted to talk to the kids. She' run with them as much as possible and they would all collapse at night, maybe lay blankets outside and watch for shooting stars.

Sharon caught Abbey and asked her. "What are you daydreaming about?"

"Hi Sharon, sorry, I was just thinking it would be great to have raised my children running form barn to pond. It's awesome. Maybe a little lonely after a long period of time, but kind of wonderful, too."

Sharon looked pensive, "Country kids are different. My kids, raised in the city, by the way are amazing and wildly successful. But country kids are closer somehow. Maybe it is all the alone time outdoors. Maybe they come to appreciate family when that is all they have. Who knows? You could ask Frieda. Her boys are really great and super close."

"You know I don't think I've ever heard anything about Frieda's kids, she had three boys, right?"

"Yep, she lost her first son as an infant and raised Caleb and Mark, two of the best and most godly young men ever. They were raised out here. Caleb is a veterinarian and is out here a lot for all the critters. He teaches at Mercer and helps run the agricultural/ veterinary program. He is the youngest one, a very dry wit. He has three children, all girls." Sharon paused and gestured for Abbey to help her work while they talked. "Let's see the oldest boy is Mark, he has five sons and writes for *Tabletalk*, (a Christian devotional). He has published several books and makes a nice living. The boys' wives are very close, probably best friends. They have been thrown together constantly by the boys. Frieda loves the gals, they are gracious good girls but they are fantastic mothers and great wives. Frieda is a tough act to follow but they are genuine and lovely. They live about two miles apart, roughly thirty-five minutes from here. I think the cousins forget who belongs to whom? Did you ever see the shows Eight is Enough or the Partridge Family?"

"Sure, I used to watch both of those shows. Being an only child, I was so jealous of all the siblings and all the support and dedication to one another. I want my kids to be that close to each other but it seems like the world pulls them apart as soon as they hit school."

Sharon thought about that, "I know what you mean, my kids aren't very close either. But, like you I have a girl and a boy. They went to different colleges and have had very different focuses. I think they would be there for each other but I do understand." Sharon smiled, "You know what Frieda calls people like you and me??... Overachievers!"

At Abbey's confused, "Overachievers?"

Sharon responded, "Having a girl and a boy."

"That's cute!"

Sharon told Abbey to go ahead and light the sternos, she was going to get back to Lori and get everything plated up for the buffet.

Abbey hollered, "Don't forget to tell me what I need to do, remember I'm the newbie!"

With an loud, "Absolutely." Sharon ran off to the kitchen.

Meanwhile, Geraldine had readied herself for dinner and waited for her new friend. She had been pleasantly surprised at the beautiful appointments of the lodge and the way that the kids ran and played outside. She was also very excited by Frieda. Finally, a woman who understood her. Funny, this gal really seemed to love the kids and Abbey. Geraldine had always had such a hard time defining her own role. Here, she could just be a woman, and maybe even a friend. How very surprising. As soon as Frieda tapped on the door, she was ready. She popped out the door and the ladies made their way outside, chatting amiably the whole way.

Abbey, Matt, Lori, and Sharon, with probably seven others, got all the food out, bussed tables, stocked the buffet line, filled glasses and delivered cutlery and cleaned the kitchen without a glitch. They all worked so well together that it felt like a dance. Abbey was enthralled. She noticed that the kids had found a group. They ate a bit but ran around more. Geraldine and Frieda seemed to be enjoying themselves, as well. It was good to know that Frieda was resting. Her mother seemed a good respite for her. A bit surprising but great.

As the band got going, Abbey and the others made their way back to the kitchen and began clearing the remnant out. The props for the dinner would get put up last, so she and Matt readied the boxes and took an old rolling cart to the back of the buffet to get it all. She then got a cool drink and waited for the evening to wind down. Looking around at the checkered tables, the cowboy hat centerpieces, cowboy boot salt and peppershakers, the old wood picnic tables, and the chuck wagon buffet it had gotten past her how perfect the setting was. Even the old fans made it just feel right. As Abbey looked around she couldn't help but notice that her mother and Frieda were making their way down a path to the side of the lodge. They were arm in arm and chatting like schoolgirls. It looked like they could be sisters, or the best of friends.

She couldn't remember the last time she had seen her mother with someone she could relate to.

For the first time it occurred to Abbey, that her mother might have great need of a friend. A single tear fell down her face and touched her lips, was it possible that her mother had given up her own connections for Abbey and the kids? Her mom constantly criticized her and seemed to find nothing but fault with her. However, since arriving to help, Geraldine hadn't really had anything just for her. Feeling selfish, and disgusted with herself, Abbey watched as the two friends disappeared around the bend. Abbey wiped her face and tried to figure out what job she could accomplish next.

While Abbey had been watching her mother, Matt had been watching her. He recognized some unhappiness but figured it's be easier to pray for her than to possibly intrude on something he didn't understand. He prayed for Abbey and then got back to work, he took buffet containers back to the kitchen to scrub.

Finally, with all the pots scrubbed and the tablecloths sent to the laundry, Matt got in his truck and switched the radio on. An old preacher out of Dallas was on, one of his favorites, so he listened as he drove home.

Abbey got the kids into their beds and read them a story. She heard her mom come in next door and wanted to let her know that she was going to head back downstairs and see if there was anything left to do.

She approached the door to her mom's room. Tapping at the door, she heard her mother pad over to the door. "Yes?"

"Hi mom, I'm gonna run back downstairs and help get stuff out for the morning. The kids are next-door and just about asleep. They are fine. This country air or something." Abbey realized she was babbling, she was nervous, maybe her guilt?

"Oh sure, I'll peek in on them and give them a kiss goodnight. I'm really glad we came; I can see why you love it here. Thank you for bringing me. You did a real good job tonight. Goodnight."

"Yeah, thanks, um goodnight mom." Abbey couldn't believe it, when was the last time her mom had actually complemented her? Holy cow!

Meanwhile, Frieda was so excited. Even though, her body ached, she was elated. Geraldine was great, and she sensed the struggle of being a parent to an adult child. It must be so hard to be in her shoes. She felt like a parent around her own boys and yet her boys were grown men of wonderful character who had no need of a mom. But, she loved them still as her babes. It was just a matter of time for Geraldine; she would figure it all out. Frieda prayed herself to sleep, still excited.

Chapter 29

Abbey's alarm clock went off and squinting to read the time, she was sure it was a mistake. She couldn't quite remember why her alarm would be going off at this hour. After coming around and remembering where she was and why she had to get up, she dragged herself out of bed and dressed quickly. She tried to apply mascara and some eye liner, but her eyes were barely open, she was pretty sure she was going to look odd but she had forgotten to ask last night what time to be in the kitchen. She was hoping that coffee was going, because those giant machines perplexed her. Making her way to the kitchen, she smelled coffee, raising her fist in the air, she softly said, "YES!"

A gorgeous woman darted out of the kitchen and almost knocked smack into Abbey. "Whoa, sorry about that, can I help you?"

"Oh, hi I'm Abbey, I came down to help with the breakfast. I just wasn't sure what time to get down here to start. I guess you get here," Abbey paused and looked around, half the buffet was set up., and this woman was carrying a pitcher of water. She guessed, "Four in the morning?"

"Well, Hallelujah and Praise God, I am Celia and I am always up at the crack of midnight"...she chuckled, "I am not much of a sleeper, so I just come on up when I am out here to work. Frieda called me a couple of weeks ago and asked if I might be able to work in June. I guess the team of missionaries that had planned to come and work this summer got delayed. All the natural disasters have had the various mission boards hopping."

"Sure, I can well imagine that. So where would you like me to start and what are you doing with the pitcher of water?"

Celia smiled, "The water is for the chafing dishes, we fill to the line, walk with me and I'll show you, then I will put you on egg duty."

Abbey dutifully followed Celia, she was so graceful and beautiful. Also very down to earth, it'd be fun to work with her, although Abbey wished she had taken a bit more time to fix her face.

Celia demonstrated how to fill the chafing dishes with water, and then explained that they would light the sternos at five, fill the buffet with food by six and begin serving. She showed Abbey how to arrange the buffet and they headed back to the kitchen.

"So, the most time consuming is the bacon, but getting the eggs to the right consistency and of course cracking all of them takes a little bit, too. We pretty much keep cooking eggs all morning, the real rush will begin around eight fifteen. That's when the kiddos rush in, their poor parents dragging along behind them. The teens will be along at the very end, but most of them just sit and stare at their drinks. Our second rush is right before we close up breakfast. So we keep the eggs coming. I cook all the bacon first, and then we keep it in the steam warmers. The hash browns, are next and we whip the waffle mix up right before we serve. I like to get all the eggs beaten and in pitchers in the frig before we start on the waffle batter. To me, there's nothing worse than sweet eggs."

The two women carried about twenty-four dozen eggs from the walk-in refrigerator over to the biggest mixer that Abbey had ever seen. "What in the world, that is the biggest thing!"

"I call it Hobo, it is a Hobart mixer, and the best there is. I love the thing. Wish they made mini ones for the house. It is very simple to operate and just goes and goes. First, how are you at separating eggs? I have a separator but it slows me down."

Abbey responded, "I think I'm pretty good at it, I've never done three hundred at once, but I believe I can manage."

"Okay, so you get Frieda's first trick for the fluffiest possible eggs. Separate the yolks and put them in these great big pitchers," Celia explained while she reached up and grabbed huge plastic pitchers from a shelf above the Hobart. "Then you turn the Hobart on slow and drop the whites into the mixer. By the time you get all the whites in there, it'll be starting to whip up and stiffen a bit. We will add a half-gallon of heavy cream to the whites, and then when it gets super stiff, we will fold in the yolks. I'll show you how to change the blade on the mixer. You'll see, …. the lightest, fluffiest scrambled eggs ever."

"That's a nifty trick," this might even be a fun, "Thank you Celia. I'll get going."

"No, thank you Abbey. I am thrilled that you are here. Frieda feels strongly about you, you made some impression on her. We all want to help her but others won't be here until five forty-five," Celia gave a wink and a smile, "we've got the jump on all the big guns…I've got to turn some bacon and get started on the fruit."

Abbey worked hard all morning and enjoyed it. The machines and ovens made things fun. She particularly liked the toaster, this marvelous merry-go-round machine and a vat of melted butter with a paintbrush. She covered herself and over a hundred pieces of toast and between the smell of the bacon and the butter she thought she might be in heaven. She curiously watched while Celia first peeled the cantaloupe and honeydew and then cut in half, seeded and sliced in thin horseshoe slices. It was a different approach and it seemed to make the melon not only more appealing but also a ton easier to eat. She was also fascinated when Celia showed her the scrap bucket, they used it for feed and also buried in the gardens. Less waste and less trash. Made a lot of sense. Apparently, the eggshells were a particularly good fertilizer for the vegetable garden. All the coffee grounds went in as well.

Once breakfast was underway, Abbey marveled at the smooth and appealing spread. It was one thing to come in and eat, entirely another to have created it. Abbey felt really good. By the time breakfast was over and cleaned up, Abbey was really tired. She decided to take the kids down to the large pond to swim, but wanted to relax for a few minutes. She approached her mom, and was greeted with a surprise.

"Abbey, I'll take the kids. You rest. I have never seen you work so hard as you have the past tow meals, and you have done a good job. Besides the kids want to show me something. We'll see you later."

Surprised, and thrilled, "Okay, thanks mom." At first glance she was pleased, but then she started to over analyze…what did she mean *she's never seen me work so hard*, all I do is work. Laundry, food, dishes, oh never mind. I am too tired to deal with that attitude. Abbey fell asleep, when she awakened however she realized that she was going to need to learn better time management, dinner would be on before she knew it. She wanted to figure out why her mom couldn't see her work as real work. Would she never approve of her?

Abbey wandered out towards the barns and asked Jess about Geves and Bug. Everywhere she went, someone had seen the kids earlier or recently but no one knew for sure which way they had gone. It seemed that Abbey was at least ten paces behind them no matter where she went. She was told that Philip and Janna Kay were with them, so she wasn't really concerned. She just wanted to see them.

Eventually, She gave up and wound her way back to the kitchen to see what tonight was about. When she got there, she smelled

Mexican and was immediately excited. Sharon and Leah were working at grating cheeses and jalapenos and the ovens were full of meats and chicken.

"MMMMM, Fajita Heaven," Abbey smiled, "Where's Lori?"

Sharon responded, "Just in time abbey! You can start out in the hall. It's time to get the piñatas filled. To answer your question, Lori is running into town. She wanted something for tonight, but I have no idea what."

"Wonderful, I love piñatas, does everyone get to play? Do you film for <u>America's Funniest Home Videos</u>? Or is just for the kids?"

"Believe it or not, Frieda has one for every family! She lets the kids make them at the craft shop. It's really a fun project. Although, honestly, some of them are nearly impossible to break. If I had to guess, I say the kids make them that way intentionally, but either way it is always fun to watch. The kids get such a kick out of watching their family attempt to break into the creatures, of course they name them too- might be why some are nearly invincible." Leah laughed.

"Sounds great, well I'll get right to work!" Abbey said excitedly. She stepped out of the kitchen and right back in, "Where and How do I hang, said piñatas?"

Sharon smiled, "To begin with, they will be the centerpiece for the tables, you should see a name attached to the piñata and you can use the table stanchions to put the place card out. The table clothes are marked and you'll see the notebook."

"Perfect!" Abbey headed to the storeroom. The smell from the kitchen was making her really hungry; she'd start with the tables and then beg Sharon for a sample.

When she reached the storeroom she found 27 piñatas stacked on a rolling cart. She was beginning to realize how much she had learned, when she went around the corner and brought back the table stanchions. They were the long stands that sat on tables, held numbers or names and could be seen easily. She felt like a real pro. She grabbed the Notebook with the layouts in them just to make sure she didn't forget anything. The table clothes were very decorative in bright yellows and golds with decorative ribbons and beads around the edges. They made the whole place feel festive immediately. By the time Abbey had added the silverware, the piñatas and the chip and salsa bowls, the whole room started to come together.

Using the notebook as her guide, she brought out the boxes marked Mexican Fiesta and found the light up peppers, brightly colored plates and napkins. She laughed at a whole box of mini sombreros and a large box filled with burrito shaped candles. Abbey couldn't contain herself, she practically danced as she placed the sombreros over the light fixtures and hung the peppers around each of the windows. Abbey was recalling good times at one of her favorite Atlanta restaurants, La Paz, she kept thinking about her favorite cheese dip, all gooey and creamy, and a bit spicy. It was time to go begging in the kitchen. Abbey couldn't take her own imagination.

Abbey surveyed the room and adjusted a couple of the candles. She could not wait for the guests to see this, it was wonderful. There was a crash in the kitchen, so she headed that way.

Lori sheepishly looked up, "OOPS, as my grandson says, My bad!" Sharon and Lori were laughing and picking up about a million little pieces of tortilla chips and a large metal pan. Lori saw Abbey's look of concern and assured her that they had ample chips for about seven functions like this. Thank goodness it wasn't a wet dish….

Abbey joined Lori and Sharon as they cleaned up the mess. The three women cleaned and giggled. As they chatted about their lives, Abbey realized that she had grossly misjudged their ages. Each had grandchildren, and not even little babies, but a couple of grade schoolers. Abbey was surprised.

Sharon gave her a look and directed Abbey to go to the walk in cooler; she followed behind, "Let's get these out," as she pushed a large Queen Mary cart that held tray upon tray of what appeared to be salted margarita glasses.

Abbey looked quizzically at Sharon, who just laughed, "Don't worry hon, frozen limeade with sugar round the rims. Just the right touch, donchya think?"

Nodding, she smiled, "Naturally!!" They really were awfully pretty. So Frieda had found someone who loved to thrill as much as she did. Abbey wondered if Sharon didn't do it for Frieda, as well. All these women, with a desire to wow the guests.

Lori came over and beamed at both of them, "It is just impossible to leave well enough alone. Frieda has come up with wonderful things, and we just have to keep adding to it…what is the old expression? …if a pound is good let's add a ton."

The women grabbed the candy filling for the piñatas and all headed back to the dining hall. As Abbey contemplated some of the curious piñatas, she took note of the two with her last name on them. She wasn't sure what they were supposed to be exactly, but she could tell that one had to be Bug's, it was more slapped together with pieces hanging down. Geve's must have created the white one. She started to wonder about her mother and the kids and what they might be up to. They hadn't mentioned a thing to her. A moment later she saw her kids and her mom saunter in, as if they owned the place.

The kids laughed, while Geraldine seemed very pleased with herself. Bug started to race off again, but Abbey caught him. She reintroduced everyone to Lori and Sharon and proceeded to ask them, "Tell me what this piñata is all about, is there a story here?"

"Yep," the ever-pensive Bug was about to launch into a detailed description of the construction but his sister cut him off. "Mom," she said, it's a contraption to hold candy, and Bug made it too easy to get into. He hardly put any layers! Now mine is gonna be tough. But can we please not hit mine? It's supposed to be Moses."

Abbey realized at that moment that the one she thought was a ghost or some cloud formation was her daughter's. "Wow, Moses, huh? Well I bet he's mighty proud that you chose to make hi into a piñata. Yes, let's leave Moses out of it tonight. I cannot imagine hitting Moses. Why don't you all go get cleaned up, dinner is in twenty-five minutes."

As always, the food was spectacular- Lori and Sharon had the flavoring down to a perfect science. Everyone was genuinely happy, and the children just loved presenting their parents with sticks to destroy their creations. The Mexican Hat Dance finished the evening, and then the families all took their bags full of goodies and dispersed.

Abbey's family made their way tiredly to their beds and nearly collapsed in their sombreros. It was a good feeling, though, the physical exhaustion. The satisfaction of a job well done. Abbey slept like a baby.

Chapter 30

Abbey rose at four thirty again, she made her way down to the kitchen, where she got the eggs separated and started the Hobart mixer. Working hard, she enjoyed the company of Leah. Together they got the breakfast out and the chafing dishes lit. The more she learned the more Abbey enjoyed the work and the pace.

As people gathered with their families for breakfast, Abbey serviced the buffet, checked the baskets of bread and ran around filling coffee and water glasses. She had one incident with the eggs where she left the sterno under a chafing dish without a damper so the whole container got really hot. The eggs sat at such a high temp, they turned completely green. It was Dr. Seuss time, <u>Green Eggs and Ham</u>. Yuck. They had to throw out almost a full pan. Abbey assured herself, that it would never happen again. Leah told her it was a common rookie mistake.

The rest of the morning Abbey would chant, "Sam, I am" Other parents would knowingly smile and chime in from time to time. Funny how every toddler seemed somewhat addicted to that poem, showing that Doctor Seuss' stays genius. She enjoyed the whole morning, especially seeing her children tear into the foods, and even try different flavors of syrups and fruits. Nice to see them both so hungry. Geraldine smiled at Abbey, "This country air really stirs up the appetite." Abbey was gonna have a hard time going back to pop-tarts.

After breakfast was cleaned up, Abbey checked in with Leah and a young man in the kitchen, Leah introduced Zach who was a local that came in to help the putting together of several picnics and some sort of "fish fry components." Apparently if you wanted to you could catch and cook your own lunch. Unfortunately, there wasn't much for Abbey to do.

So she ran to find her family. She looked out towards the barn and asked if anyone had seen her kiddos, no one had but Janna Kay was pretty sure they hadn't gone past either. Abbey returned to the lodge and headed upstairs. Geraldine was singing with Frieda in Frieda's room, and Abbey cracked up at their not so great attempt to harmonize. While Frieda had a weak soprano voice, Geraldine had something of a flat tenor. No Barber Shop Quartet for them. Neither was gifted in the singing arena. It was actually kind of cute, though, to see two older women grinning and singing. Geraldine would change pitch often, but they would put their heads together as they finished a verse.

Abbey tried to be inconspicuous and pass by, but Geraldine spotted her and waved her in.

"Hi, Frieda and I sent the kids off with a wonderful young man named Matt. She assured me that you knew him and that you were friends. Is that okay?"

"Oh, of course, I didn't even know that Matt was here. How are you feeling Frieda, is there anything I can get for you?"

"Actually dear, I would really love to speak with you and your mother about something I've been thinking about. Is now a good time?"

Mother and daughter looked at each other and nodded to Frieda.

Good. Just so," with a determined look on her face, "How long are the children out of school?"

Abbey responded, "They go back on August twenty-fourth."

"Is there anything you need to get back to right away?"

Again Geraldine and Abbey looked at each other and shook their heads. "No we even brought the hamsters, and the fish have an auto feeder, although, I should probably get my mail," answered Abbey.

"Fantastic, it would appear that my doc wants me in bed for at least a few more weeks, I would like to offer you two a position here and it would be paid. Although, I cannot offer a lot in the way of compensation, I can at least help you keep your rent paid and naturally, you will dine and stay here. I just need you as long as you can stay. Is that okay?"

Frieda's mind had been working toward this, she felt like God was telling her something in her prayers, but just couldn't figure out what in the world it could be. All she could be sure of is that Abbey needed to be at the ranch.

Abbey wanted to jump at the chance. She thought she could squeeze an article or two out and actually get ahead a tiny bit. It also seemed to be a great solution to her ongoing expenses with daycare and summer camps. The kids were thriving. She looked to her mom for approval, and when she got it, she decided to leap. "We're yours as long as you need us, I'll just need approval from the two short bosses."

Both older ladies cracked up. Finally Geraldine answered her concern, "Oh Abbey, they've already begged to stay and never leave."

"Super, then it is all settled. I put a stop hold on my mail, so I guess I'll just need to send an order to forward the mail for a month or so. I think our landlord could probably stop and check the fish feeder, even refill it possibly, Cool! You know, Frieda, you may just find me irreplaceable."

Frieda smiled and thought to herself, I'm counting on it. She told Geraldine that she would nap for a while and suggested that

Abbey do some work or get a bit of rest. Matt would be taking the kids to catch their own lunch. After lunch, he had promised to get them cleaned up and ready for New York night.

Abbey was ecstatic, this would be a blast. New York, New York was unreal. She couldn't wait to see it. Also, it would be nice to see Matt. She hoped that her kids behaved but figured it was better for him to see what they were all about. He had been to the ranch so many times as a child; he would surely understand their perspective. She hoped that no ducks were off wrestling, and smirked. Abbey excused herself and went in to lay down, but she couldn't stop thinking about everything she had participated in. She thought of the kids with their amazing piñatas and the way that all the women around here laughed together. She was even a bit awe struck by her mom. Watching her mother laughing and singing was so out of character for her. It was like she had gone into a wonderland. Maybe Disney had it wrong, maybe Sweet Silver Ranch was really the best place on earth. She felt like a different person. She felt peaceful, and as if what she did mattered.

Abbey got back up and decided to try to write, she wrote a couple of ideas down and jotted some notes about peace and restfulness and how they were a result of exhaustion and completion. That did it; she laid back down and fell asleep.

She dreamed of Broadway shows, and cute yellow ducklings.

Geves and Bug burst into Abbey's room early in the afternoon and woke her up to tell her about their fishing expedition and the tuna sandwiches that Matt had packed. Apparently, he had tricked them into thinking they had to catch their own lunch. Matt had told them they would have to catch something big enough and then make a fire and a pot and cook them before they'd eat. He told them how hungry he was and that he'd need them to catch an especially big fish for him to eat. They were enthused and seemed quite taken

148

with Matt, too; who had taken them all over the ranch. They had driven the Mule from Matt's lap and they had helped to repair a fence that Moses had messed with. Both kids claimed to have helped with a lot of thing and abbey hoped that they had genuinely been helpful. They could be, but she knew from her own experiences that they could just as likely have been a handful.

Abbey loved waking to her kids, even if it had been a bit startling. She had always thought that these kids were some special measure sent to keep her from going crazy. Well, maybe *half-keep* her from going crazy. Some days she felt like she'd crossed that particular bridge.

After demanded hugs and kisses, the kids rushed to tell grandma and Miss Frieda of all their adventures. Abbey freshened up and went to check out what the preparations were for tonight.

Nearing the main hall, she heard men's voices, peals of laughter, and a lot of mechanical noises. Abbey got closer to peek. Maybe there was one of those meetings that Frieda had told her about. Peeking in she saw Philip, Jonathan, and another older man pulling down screens from the ceiling. There must have been thirty separate audio/visual screens and a camera or some sort of multi-lens video thing that was lowered by a pole into the center of the room. Abbey wasn't sure how she had missed all those things being there. It was as if it didn't matter until they were in use. She did wonder what the screens were for, but then she heard the distinctive sound of Matt's voice behind her. She turned and saw that Matt was covered from the top of his head to the bottom of his boots with mud and dirt. He was a colossal mess. She snickered and then with the suddenness of a light bulb switching on, "Oh no, did my kids do this to you?"

He chuckled, "Absolutely, Bug has a gift for driving and running-he managed to find every tiny spot of mud between the pond and the bunkhouse, I feel as though I have been to a spa for one of those

special treatments! But, I cam straightaway, to help these slow men."
Matt raised his eyebrows at the others.

Abbey wanted to thank him for the day with the kids, but
was interrupted by the older man, as Abbey turned she saw a
distinguished and terribly handsome man. He was a combination
of Sean Connery and Cary Grant. He had beautiful shiny silver hair
and kind grey eyes. He was dressed in a nice cotton cable sweater
that was bright blue and made his eyes glisten. He had large features
but they were really well put together. He winked at Abbey, "You
must be Abbey, and my girl says you are the cat's meow. And that
is high praise, young lady. I'm Mark and I'm Frieda's pop." He took
Abbey's hand in both of his and grazed her cheek with a kiss.

Abbey was somewhat flummoxed. He was very handsome and
if he was Frieda's dad he had to be ancient. Before she had a chance
to answer, Mark looked into her eyes and continued.

"I am so glad to meet you. I've spoken with Geves a dozen times,
she is a bright one, you need to get her reading some poetry, and I've
got just the book. I'll bring it to you tonight at dinner, okay? I better
get cracking or my daughter will hop out of bed and jump on me.
Blessings Abbey, see you at dinner."

Abbey nodded and smiled and said, "bye" as Mark strolled
away. He had held her hand in both of his the entire time he spoke,
he had behaved as if they were the only two people on the planet.
What a charmer.

Matt found Abbey's introduction to Mark funny. That imposing
old man had more energy and more heart than anyone that Matt
had ever known. He had always enjoyed any time with Mark. They
had been really close when he was here as a child and because he had
fallen in with the two other grandsons, Mark had accepted him as
one of the gang. It tickled him and intrigued him to watch Abbey
get tongue tied and charmed by the guy. Matt had no idea how he

did it. Any woman or child in Mark's orbit was immediately drawn to him. Even as an old guy, the women still just loved him. He'd have to quiz Abbey about it. Maybe, he'd figure it out.

"Abbey, your kids are fantastic! I wasn't sure if your mom was gonna let me take them, but Frieda intervened. I hope it was okay. I got in last night and had this idea to take the kids. I really didn't have a chance to clear it with you, I am sorry about that."

Abbey responded, "I cannot thank you enough. The kids were fairly busting with details about your excursion today. They had a ball and, of course, it was super. Mom is fairly smitten with you I'm afraid. You may have to watch yourself." Abbey teased, "Mark is amazing, isn't he?" Abbey paused and struggled for words, "well I don't know. I'm never at a loss for words, I'm a writer for crying out loud, but Mark, and well he is just something else. Frieda's dad, too. Wow!"

Matt laughed, "Mark has that way with women. I will watch out for your mother, and I enjoyed the kids."

He was beginning to explain the New York theme when there was a sudden burst of sound and visual. The room was filled with screens showing Times Square images scenes around New York, and the Empire State Building. Frank Sinatra was singing, 'Start spreading the news....' It was all-spectacular. Amazing how a few screens and some film could transform the room into a city scene. Abbey looked all around her turning 360 degrees and looked up at skyscrapers, and streets filled with taxicabs, buses and people going by on screens. She was surrounded by the sights and besides Sinatra; she could hear horns and traffic noises in the background. "Holy cow, it's New York!"

Jonathan hollered down when he saw her, "Welcome to New York City, the Big APPLE!"

"This is great! I cannot wait. What are we serving?"

As Abbey was asking the question, Philip and Zach were making their way, somewhat clumsily, through he double doors with what appeared to be a huge cart. Matt raced over to give the guys a hand. Once they got it into position and began unfolding the contraption, it became clear, it was a street vendors cart, and this one appeared to be for hot dogs. They set it up under one of the screens that was showing skyscrapers from a street view.

Abbey clapped her hands together, beaming. It was all she could do; she was delighted with all of it. She felt a bit foolish, especially since she purported to be a writer, but sometimes the appropriate word is, "wow"!

Jonathan checked all the screens, made a few adjustments, cut the power and said that he'd see them all later. Matt and Philip rolled in another Queen Mary full of tablecloths, candles, and miniature skylines for each of the tables, and then the guys headed back for more vendors carts. Matt told Abbey there would be an abundance of foods on the carts and vendors yelling, 'get your hotdogs' or 'pizza' or whatever they were serving. Abbey started working on the individual tables.

Abbey was glad Jonathan had cut the sound and video, she was still awestruck by the look and feel of the room. It was really exciting. She stood in the center absentmindedly folding one of the paper skylines that would serve as a centerpiece.

Leah arrived within a few minutes and saw Abbey just standing there.

"Hi Abbey, you okay?"

Abbey was glad to see Leah, "Fine, I'm just daydreaming. I haven't been to New York in years; I've never taken the kids. I am pleased and it looks like I'll be staying for the summer."

Leah grabbed Abbey and hugged her, "I am so glad. What a relief. I cannot tell you how happy that will make Frieda. I am very happy that you are here and I think that we work really well together."

"Absolutely, just don't forget, I'm still a novice. So, will we really be serving hot dogs, hamburgers, popcorn, pizza, and pretzels as the carts are labeled?"

"Of course, no false advertising here! We will also have a fruit vendor and some cupcakes and cookies in the center under the cameras. Which street vendor do you want to man?"

"Seriously? Well I guess you'll have to find the one that is least difficult. Or at least what you think I can handle."

Leah and Abbey spent the rest of the afternoon setting up the tables, checking out the carts, and putting supplies like buns and ketchup out. Abbey thought a lot about how a bit of effort transformed the whole place into other worlds. She decided to be the hamburger girl and set her cart up from start to finish, so that she would know where everything was. She got her shirt, apron, and paper cap and took them with her; she'd clean up before dinner and come down ready. Sharon and Lori had the kitchen and the guys were cleaning up and laying low for a bit. Leah said that she would stay downstairs and heat all the carts. She sent Abbey up to shower and find her kids.

Abbey spotted her kids on and around the porch playing with a bunch of other kids, they even had a few goats in the mix. It appeared to be a game of tag, Abbey was tickled at the way the goats would follow the kids around and then bump them from behind. Apparently the boys in particular liked it, too. Some of the girls sat on the porch watching. They were all giggling and Geraldine was seated nearby with Frieda, they smiled and waved. All was well. Abbey waved back, tapped her watch and showed the women her hat and apron, then proceeded to go to her room for a quick shower. She couldn't wait for the kids to see New York. It would be fun!

Abbey got back down to the hall; she helped haul food out to the heated carts and got some further direction on her stand. She was in place tongs in hand when the dinner whistle blew. Funny, with the lights down, the screens were even more prevalent. The music, the hustle and bustle of all the people streaming in and the cart workers were each hollering 'get your hot dogs' and 'hot pizza'. Abbey decided to try her voice out yelling, "Burger, Hot and Ready!" She was so grateful for her family, grateful for the guests. They all came in and just 'oohed' and 'ahhed'. Many families were struck, as Abbey had been and stood off to the side, looking all around them, not sure quite what to do. One near Abbey's cart was near tears. Saying quietly to one another, that they could never have done this for their children. The parents looked at each other and said, "Praise Jesus". At the same time, Abbey felt like she had intruded. When they saw her, they said, "Bless you and thank you so much." Abbey smiled and was nearly in tears herself. Yes this was a gift, and it was so great to be part of it.

Towards the end of the meal, she began carting the food to the kitchen. Then cleaned up her workspace. It was then that she noticed some folks at the door. Disconnecting the electric from the cart, she continued to clean. Satisfied that the cart was shiny, new, and ready to be put away for the next time, she cast a glance at the people at the door. They were strangers to her, and actually looked to be a group of overdressed older folks. Not sure if she could help or do anything, she wondered into the kitchen to ask Lori.

Lori turned to Sharon, and with shrugs, they all headed out to see who it might be.

Out of nowhere Jonathan appeared and he was greeted with kisses, handshakes, and hugs by the newcomers. Jonathan grabbed Philip, (the former hot dog vendor and self proclaimed 'king o the

Bronx'), and they moved a piano onto the stage area. The curtains were closed, it seemed a show was about to begin.

Standing towards the back, Lori, Sharon, Leah and Abbey waited curiously. The screens went up in front of the stage; all the rest had been dimmed. The light son the stage came up and Jonathan introduced the Barn Raising Players, were a performance troop of retirees. The women all looked at each other as the music began. A man of at least eighty, not terribly fit sat at the piano, with a slump. He didn't look well, but his smile was huge, he clearly loved performing. Coming up behind the piano, a woman…. who had to be at least seventy, in leotards, with a cape, top hat, and a cane. She began singing New York, New York complete with the rockette-style kicks. Problem was, she was just terrible. It appeared to be a comedy routine. The whole room was exploding with clapping and laughter. Abbey was concerned that these older folks were serious, but there wasn't anyone to ask, the staff around her all seemed too stunned to answer a question. The applause was huge, with people roaring, which seemed to please the players. It all seemed a bit odd.

They did two more routines, both appalling in their poor quality. There were just too old, their voices were rather weak, their movements slow and at times offbeat. Abbey tended to be too empathetic but it seemed so wrong to laugh at them. They didn't seem to mind, but it just seemed rude. But, really they were quite a picture; the costumes were garishly old with sequins everywhere, tassels, and spats. The women actually were made up with what looked to be mime makeup, the caked on quality, with the clown like cheeks and deep red lips was somehow disturbing when combined with jowels and deeply sagging skin. It just didn't seem to go with anything else at the ranch. Maybe, that was the point. Abbey thought New York might be about as far as you could get from Sweet Silver, who knew? Very odd.

Jonathan got up thanked them, and explained that the Barn Raising Players had been together since they had performed on Broadway in the late 1930's and 40's. There weren't many of them left, but they wanted to come bless the pastors and their families. And that they had volunteered to come and perform. Everyone gave a round of applause, and they took a bow.

Stifling a yawn, Abbey asked the Lori and Sharon what else needed to be done. They all retreated to the kitchen to check and Leah left to get some rest before breakfast. The boys would get all the carts put away and set up for the morning.

After finishing the last of the dishes, Abbey said good night and trudged on up to check on the kids. She saw that Geves was fast asleep. She seemed really peaceful. She wondered if the restlessness that her daughter showed normally, wasn't dissipating somewhat. There were no covers on the floor; no pillows askew and the bedding looked half tucked. The ranch was wearing them all out, but in a restful and peaceful way.

Chapter 31

Abbey yawned and stretched, something had woken her up. What was it? Looking at the clock, she had forty-five minutes left to sleep. And then she heard it again, a horrible sound outside. Maybe this was Frieda's screaming rabbit. Abbey tried to ignore the sound but within minutes Bug and Geves were by her bed, "Mama, look outside. Please we have to do something!"

Abbey reluctantly looked out and saw a cat dragging itself, low to the ground and an owl attacking it. She saw the horrified looks on her kids' faces and hurriedly put her shoes on. Abbey was an animal lover, but not to this degree. She needed a weapon. What did one do to fight off an owl? She went out the side door, the children inching behind. She wielded the book she was reading and a belt.

Matt rushed out first, he ran at the owl, and the owl flew away. The little cat had blood all over it, yet it was looking up at it's heros with unflinching awe. Matt, seeing the kids' distress, gave them tasks.

"Geves, go and get a pillow. And Bug you get a towel. We'll take the little guy into the mud room."

The kids raced to do Matt's bidding. They appeared within moments with the materials. Abbey was fidgeting, trying to tamp down her hair and rub the sleep out of her eyes. She was embarrassed to be out here with Matt in her robe with her book and belt. She was really grateful that he was there, though. She looked at the small cat and wasn't sure what to do.

Matt gently scooped up the cat onto the pillow, using the towel, and transported it to the mud room. Once there, he gave the kids more directions regarding antibiotic ointment and some peroxide. He gently stroked the cat where he saw no blood, and spoke to it tenderly. Abbey was impressed but had no idea how to help, but Matt quietly explained to her that he would need her help, cats were notoriously bad about being doctored.

He wound up holding and stroking the cat, while Abbey actually performed the clean up and applied a ton of antibiotic ointment to it's wounds. It appeared that the owl had actually been holding the cat. Probably in the air. And had dropped it. The wounds were puncture-like, and the cat had a little trouble getting it's back end straightened to stand. Matt told Abbey that the cat might heal, but not to get her hopes up. It was one of those barn cats, he thought, and with its slight build, probably a juvenile.

The kids had to know everything. They had agreed to name the "little guy" as Matt had referred to it earlier, "Lou."

Abbey hated to burst their bubble, but she was pretty sure that the cat was a female.

Realizing that she would be due in the kitchen, Abbey rushed ot get ready and ran to the kitchen. She and Leah managed everything well. While working together, Abbey relayed all the excitement of the morning to Leah. Both women planned to check on the cat after they finished breakfast. Leah loved cats, but had always been allergic to them, she planned to help when she could, and until she couldn't breathe. She also assured Abbey that Frieda would have no problem with this little cat being nursed in Abbey's room. Abbey just hoped there was enough allergy medicine for her to manage. Geves and Bug were certainly getting an interesting education and quite the experience.

Chapter 32

Routines began to take shape for this fifth day at the ranch and Abbey was more of an asset than she ever thought she could be. She definitely felt as sense of accomplishment and couldn't wait to see the next event and take part in creating it. Even after repeating a theme evening, it was fun to see how the new guests would respond. That was the complete and total magic of it. The transformations. Waterless waterways, ice swans, street carts, bands, and fabulous foods. Abbbey couldn't imagine creating and planning but she could feel the excitement as each new group entered. It was like showing the world to some gentle people. The other thing that surprised her was that she really appreciated working with these servant types. Lori, Sharon, Frieda, Matt, all of them were just thrilled to be doing the work – each and every one of them felt genuine love for the people, and even the people they had yet to meet. And when a family returned, my goodness, you would think that the greatest of friends were uniting.

Years ago, Abbey, had had a roommate. It was college for Abbey and she met this woman, Judie, who needed a roomie in some apartments near the school. Abbey and she became the best of friends. They genuinely loved each other's company. They didn't part until they each got married, but Abbey could remember times with Judie that seemed like special events, even though they lived together. Every time a family returned to the ranch, it was just like that, a celebration. Lori and Sharon would rush from the kitchen to embrace and kiss the families, then would spend time gushing about changes, or the lack of changes (for the older sets). Frieda knew everyone by name and could tell you some small thing about each and every one. She always remembered an event from their travels here. No one went unaffected by Sweet Silver.

Being here felt like relaxing, maybe the opportunity to be wowed and awed, the peaceful nature, the physical aspects and healthy living all purposed to make it possible to just be yourself. Abbey couldn't detect any fascades or masks. She recognized for the first time that being here was more like coming home to yourself. No compromises, no worries. It didn't matter what was happening at home or at work. If the roof leaked, or the carpet smelled. No one had to think about those things. They could merely focus on what was happening around them from one moment to the next. It gave them a peace, and one that they all seemed to share. Abbey wondered if it was the all the ranch or if these people might be the same way at home. Do they even know what brought them together? It still seemed to Abbey, that there was something magical about this place. A place where even her mother became delightful. Who knew? Abbey would continue to try to figure it out.

Abbey found that she herself was sad that this week was coming to a close. Many of the families that were here, would be heading home. She worried about how her own children would respond to losing the new friends, and having to meet a whole new set. The natural ebb and flow of the camp. One good thing, Lou, or as Abbey was now calling her; Loulabelle, was healing and had taken up with Shasta. It was hilarious, the dog seemed to want to care for and protect the cat. Shasta was constantly watching for anything or anyone approaching the cat. No one could touch her without approval. Once again, the ranch seemed magical and surprised Abbey. Only here could a dog be the owner of a cat.

Lori stopped to check on Frieda and noticed Abbey standing in the hallway petting Lou and Shasta. "Hi sweet girl, how are you? How's the little cat-what are you calling her?"

"Hey Lori, I was just checking on her. This little gal is Loulabelle, and she's coming along quite nicely. She's walking, although her backend is still week. She isn't able to get up on things yet, so I'm kind of glad that Shasta is so protective. I don't think the little thing could even get herself out of the way, is she needed to. How are you doing? Tonight is sianara night, right? I am excited to see your Japanes chefs. How fun! When will we begin the prep?"

"Oh tonight is insanely easy. The meat is all in the refrigerators in marinade, and the Japanese chefs do almost everything. The cooking tables will be set out by the guys and then we just stock them. Then we will set up the tables like usual. We have all the desserts ready, and otherwise it's more about the show of it all. I hear that your little Winston has charge of the gong. Is he excited?"

"You have no idea. He actually asked Frieda, if he could do a Samari performance. Frieda explained that due to the insurance and rules, that it had to be done by professionals. He was so disappointed, but I am just thrilled. Frieda was able to tell him, "no," in a way that saved his 'little masculine boy toughness.'" They shared a conspiratal wink. Every Mom understood the need for their little boys to be macho. Lori started talking about her grandson, Wyatt, she flashed a picture of a really cute young boy. Wyatt had always been a mama's boy but he also wanted to be tough. Lori agreed that it was a tightrope for a mom. It was nice to be with so many people who got what it meant to be a parent.

Abbey had worked in a world where most where most weren't parents or spent no time with their own kids. She had tried to be a stay-at-home mom, but when her husband had checked out, she got a job free-lance writing to try to make ends meet. She longed to be with her kids as much as possible, and day care was an impossible cost.

Lori went on to see about Frieda, as Abbey headed toward the dining hall. She left the dog and cat in the hall, but made sure that her door was blocked open for the cat to get back in. Abbey was hoping that she could get the dining hall set up and then run and swim with her kids for a bit. The pool looked particularly beautiful from the window.

After working hard for over an hour, she was happy with the way things looked. Te food couldn't be delivered until the tables were plugged in and the chefs were getting set up.

Abbey ran to her room, got into a bathing suit and a nice cover up and flew outside to find the kids. She located them in the hen house with Geraldine and Frieda.

"Hi dear, grab a baby chick and help," said Frieda.

Delighted, Abbey complied. She placed two of the softest little chicks in the pockets of her wrap, and gently getting a third in her hand, she followed the others. Everyone had at least two chicks and they all walked out to a small yard that had a coop and some adult hens. The chicks were placed with the hens and ran around pecking at the ground and some food. They appeared to be playing a complicated game of tag. After watching them for a few minutes, Abbey looked at her mom and Frieda then asked, "So how come you are out of bed?"

The older women shared a look, but Frieda answered. "Doc says I need to get out a bit. Do some walking and get a little sunshine. I'm better Abbey- it's just that I must take it a great deal easier than usual. I always think I am tougher than I am and I guess I've been ignoring the signs for a while. I have been tired for quite a while. Symptoms that I chose to ignore should not have been ignored. But I promise, I am paying attention now. Besides, you and your mom have been terrific. You have taken over for me in the kitchen and dining room, and your mother has made the time pass by so easily." Frieda held up her hand and crossed her heart, " I promise you Abbey, I am listening and I cannot thank you enough."

Abbey smiled at Frieda and looked over at the kids, "hey you two, are you up for a swim with your mama?"

They beamed and jumped and nodded and ran for the lodge in seconds. Meanwhile Geraldine and Abbey ushered Frieda back inside and up to her bed. Frieda was much slower than Abbey remembered. Just a month or so ago, she hadn't been able to keep up with the woman. It was sad really to see such a decline. Abbey sincerely hoped Frieda was getting better.

As soon as the kids appeared, in bathing suits, Frieda told Abbey to go and not worry but that she needed to discuss the upcoming week with her later. It was going to be unusual. Abbey was pleased that Frieda was going to allow her to really help. She hoped Frieda knew how hard she was working, she really believed in earning her keep.

In a blur of two blonde headed kids, towels, and inflated pool toys, they were off. The water was crystal clear and the soft whirring of the motors was peaceful. There were only a few people sitting around the pool, most were reading, one snoozing. Bug, being a boy, had to be the first one in. Geves and Abbey looked at each other laughingly. Geves eventually jumped in, too. Abbey was more of a slow entrance. She slowly got her feet wet, sitting on the side watching her two little fish. They loved the water and were so natural in it. Abbey had slowly gotten to the steps and made it to where the water was lapping at her knees. This was not working, she realized…the only way was to jump. Spying the diving board and checking to see who was around, Abbey decided to go for it. She leapt, unceremoniously, and not gracefully off the diving board and swam up from underneath to her two squealing kids. They splashed, raced, and did summersaults in the pool for over an hour.

By the time they got out, they were all pruned and exhausted. Each got a cold lemonade from the small refrigerator near the pool, and dried off for a bit on the lounge chairs. She realized that she did recognize one of the families by the pool. She imagined that they were probably relaxing on their last day. ..

After getting dried off, they headed to their rooms to get dressed. Both kids were supposed to go back and help Jess with getting the chicks in before dinner. Bug was then going to go with grandma and make sure he was ready for his 'gong duties'. After delivering the kids, Abbey grabbed her steno pad and headed to see Frieda.

Frieda was up and looked really happy and relaxed, "Abbey, come in how was your swim?"

"Wonderful thank you. I am thoroughly tired, but it feels really good. It's funny the more I do the stronger I feel."

"Oh yes, there is something so great about good old fashioned physical exercise. It's funny, we look at kids and think, where do they get all that energy, well, it's from constantly moving, of course." Frieda was grinning and continued, "Lori and Sharon keep gushing about how natural and easy you are to work with. They say it is more like dancing than working. I hope you sense our joy over you – not many people can jump in the way that you have. How do you feel about all of the work here?"

Abbey had to smile, dancing, yes, that's right, it is one movement and a counter movement. She had never been particularly graceful, but this did seem easy and natural. Just like being a mom. Holding her babies had been the most natural thing in the world.

She blurted out, "Truly wonderful…you know I just love the work. I really do. There is something magical about this place, and I do find the work fun. I thought it would get dull after having seen the set ups and then setting them up, but really I keep imagining the way the new people will feel, and how I felt the first few times. I get carried away, it's my imagination, I suppose. This all just feeds right into a writer's imagination. Lori and Sharon have so much talent and direction, it is just easy. Leah and I have an easy comraderie, too. But it's really more them. I also think I am getting stronger, my feet still hurt sometimes, but I am learning. Thank you for the opportunity and the encouragement." She hugged Frieda and then sat down to take notes.

"You are so welcome. I saw that you loved it, as I did the first time you were here. I tell you, when I was in college, I worked in the food service industry- once it is in your blood, I am afraid it stays there. I need to tell you about the upcoming week; sadly our families are getting ready to pack up and go home and tomorrow will be a little crazy we'll have cars, vans, and all manner of transport coming and going. Oh the Wallaces from the Philippines will stay on. We will be hosting one of our scholar weeks next week where we attempt to assist the pastors with some basic business courses and quiet fellowship time. The meals will be much more basic – meat and potatoes, with lunches added. We also keep to a very conventional buffet. The men seem to like the regularity of it, but we women crave the extras, the variety. The guys seem to like to go through their routines. We won't do all the decorating and entertaining. My dad, will do quite a bit of speaking, as will a few others who consider the ranch a second home."

Frieda took a sip of water and continued, "What I am hoping for from you, is a bit more of your writing skills. Since set ups won't be nearly as involved, I am hoping it will free up some time for you to sit in on some of the talks. We really need to get them documented. I spoke with David, he's your editor, right?"

"Yes Ma'am, we call him Ed at the office, short for editor."

"Well that's clever, anyway, he agreed that you could possibly to a series on our business courses. So many pastors cannot get here but really need the information. We cover a myriad of topics. Human Resources and the law, marketing, and employment issues as well as not for profit tax issues. It seems that my dad has a way of putting great nuggets into the marketing sessions, and the guys have a hard time capturing all of it. For our purposes, you would be creating something of a handout. Obviously, I know this is a strange request. We just need someone who can capture some of those nuggets. You can use recorders or anything else you wish. Dad as some materials that he makes available. He just has so much in that head of his. So many questions come up and he seems to just dig a new great insight out each time. As you know, he is no spring chicken, although he's quite a bit more spry than I am these days."

Frieda drank more deeply and continued, "He is a wonderful gift, but many of these pastors haven't ever been to business school and I'm afraid that he blows past them quite a bit. He does give them a great overall sense of what the individual church Brand means and he is wonderful at conceptualizing ideas for the guys. So, is this something that interests you?"

Abbey tried to take in all the information, tapping her pencil on the pad, "Of course, I would love to try." She thought about her own miniscule marketing knowledge and hoped that she could get it. She started worrying and asked more questions. "How many sessions are there a day? How do the men pose their questions? Is it videotaped? Is there a schedule or notes that I can preview and how long are the sessions?"

Frieda raised her brows, "Umm...let's see there are three meetings a day and then several breakout sessions for the pastors to get together by region, by size of church, and by years in ministry. We are trying to get them all acquainted and to create a source group for each of them. Each program is about an hour and the conference is three days long. We will do two groups...Monday-Wednesday and then repeat the conference on Thursday-Saturday. The second group will have some stay on, with their families joining them on Saturday night. The repeat of the process may give you a better handle on the whole of it. Next week we'll only have thirteen families here totaling forty-eight people."

"We will do all the fan fare, but it'll be a smaller crowd. I think you'll enjoy it, and I am hoping it'll give you a bit of time to work on your writing. The ranch is always this way; ebbs and flows. We try to make it available, and we do our bookings fairly loosely. But, as with everything, it is a matter of the pastors being able to come, both financially and take time off. Our missionaries will arrive in late September. They need the church members to be at church when they come in to request funds. Otherwise, you are welcome to look at the scheduling book in the office or in the kitchen, it's computerized and printed. Lori has it memorized and Sharon keeps a copy at all times. They are the hearts of this place. They keep our tummies and taste buds delighted. Did I miss anything?"

Abbey looked at her pad. While she couldn't think of anything to ask, she was kind of excited. She was intrigued by Mark, Frieda's dad, and the seminars would be a welcome respite. She was also thrilled because she'd have a week to look forward to Italy, New York, and Paris all over again. She felt ready. "Well, no I can't think of a thing but can I ask you a personal question?"

Frieda was an open book, "Of course, whatchya wanna know?"

"Did you really home school your children here? What was that like?"

That was out of left field, but Frieda loved to talk about her kids and home schooling. "My yes, I did. It was something else. I think that it was a gift, and a chastening from God. I was just a very selfish, goal-driven woman with little understanding of what it took to raise a child. Abbey, did you know that my first baby died as an infant?" Abbey shook her head. "Well my first little guy, Dan Junior- we always refer to him as DJ, was born prematurely. I was devastated and totally shocked...I just never expected to have any problems having children. Anyway, it made me a bit deperate about having a child and caring for it, so I was hyper careful throughout my second pregnancy, and I still had a difficult birth. My son Mark was in the intensive care unit for three days. All in all, I didn't come by my babies easily. I was so grateful for them that I was genuinely prepared to give them my all, which I hope I did. I believe all mothers do really, I just know that I was over the top with my dedication to my kids. Probably to my own detriment. But I didn't care, I was just going to make sure that nothing happened to my boys that was within my power to control. The home school thing was more about the individual needs of my boys. You know schools are set up for a particular type of child-lines of desks all facing a chalk board, with little activity and less excitement."

"Mark is a very sensitive and creative guy with some slight focus issues. I think all boys need movement, you need to wear 'em out if you want them to just sit quietly, they just need to be boys. Anyway, home schooling started for us when he was sick, he missed twenty-one days of school and I had to catch him up. The sum of work that we needed to do, was paltry. Not only did we knock the work out quickly but he really understood it. At the time he was enrolled in a private school, upon returning to school, he started to slip behind. Had I known, I could have been working with him. By the end of the school year, there was some real question as to whether or not he should be promoted to the next grade. He was really smart then, and now. I ordered some school materials for over the summer, and we had a great time. His reading level went up by two grades in two months! I couldn't ignore that, so I ordered the rest of the year and wound up home schooling all the way through high school. We tried a variety of schools and programs over the years, but he just worked better one on one. Mark attended an Ivy League school and is a professional writer. He writes for Ligonier Ministries and does free lance for several apologists. He writes speeches, and has even ghost written seven novels.

Mark has five sons and his wife is perfect for him. You will see him this week, he is one of the speakers. My youngest, Caleb is a vet and has a terrific wife and three daughters. I home schooled that boy up until high school. Caleb was such a football nut, that he had to get to school. Caleb is Mr. Social—and he is a fierce competitor he needed the whole high school scene. He did well there. He is still a giant kid, thirty-nine years old and still my baby. He should be by here towards the end of the week. He'll speak at the second conference in place of a regular speaker, and mess with his brother. They are very close."

Abbey could see that Frieda was happy to talk about her boys, but she was clearly exhausted. So she decided to get out and let Frieda rest. "You've given me a wonderful idea on how to get started. I'll be happy to document as much as I can, but I had better get ready for tonight, and make sure that Bug is bathed before becoming the gonging Samurai. Oh, and thank you so much for that, he is really excited 'cause he's still trying to be the man of the house. It's just tough for a six and a half year old to assert his maleness in a home full of women. Bless you Frieda, get some rest. We'll all see you later." With a quick hug, Abbey left and headed down to find the kids.

Frieda smiled and recognized the parting works, Abbey had said 'Bless you', she had come a long way. She was beaming as Abbey left to tend to her son and dinner. All was right with the world.

The dinner went off without a hitch and abbey was able to sit down with her kids and enjoy the Tandori steak and veggies with her kids. Even Bug consented to catching some vegetables that wer flipped to him by the chef. It turned out that all of the chefs who came were provided, and paid for, by a Japanese Christian in Atlanta who owned a famous restaurant. The chefs and the fluid and beautiful swordsmen moved with such grace. Bug, naturally, made the decision then and there to become a professional Samurai and to return to the ranch to perform.

Thankfully, the whole day served to wear the kids out and they went to bed with no arguments. They were asleep immediately and Abbey returned for the quick clean up and to say good-bye to many of the families, who would leave before breakfast in the morning.

Chapter 33

Seeing so many families packing up and heading out, Abbey felt a bit sad. She had come to enjoy serving them and got such a kick out of their stories. She would really miss them. Seeing them with their families, hearing about their days—they had connected, that made the thanks yous' so much sweeter. Abbey was even given a handful of notes, and one handmade wooden cross. She would cherish them all. Leah came over and gave Abbey a hug, recognizing that they were both a bit sad to see the people go home.

Leah frowned and tried to explain, "It hurts a little each and every time. No matter what. Seeing these people go home after taking care of them for a week, sometimes longer." Leah paused, "but still it is absolutely worth it."

Abbey watched as the guys and young gals all chipped in to help the families empty the trailers and cabins. It was funny, in so many ways, the ranch was simple and yet the opulent and extravagant dinners lent this wild flair. It was a glorious summer camp with a twist.

Trying to get her mind wrapped around the intinerary for herself, Abbey prodded Leah to explain how the week with seminars would be. They had only a day to get ready, but as with most everything else, Abbey expected there would be a fine system in place.

"Basically, we will do breakfast from six to eight in the morning but it will be an abbreviated version of what we always do. Guys tend to like their sweets, so we hae an abundance of pastries, and donuts. We essentially leave the silver chafing dishes out all week. We do breakfast in the morning and lunches are usually soups, sandwiches, and salads. Then your standard guy fare; country fried steaks, mashed potatoes, London broil, and what not. We will vary it, and we always have a heart healthy dish like grilled chicken. However, you'll see a lot of it wind up in soups the next day. The men take several breaks and go into groups. So we keep coffee, water, soft drinks, and snack items out in the back of the room. I like to surprise them each day with something late, usually some warm cookies, or brownies, or something. It is a super easy week though and our numbers are not so great that we spend hours in prep. You'll have a ton more free time this week. The pastors become fast friends and Frieda has found some ingenious ways to place them in different clusters throughout, so that they all get to know one another. You will also notice that Frieda's dad, Mark, is hilarious. He genuinely loves people and is so fond of pastors. Mark does his best to share info with them in ways so they can absorb it. He is a consummate teacher, but he really just loves and appreciates people. It draws them to him. Mark is so accomplished, the guys love him right back. Oh, wait till you see him working in tandem with his namesake. Although he is forty-three, Mark still acts like a kid around his grandpa and they rib each other endlessly. Mark is brilliant, both Marks are really. Anyway, it's really a nice quiet week, did I cover everything?"

Abbey realized that Leah didn't know about her other duties this week. "I'm sure that you covered more than enough. I will try to keep up with you. I will also be attempting to document the sessions. So during the break outs, I won't be a whole lot of help to you."

"Oh, no worries, it's pretty much a one person job anyway. Don't worry about lunch either. Jess will be around and you will be a marvelous extra set of hands when you are available. Lori and Sharon are taking the week off to visit with grandbabies. My guess is they are spoilin' the heck out of those little ones. They are two God-honoring women; however, they are both positively smitten with their grandkids. Oh my gosh! They are still such a blast, I always giggle with them. Did you know that they lived next door to each other as young moms?"

"I had no idea. Is that how they met? How did they meet Frieda, then? At first, I assumed that they were quite a bit younger than Frieda, but I think it's just cause they are both short. Shorter women just always look younger. Too bad for us, huh? What are you Leah, five ten?"

"Yep, there about, I wind up reaching a lot for the shorties. It's a curse but I can always eat a lot more than they can."

Abbey laughed, "As can I at five nine. It's a blessing and a curse."

They finished cleaning up the breakfast. It seemed it was a fend-for-yourself day for the staff. There were a ton of options and Abbey planned to dig into some more of the left over Tandori steak, she and the kids loved it. With the rest of the day and half of the next free of kitchen duty, Abbey started making some plans for herself and the kids-hoping they could spend time wandering the ranch, she really wanted to explore a bit with the kids.

Geraldine was delighted to have the kids out from under foot, she planned to spend the whole day with Frieda. Bug and Geves liked their mom's idea, they also talked to Philip who showed them how to operate the Mule. He showed them how the red fences ran the length of the property and the fences with gray metal gates all ran across the property. He also told Abbey about the cellular service throughout the property and gave her a working cell phone that they used for guests. He made sure the Mule was all gassed up and showed her how to check the gauges. Abbey thanked him, ran back to the lodge and to pack a picnic. She also gathered treats for Moses, and some bug spray. She was just thrilled to be able to do all these wonderful things with her kids.

As soon as they got into the ATV, the kids began laughing and telling Abbey stories of pasture paddies, pot holes, and an old Indian mound. It was a thrill to see it all through their perspective, overall a very pleasant time. There were some beautiful birds, although Abbey couldn't have named them. It was like the world's best view. The Appalacian trail started at the base of the far off mountains, leading to thoughts of the early settlers, perhaps the American Indians. What had they seen from here? Abbey had never been particularly interested in history, but she loved Georgia. When General Oglethorpe founded the colony of Georgia, he forbade three kinds of people: murderers, rapists, and lawyers! That always made her laugh. It was one of those things that you shared with people new to the area. In reality, Atlanta was littered with lawyers. While Abbey had had a good experience with her divorce attorney, she had been happy to avoid lawyers thoughout most of her existence. The ones that she met in the dating and working world had been horrors.

Geves said, "Mom, I'm getting hungry, can we go back now?"

"Sure, I suppose. What do you want to do Bug?"

"I don't care, but I wanna see Moses."

"Okay, I do too. Let's go see if we cans pot him, and then I have some sandwiches packed in the cooler. We could eat with Moses." Geves and Bug agreed, and they drove around without spotting him. No fences were down that Abbey could see, but they were unable to spot him anywhere. They stopped and ate their sandwiches.

Abbey was genuinely disappointed, but didn't want the kids to be. "Have you guys seen Grace and Faith recently?' They both shook their heads and and everyone agreed to go see the twin fillies.

After a bumpy ride to the barn and giving the kids all the treats that had been packed for Moses, the kids wanted to check on the baby chicks. They were really enthralled with anything that they could handle. Abbey thought they might be a bit intimidated by the young horses.

Abbey dropped the kids at the chickens' are and went to return the ATV. She was looking for Philip to thank him, wasn't exactly sure where the cell phone was kept. Turning a corner abruptly, she ran smack into Matt.

"Whoa there!" Matt winced because Abbey had knocked him into the barn's side, "Are you taking lessons from your little cat? You've gotten quite stealthy, Miss Abbey, " he said smiling.

"I'm so sorry. I was just thinking, distracted, and maybe a little determined. Didn't mean to run you over, but I didn't realize you were even here. Have you been here long? Do you now where they keep these cellular phones for the guests? Philip loaned it to me, but I don't know where he is, do you?" Abbey was rambling, and must have sounded like an idiot.

"No problem, happy to see you, but you can give me the phone, I'll put it in the office. Looks like it's about ready for a charge anyhow. I actually never left this week, and I'll be going home in an hour, so I can be ready for services tomorrow. I won't be here next week. But I'll be back in time for the new families, Frieda would have my hide if I wasn't back here."

Matt continued talking, to fill up the space, "I have two sermons to prepare and give. DO you remember I told you about Julie, she's the one who lost the baby? Well, she wants to speak next week to thank the congregation and share what's going on in her heart. While I am thrilled and commend her, her husband isn't ready and I am trying to put the brakes on them carefully. I don't want her enthusiasm to wane but I don't want her husband to think that his raw hurt doesn't matter, either. It's a tough balancing act." Matt walked and Abbey followed and he continued to talk out his concerns.

"While Julie is able to be grateful for the little life, the short burst of joy, all her husband can focus on is his failure to protect. He is a great man, but this is taking a toll on him. I worry because so many marriages fail after this kind of trauma. I want to be a great support to both of them, but one is thriving, the other is not. It's just hard to know the best thing."

Abbey thought for a moment, "That sounds really tough, tell me, and you don't have to answer this, do you ever run the risk of having a woman in her situation or any rough one cling to you instead of to her husband?" Seeing Matt's obvious respect, she couldn't believe she was almost jealous of Julie.

"Yes, it is something that we have to guard against as people. Not just pastors, but we were all trained in seminary to be especially careful never to be alone with a member of the opposite sex- it just leads to problems. IT's even more difficult when you are a single man, but you are correct, I have to be careful never to encourage a vulnerable woman. I am very careful. I also happen to love her husband. He is salt of the earth. Ben and Julie are perfect for each other. They truly belong together."

"I've never been a real church type person but you always here about the leaders that are exposed. Probably just because those are the only ones on the news. It seems sortof natural too, Pastors are very often in a position of authority and counsel, much like a good friend or lover." Abbey was mortified, and probably blushed, she felt hot and wanted to end this conversation, but her embarrassment made Matt think she needed more information.

"Abbey, let me tell you churches are filled to the brim with hypocrites." At her bizarre look. He rushed to continue, "We are all hypocrites. Event he apostle Paul said, 'Why do I do the things that I don't want to do and don't do the things that I should, I am at war with the flesh.' I am paraphrasing of course, but really, sinners need to be in church, don't ya think?"

"Sure I suppose, but why do they always seem so judgmental and cold?" Abbey's own experience had been one of condemnation and disapproval. Who would want to be there?

"It is truly the pain of every pastor to hear that. Let me put it this way. To be physically fit, you have to constantly eat right, exercise, and get enough sleep. Well it's the same with our faith journey. To be accepted by God is easy. You pray for forgiveness and receive it because of what Jesus did on the cross for us all. His resurrection is our promise and future hope. But to know God, that is a practice. It is a constant. I have to pray, stay in God's Word, and never take my eyes off of Him. It is work You cannot 'catch' health, you have to work at it, in the same way you cannot catch 'faith'.. You can have 'aha' moments and some glorious emotional times with God, but you must be intentional about it. You have to make His Word your own. You have to spend time with God. As in every health club, you will see the dedicated, and the guys who will go in irregularly. The difference is that instead of looking at huge biceps we are looking for huge love. Jesus said, 'I will know them by their love.' When you really know Him and love Him, it flows outward. Surely, you see it in Frieda."

"Well, naturally, Frieda is a loving, dear woman and yes I understand all that but I guess when youg et knocked down by Christians, it's hard to give them a pass. They just should have a much higher standard. Too bad you cannot test their 'spiritual muscles' before you join their church."

"Ah but here's the question. Who needs to be in church more? The believer goes to church to worship God corporately, to be obedient, and to be surrounded by fellow believers. But the believer also needs the teaching, the time of prayer and the support of the church. The unbeliever goes looking for something to fill the vacuum in their life. Both need to be there and each will get something that they need based on what they can take in. Half the folks in church don't read the Bible, a third of them don't pray, another two thirds don't tithe. All I can do is encourage them to be whole authentic Christians. I offer opportunities, try to be an example and pray like mad. Does that make sense? ...I'm sorry you asked me a question, and here I gave you a sermon..."

"Well, you definitely gave me something to think about. Meanwhile, I'll be sending up some good thoughts for Julie and Ben. I hope it goes well. I do think she should tell her story, you never know who she might help."

Matt felt like she had missed the point, but at least she heard the truth from him. He was going to pray for her, he just hoped someone could get her over the hurdles. "Well, I am sure that whatever happens God is in control, I try not to accept full responsibility and lean as much on Him as I can. I really need to get going, I already said goodbye to Geves and Bug, Are you checking email these days, I may wanna keep you posted that way?"

"You know I have been so busy, I haven't been checking. I need to, though. It has been really freeing not being tied to the computer. Please do email me, I will look forward to it. Good luck Matt."

They had a sortof awkward hug, as if they were both in full football gear and couldn't quite reach, then separated. Abbey wasn't sure if hugging a pastor was appropriate, and Matt didn't want to be attracted to a woman that wasn't sold out for Christ. It was a weird relationship.

Abbey headed for the "chick barn" to claim her own little chickens, noticing that it was such a lovely day. Pretty overcast, but really comfortable. Abbey kept thinking how much her kids were thriving here, and she wondered if this wasn't a much better way to raise your children. Too bad there weren't any permanent jobs here, although, the school thing might become an issue. Her mom was really happy, too but it was time to quit daydreaming, she scolded herself, 'Abbey enjoy what you have while you have it!'

She and the kids had a wonderful day playing and goofing off, they swam, ran, played games, helped with a variety of animals and the kids showed Abbey all their favorite spots. Geraldine spent most of her time with Frieda. But late in the day Abbey found he r in the kitchen laughing with Jess and Leah. They had apparently decided to make some snacks for dinner, having a grand old time. Since this had been her domain or the past week, it was kind of fun and a little bit uncomfortable seeing her mother there. Then again, it was good to see her mom laughing. Apparently artichoke dip and potato skins, buffalo wings, garlic bread and pizza sauce and cheese were for dinner. Tandori steak fled Abbey's mind as she saw all the guilty pleasures. The all ate early out on the porch and everyone was in bed by eight. Abbey actually read a book, and spent a short amount of time writing descriptions of some of the events, mainly the dinners at the ranch. The food was so beautiful that it lent itself to word pictures like the lemon boats stuffed with lemon sorbet and mint, the colors, textures, and smells.. she enjoyed writing it all down. She slept soundly.

Chapter 34

That Sunday morning, Abbey felt fantastic. She had only been able to sleep in until five thirty but it sure beat her regular time. She spent the morning leisurely showering and dressing- it felt good to spend some time on her hair and to paint her fingernails and toenails. She didn't really have anywhere to go, but it just felt good. She planned ot spend the day driving to town with the kids and doing some laundry at the great big laudromat, (it would be good to get all the loads of clothes done at once). Then she planned to take the kiddos to McDonalds for lunch and maybe catch a movie. It might be the last day she could do this for a while. She caught her mom in the hallway, to let her know. Her mother was on her way to see Frieda, so Abbey decided to head out with the kids.

Frieda was sitting in her room with her Bible, but she was gazing out at the hummingbird feeders. She had a funny smile on her face and seemed to be well rested with really good color. Geraldine watched for a few minutes not wanting to disturb her.

When Frieda looked up, she said, "Good morning Frieda!"

"Well good morning to you, how did you sleep Ger?"

"Oh very well thank you. I wondered what you thought of our dinner last night. I had such fun in the kitchen with those two young uns. You look really great today and your color is back. Do you feel better?"

"Absolutely, I think I am truly on the mend. But about dinner, honestly appetizers are my favorite. Was Abbey in on all that too? Frieda saw Geraldine shake her head and seemed truly disappointed. "I hear that your Abbey has a real way about the kitchen. Leah and Jess absolutely adore her. And my dearest friends in the world Lori and Sharon have come to rely on her. She is really a joy. You have done so much for her and I know that her behavior and attitude is actually a tribute to you."

Geraldine tried to remember a time when she and her daughter had done anything together that wasn't around the kids. Even going way back her daughter and she had always danced around one another. They didn't share interests or abilities…

She always felt like she was tip-toeing around trying not to offend Abbey. It bothered her that she wasn't closer to her daughter, but she was just so sensitive. A mother's job was to offer her wisdom and share her knowledge. The simplest suggestion got her back up. Geraldine wasn't sure how to repond to Frieda's remarks. She loved abbey and was proud of her, but she just didn't feel like congrats were in order. She decided to just change the subject. "Have you ever had a bar night here? I don't mean serving alcohol but making it like a sports bar?"

Frieda recognized the subject change and decided to go with it. Time enough to plant seeds. "You know I have been working on a Casa Blanca Night and of course that was set in a bar. Okay, tell me what you think: a piano player playing, <u>A Kiss is Just a Kiss</u> to begin with, small dark lamps on each table, we could utilize the booths from pizzeria night and a Moroccan skyline on the buffet. I would also like to show the movie in the auditorium so that the kids could watch it with their parents. Especially, all those who've never seen the movie. What do you think?"

Geraldine thought she could picture some of it, "That movie is in black and white and we could put up movie posters and wear bowler hats… what is the food like? Oh I don't think I'm very good at this," she threw up her hands.

"WRONG! You came up with the bar and appetizers, actually that's a great idea. For me, this is a fun right brain kind of thing, I do this all the time. You cannot and should not expect to come up with an entire night in one moment; I love that you are contributing and I love that I can say anything to you. It's fantastic to bounce stuff off of others. And seeing that you don't get a crazed look in your eyes is a huge blessing. My husband used to roll his eyes and look dazed when I started to describe my vision. I would get so excited and poor Dan just couldn't get it…you are a breath of fresh air."

Frieda continued, "The food will be Mediterranean, so orzo with artichokes and cucumbers and tons of oregano, Chicken Schwarma, rices, Kefta, sortof a spicey meatball with eggs on top. Hummus and perhaps a Couscous with veggies and turkey. Oh and Tuna could be a nice option, that is common there. What I love about the food is that it is so colorful. What do you think?"

"Oh that sounds fantastic, I can almost see it." Geraldine was so pleased to be part of this. There were so many women her age and they were so accepting of her. Instead of being an extra in Abbey's life, Geraldine felt like she was front and center. She really had a place here. She felt important and like someone really cared about how she was feeling. It was not natural for her to confide in someone, but here Frieda sat…She pressed forward, "I'd like to discuss something with you. I don't share your love of God's people. But I was saved as a little girl. I turned away from the church and God because I was hurt very deeply by an uncle. He was a big man in at our church, a deacon, I was only eight years old, … he sexually molested me. I never told my mom, I expected her to know. You remember how it was back in those days, it was always the woman's fault, but I was only eight years old. I don't know"…Geraldine lowered herself into a chair and dipped her head, it felt good to tell Frieda but it still hurt all these years later.

Frieda reached out to Geraldine, and told her to go on, she knew there was more.

She continued, " I guess I know now that he was a stupid sick man, when I look at Geves, I cannot imagine any man touching her, so I sortof understand why my mom couldn't see it. Being here, with you I am recognizing for the first time in my life that my anger with my mother was somewhat unfounded. But why did God let that happen to a little girl? Why?"

Frieda moved slowly, but she lowered herself to the floor on the pretty braided rug in front of Geraldine, her legs creaking and popping the whole way. She looked up at Geraldine seeing the tears in her eyes and said, "God has allowed free will, which means that bad people are still going to do bad things. I have had this conversation a million times, even with myself. God can take your anger, He understands and I believe that it pains Him every day; what bad people do. The thing is, God can heal you. It is terrible what happened to you, I bet you watched Abbey like a hawk when she was little, and now Geves. Ger, is it possible that what you went through prevented that from happening to your daughter and granddaughter?" Geraldine looked shocked and appalled at the thought, but she was really listening.

Frieda continued, "I am not saying that it is ever okay, but would you accept that pain so that it won't happen to them? Isn't that what Jesus did for you? He took that pain and death on your behalf. Again, I am not excusing, I am not saying it is okay, but maybe just maybe, God was preventing something far worse for Abbey and Geves. I don't know, we cannot; but you see the news…it is inhumane the way people treat one another. Regarding your mother, she may not have known, but it was a different era. We didn't discuss these things. So much went on back then that none of us discussed."

Frieda reached up to hug her and stated to pray, "Father God, thank you for this beautiful lady. You know Ger better than anyone. Strengthen her, wrap your arms around her so that she knows you are right here. Help her broken heart to heal completely. Show her how you can turn the bad to good for those who love you. You are our healer and our provider. We pray for great leading for your daughter Ger. She received you so long ago, revive her love for you, O God. Restore her faith."

Frieda tried to get up, her knees were not doing well, she got help from Ger and stood up, she wanted to continue to pray and asked Ger's permission. Ger nodded, tears on her face.

Standing together, holding hands, Frieda prayed on, "Father we ask also for forgiveness for our sins and our departures from you. We pray for forgiveness, gor Ger's mother and even for her uncle who did this horrible thing. We pray a blessing on this family. We ask for safety for Geves and Abbey, that they might never be harmed. We love you Lord and thank you for putting us together here. In the precious name of Jesus the Christ who is our Savior, amen." Frieda grabbed some tissues and tried to clean up Ger's face and her own. It was such a blessing to minister to someone who had been ministering to her.

Geraldine recognized the tenderness of Frieda's prayer and she was awestruck that her vigilance throughout Abbey's and Geve's lives had been a blessing. Abbey never saw it that way, she always thought her mother too strict. Ger blamed herself for Abbey marrying the first guy she could to get out from under her mother's hard rules. But, in fact, Geraldine was pretty sure that she had kept her safe. It was kind of a kick in the gut to think that her "cross to bear" was indeed a sacrifice of her safety for those of the girls she loved. She knew that it would have crushed her to have anything like that happen to one of them. She also recognized that she needed some time alone to digest. She was emotionally drained, but relieved, too.

Geraldine made sure that Frieda's knees and back were okay, helping her to settle back into the chair that Geraldine had vacated. She thanked Frieda profusely and suggested coming back in for lunch, she needed to rest.

Geraldine walked back to her room, feeling somewhat lighter and a little raw. She was running so many things through her head, she laid down on top of the bed and for the first time in years, attempted to pray...she fell asleep thanking God.

A few hours later, Geraldine awoke feeling stronger. She met Frieda and took her downstairs for a light lunch, at which, Frieda presented her with an old Bible that had been hers. It had notes in the margins, stuff highlighted and underlined, it was unlike any Bible that Geraldine had ever owned. Thoroughly used. Frieda hoped it was make it less intimidating. The day allowed Geraldine to really focus on what she had experienced with Frieda. She knew one thing that just couldn't wait; she needed to go and see her mother.

The two ladies made their way out to the porch. Frieda wanted to sit outside and enjoy the day, she claimed a little vitamin D would go a long way. While Geraldine collected Frieda's things for her, and made sure she had everything she needed she sought her advice on speaking with her mother. Frieda was thoughtful. She was all for it...her perspective was that it would be beneficial for both and that Geraldine would never regret visiting her mother. She told her that if it felt right to tell her about her uncle, that she could but to tread lightly. "Imagine how you'd feel if Abbey came to you." She had said. Frieda believed that it was more important for Geraldine to be forgiving and loving than to necessarily explain why. But, she was also crystal clear that she should go and see her mother...just see where it led.

Her mother lived at a retirement center in Atlanta, so she called and made some initial plans. It was the perfect week and the easiest on Abbey and the staff, and Frieda had even had her car checked out and gassed up for Geraldine to take. She decided to wait for Abbey and the kids to get back, and then explain that she needed to run up to Atlanta to see her mom and grab a few more clothing items. She would also grab mail and feed the fish and then return in a day or so. She planned to reassure abbey that nothing was wrong and then after she got back, perhaps she could explain to Abbey.

Geraldine couldn't remember where to read in the Bible, being raised in the church she knew the books in order and could recite the usual passages but she was trying to remember one of the stories that she had performed in a play, Shaddrach, Meshach and Abednego, so she looked in the appendix of the Bible and decided to read that one. It was in the book of Daniel. She was shocked when she read about the fiery furnace and the fourth man. Funny, she never thought about it...she, too had been in a fiery furnace, had God really been with her? She thought and thought about it as she packed to head to Atlanta for a few days.

As the day dragged on, waiting for Abbey and the kids, and considering all that she had heard, read, and felt. Geraldine imagined her conversation with her mother. She knew her mother would be delighted to see her, and that she would be thrilled to hear where she had been and what she was doing. But, could her mother take the truth, would she turn it around on her? Geraldine was working herself up and decided to heed Frieda's advice. The only thing she could do was pray. She had prayed when she was a little girl, she'd prayed several times when Abbey was a teen, and even a few times here but never like Frieda. She tried to think, Frieda always called God Father and Daddy, maybe Geraldine should try it that way.

She prayed to herself as she aired out and picked up the kids' rooms.

Meanwhile, Abbey and the kids were having a blast; they saw an animated movie, ate tons of popcorn and played putt-putt. She got all the laundry done at a place called *Suds and Duds* where the kids could drink fun drinks and watch television. The kids were great but actually missed physicality of the ranch. Abbey could tell they were getting restless, (running jumping and playing with rabbits and baby chicks was very much their speed),but they were mostly well behaved. Geves was pretty good generally, but she was especially complimentary of her brother, who was quite the little gentleman; even holding doors. By the time they were pulling back through the ranch gates, it was close to seven at night. No one was particularly hungry, so they agreed that the kids would go straight to the chicks and then meet their mom in the lodge to help put away all the clean laundry.

Abbey was thinking about the week ahead, it was going to be so different. But she had enjoyed everything at the ranch so far, so she looked forward with excitement.

When Geraldine finally saw Abbey, she was tied up with the kids, so she decided their conversation could wait til morning.

Chapter 35

Breakfast was really easy, very few of the guests had arrived and the ones that were there were happy to hit the pastries. Abbey went back to the room to grab her notebooks and pens when her mom popped in.

"Hi Abbey, do you have a moment?"

She nodded, "Sure mom...everything okay?" Abbey couldn't put her finger on it; but her mom looked different—happy but with a nervous energy.

"Well honey, I need to head back to Atlanta for a day or two; because I want to check on my mom, the fish, maybe grab the mail. Frieda and I have a couple of things that I may be able to find in the city, too." She barely paused for breath, "I spoke with Jess, she and Philip can help with the kids and Frieda is doing much better. Do you need anything from home?"

"Umm, the mail is being forwarded, and the fish should be fine...wait is Grandma okay? And what in the world do you and Frieda need, I asked her before the kids and I went in to town and she said she didn't need a thing."

"Sure, your grandma is fine, I just feel the need to check. It'll be good and I'll be back in a couple of days. Actually, Frieda and I have come up with a new theme night, and we are excited to work on it. We only came up with it yesterday and believe me I doubt I can even find it in Atlanta. We are looking for a Moroccan skyline and Casa Blanca movie posters. I am also checking prices on pool tables and foosball. It'll be a fun excursion for me...Oh, and I am taking Frieda's car, she is insisting, says it doesn't run near enough."

"Well, there isn't anything I need, say hello to the fish. Keep in touch, is your cell phone charged? I am excited about a new night, that's really great. I love you, mom. Tell grandma hello and we all send our love. I am really glad that you came with us, we will miss you."

Surprised by Abbey's sweetness, Geraldine tried ot respond appropriately. "Abbey it has been the very best thing for me, too. I love seeing you working with all these people. I am so proud of you. I have always worried about your writing, it is so hard to make a living that way. And you are so gifted with people. You are so lovable and I am so proud of you. I will be back by Thursday." They hugged and Geraldine was wiping back tears as she grabbed her bags. While she was nervous about seeing her mother, she believed it was going to make her feel even better.

Abbey headed into the first session, she was shocked when Mark kissed her cheek and introduced her to all the men. He made her feel special, it was a little bit embarrassing, but at least she wasn't just sitting in the back feeling like she didn't belong.

Mark was very engaging, he was a real talker. He began with some disastrous marketing tales, the first about "Jet Cola" a soft drink that had been invented and put into a test market. The story got hilarious as Mark went on to describe how the bottle shape and the extreme carbonation were a hit with the inventors...the issue was that it was put into a test market in Denver Colorado. The altitude proved to be a nightmare as case after case after case exploded in the bottling plant. The plastic bottles proved to be shrapnel all over the factory floor and walls. It was a total failure, as it never even got into the hands of the intended teenagers. Mark used the story to explain that even a great concept a wonderful idea needs to be seen from another perspective. You need to consider from other "altitudes" or perspectives. He was so engaging, the Pastors were chuckling along and sitting on the edge of their seats. Abbey was glad she was recording because she realized that she had stopped writing.

Mark then launched into a Brand Equity lecture. He explained that a brand has it's own meaning. He took a common household name and began on a whiteboard having the pastors call out meaning of the product and it's name. The pastors were engrossed and were shouting out all sorts of possible meanings. Mark went on to explain which ones were actual equities. He showed how a brand had a really common meaning to others. Sometimes that meaning was created through advertising, sometimes through use. He showed one example of a really strong mouthwash having a meaning that the company probably hadn't intended. Once they had a solid idea about what Brand Equities meant, he went around the room and unfolded a single giant piece of flip chart paper that had been papered around the room, once unfolded they each revealed the name of the pastors own churches. Mark asked the pastors to first write equities that they thought the community outside of the church would say, and then move inside the church and what those equities would look like. The pastors all got up, went to their church chart and started writing with Mark walking around and generally being available to all the men. After several go 'rounds with each, Mark closed the session asking the men to really consider the equities, whether they needed to change and how to change them. He planned to hit the actual marketing in session three giving them some time to consider.

The men all took a break and got some drinks, there was a hum with all the men's voices speaking and they seemed excited. For Abbey, it was so different from what she imagined, but that was true of everything at the ranch. Why not. As the men returned, Mark took a few questions, and then announced the second session, a new man entered and walked straight to the stage, apologizing for being late. Mark beamed and announced his grandson, Mark. It was cute, they were practically elbowing each other... Abbey could imagine them wrestling without too much imagination.

Mark, the elder, introduced his grandson as a really tall Christian apologist writer. The younger proceeded to put his elbow on his grandpa's head, using him as for an arm rest. When the younger began to speak he introduced the topic of human resources and the law. He was very articulate and funny, clarifying the law and then making fun of it. He explained how easy it was for the churches to get in trouble with hiring, firing, work hours, and even the employment applications. From church secretaries to the accountants who often served on staff, the church's human component was being attacked.

Abbey took copious notes of his talk, but no written word could hold a candle to his genuine fun personality. She glanced around the room from time to time, and noticed that the pastors were also writing at her pace. Abbey believed that a few days under these people's tutelage, and she too could run a business.

Jess and Philip popped by with the kids, during one of the breaks, saying they were going to be working the rest of the afternoon. Jess told Abbey that they were charged with the animals all day. But that the kids were having real fun. Jess gave a conspiratorial wink about the work and the kids bounded off as happy as ever while Abbey made her way to the kitchen.

Session three would resume with the pastors being broken down by church size...there wasn't a good way to cover that, so Abbey decided to check on the kitchen.

Leah had all manner of things simmering and roasting; and it smelled so good, layers of garlic and sage, rosemary and onions.

Abbey's mouth watered. Leah waved her off and told her it was far too soon to worry about the sternos in the dining hall.

She told Abbey to take a break.

She complied and wandered up to see Frieda, who was on her knees in prayer. At first Abbey thought she may have fallen, but thankfully recognized what Frieda was doing and didn't interrupt. Actually, she may have been singing…

"May I run the race before me. Strong and brave to face the foe, Looking only unto Jesus as I onward go."

It was a somewhat familiar tune, but the words were different. Her grandma used to run around singing hymns all day.

Abbey wondered how her mom would find granny. She had been in an assisted living facility in Atlanta for years. It was a difficult place to visit, because of the kids. They seemed to frown on the youngest visitors. The were viewed as loud germ machines. She was aware enough to realize that Frieda had risen by the chair, so she entered.

"Hi Frieda, how are you?" Abbey noted that she was moving a little better and her color was good. "You look great, what song were you singing?"

Frieda responded, "Hello sweet Abbey; let's see, I *am* feeling better, I would like to go for a walk a little later. The only thing about sitting around is these old bones and joints get stiff. Oh and I was singing May the Mind of Christ, My Savior. It's a really ancient tune, but it came to me this morning. How are the notes going from the seminars?"

Abbey chuckled, "Well, taking notes during your father's talks is sort of like drinking from a fire hydrant. He is a wonderful speaker, though, and your son is too. I had no idea he had such a broad knowledge of the law. He did a fantastic job and I was suitable impressed – every pastor leaving this conference will have learned a ton."

"My Dan was an attorney, and one who could analyze and pick apart almost anything. He used to teach that part of the conference, but that was before he became sick. However, my boys watched him for years and learned all of it from him. This part of the ranch was his dream—what he brought to the ministry. Pastors are never taught many of these things, and yet they have to put them into practice in their churches. This is our mini law school, business school, and accounting training. A few hours gives them enough to go back to their churches and take a good look at everything from their employment agreements to their advertising. Once a church is big enough, they usual have their own bookkeepers and often there is a member lawyer who can help with contract stuff...until then, these poor young men are left holding the entire bag. Seminary gives them extensive training in counseling, apologetics, and Bible study but the business end is woefully lacking."

Abbey considered what Frieda said, she thought she should give her a sampling of what she had but really wanted more time. "Well, I hope to put together some stuff for you to look at, but only once I've attended both conferences. I am not always sure where your dad is going sometimes. He is fun to listen to, though. I cannot believe some of his business stories. So funny, and I'd like to see if I can find any reference to his stories anywhere else....did you tell me that he had produced some hand outs in the past?"

"Oh, sure he had some years ago; for sure on his computer—he saves absolutely everything. Have you ever noticed a gravel drive just off the road coming into the ranch? –off to the right? Well, back int eh woods down there is where my dad lives. Just holler at him and be patient in the front, he'll be able to find his handouts...I am afraid that if you don't go out there and get them, he'll forget. He still as sharp as he ever was, but he tends to get distracted, always has. Just run on down after the seminars or dinner. He'll be up, just tell him I sent you."

Abbey was a bit reluctant, but he was a sweet guy. It'd be okay, she figured, " Alright, I'll head down before it gets dark, you know he reminds me of one of those old actors, like Cary Grant."

Frieda cracked up, "He has always said he looks just like him. Oh, don't you dare tell him that, I will never hear the end of it. I would make sure that you don't go to late, he will wear you out chatting. The man can talk, it's where I get my special gift." Frieda was shaking her head and grinning.

Abbey thought it was really cute, she wanted to make certain that Frieda had what she needed, she was glancing around noting the full water pitcher and her cell phone and note pad. She was about to turn to go when Frieda asked a question.

"Abbey did Geraldine get off okay? Did you two get a chance to talk before she left?"

Abbey nodded, "Yep, she did." She was couldn't figure out what Frieda meant, "What should my mother and I talk about? What do you know that I don't?"

Frieda just smiled, "Abbey, your mother and I have formed a very nice friendship, I think I might remind her a tad of her mother and maybe that has more to do with her sudden desire to see her mom than anything else. I just hoped that you two could somehow voice what I see. I see a young woman who loves her mom, but is always waiting for disapproval. I see a middle age woman who adores her daughter, and wants the very best for her. Both of you are so blind, deaf, and dumb when it comes to each other, that just makes me crazy. Forgive this old woman, Abbey, but you need to live with as few regrets as possible-you need to speak with your mother. You need to say what is on your heart. I see you genuinely pleased when your mother looks happy, you love her and you want her happy, YOU care! Please Abbey, spare yourself the "if onlys" and the "what ifs". Tell your mother how you feel about her. I can tell you, as an old woman, you do not want to wish you had done something later that you can do now. Abbey I have come to love you – you are a darling young woman, but I see a depth of pain and sadness that just doesn't have to be. I may never truly know all the pain and frustration that you have lived with – I don't know a lot of things Abbey- but I know that the answer to all of it is Jesus Christ. You will come to Him when you are ready. But don't let people in your life get away without knowing how much you care. It's important."

At first Abbey was a bit miffed, but because Frieda always dealt with her in such a genuine and loving way, Abbey took in what she had said with real thought. She nodded, recognizing that it all rang true. She would need to communicate better with her mother, even she recognized that.

She answered simply, "I know." After a couple of moments, what seeled like a really long time to Abbey, she finally said, "Frieda, I understand, I really do. I love you and my mom and I am tickled that she has this relationship with you – so I promise to try with her. You have to understand that our....we're complicated." Abbey stuttered.

Freida knew she had struck a chord with Abbey, she told herself to go slow. "Dear, we are all complicated. But most of us are wrong about others. We are always looking for people who are the same as us. Life is so boring with a bunch of people just like us. Take Lori, Sharon, and I. We have been friends for more than thirty years and have so much in common. We are more different than alike, though, we each bring our own peculiarities to our relationships. We also bring a lot of love and variety. I couldn't imagine the last few years without these ladies, who I count on. Lori is our cheerleader, she's the one with all the innate abilities, she can grow a garden, create a bouquet or a bow, and sew like you cannot imagine. Sharon is our Proverbs woman, entirely capable, but so gentle and sweet she just keeps things smooth. Both are good kind people who mean the world to me. It is their uniqueness that makes it such fun, and it takes the two of them to keep me from going off the deep end with my over-the-top ideas. They ground me and yet they are the ones that make my visions become reality. I'm boring you, I only tell you that your mother loves you. She is so proud of you she just struggles with the verbiage."

Abbey hugged Frieda while smiling. There just wasn't much left to say. So, she helped Frieda to the chair and excused herself.

The sessions were wrapping up and several of the men were taking a run out to fish. Several were trying to grab Mark and ask questions. Two of the men were sitting with cookies and their cell phones. Abbey checked her watch and realized there were two hours left before dinner, she checked in on Leah, who not only had everything under control but was on the phone. Leah held up her finger, asking Abbey to wait one minute.

Abbey looked around the kitchen and the wonderful meats were getting very close to done, the thermometers were nearing ideal temps. She couldn't help but overhear the phone conversation. Leah's squealing and "oh I cannot wait," had Abbey thinking "what? What?"

Leah hung up the phone and clapped her hands together, she was grinning and came towards Abbey. "We have a huge surprise coming for Frieda, three of the best doses of medicine are on their way!"

"Oh, that's good, who or what?"

Leah explained that in two weeks three of Frieda's oldest and dearest friends were coming to the ranch. Word had gotten out that Frieda was ill and the "ranch family" was determined to come see her.

Leah started, " Apparently Jeanette was Frieda's very best friend and though they didn't spend a lot of time together, their friendship was always there. Frieda had nicknamed Jeanette, "Princess" and according to Jeanette, treated her like one. They raised their boys together for some of the tough years and bonded over their mothers' cancer. Both of their mothers had died within years of each other. It was something that they shared."

"Angelique was Frieda's friend for thirty years. She and her husband ran a para church ministry out of Wichita, Kansas which had tentacles all over the world. They ran an institute for Biblical counseling, helping folks overcome addictions—sounded pretty intense. They had found the keys to reaching people and more importantly, getting them through some of the toughest parts of addiction. The beauty of their ministry was the ongoing nature of it—according to Frieda, Ang is like a dog with a bone, she will not let her patients go…she follows up until she is confident that they will not return to their particular addiction."

Leah paused a moment collecting her thoughts, "Alma, well, we all just love Alma. She is Frieda's heart sister. When they met, Alma said that her English wasn't too good, but Frieda's Spanish was worse. They genuinely love each other, but Alma specifically seems to love everyone. Her work has always been in her community. She has worked with English as a Second Language kids, she has worked in the immigrant community, and she brought people together wherever she went. She has a way of making you feel like you are the only person in the room. Oh, I cannot wait to see Alma. I am so thrilled." Leah did a little spin and pumped her fist, "Frieda is going to flip!"

Leah, then swore Abbey to secrecy, but still had stories to tell.

"Anyway, apparently Jeanette and Ang don't cook but Alma taught Frieda the great Mexican dishes we have on Fiesta night.

Frieda got them all to help her in the early days of the ranch and there were stories of Ang sitting on the floor of the kitchen in tears, not bad tears, laughing so hard she had to sit. Laughter was the biggest factor in the group."

Abbey started contemplating more stories for the magazine. She wondered if she'd be able to pick Angelique's brain, the institute might be interesting. And the Latina element of Alma's story would be great for the magazine. It would be a wonderful way to get other readers, too. Anyway, it would be a happy time for Frieda and that made Abbey smile.

Leah laughed, "You do get caught up in thought, huh?"

Abbey looked at her strangely, "What do you mean?"

"You have that far away look in your eye, I was telling you that speaking of laughter your kiddos caused me some today."

"Oh, sorry about that. I was just thinking about articles I could write based on the other women's stories... what'd my kids do now?"

"Well, they were having a ball working with Philip and Janna Kay- they were out in the barn jumping and climbing around the hay bails. You should have seen them, they discovered some kittens that looked a great deal like your little cat, but I doubt that your is old enough to be their mother. It's possible, though, that she was from an earlier litter. Anyway, the funny little fuzz balls just stole their hearts. Geves began naming them all while Bug watched her rolling his eyes. Philip started to laugh when Geves turned on her brother. She hollered, 'Why are you laughing at me,' and Bug said that "there is no way on this earth that mom is gonna let you have ten cats.' Geves said, "I know that,' Pat, Janna Kay and I were trying not to bust a gut, but you have to picture this miniature adult, your little guy is so assertive. He's a ball. Long and short of it, Geves knew she couldn't keep the cats, but she thought of the perfect names for them. There were eight kittens; one was white, so she was naming them for the Snow White and the Seven Dwarfs. Problem was none of us could remember all the names, so here's your heads up, she said her mom would know."

"It's always something with those two. Yes, Bug was born old. I think he has tis incredible understanding sometimes. It is hard to see it coming out of your six; almost seven-year-old son. Let's see, Doc, Sneezy, Grumpy, um how many did you guys get?"

"Well we got those three, and Dopey, Sleepy, and wasn't there one that laughed. Out on the farm we could always name one Wheezey!!! Although, I don't think it'd fly with your Geves...ya know I think that is as far as we got."

"I wonder if there's a copy of the book around here anywhere... oh never mind, I'll just look it up online later. Seems, I am getting out of the habit out here. How did anyone survive child-rearing without the Internet??" Glancing at the clock Abbey announced, "It's time to light the sternos." She grabbed a pack of matches and told Leah, "I've got it."

As Abbey finished lighting the sternos and ensuring that the pans had sufficient water, she placed the lids on the last two. She was about to check the drink station, when she heard a peal of laughter from the door going out onto the deck. Abbey peeked out of the dining hall, seeing three of the pastors were covered in mud. Literally, she couldn't make out their clothing or their hair color. Well except for the bald one. She could tell that they were afraid to come into the hall. A whole bunch of little boys, unsure what to do and terrible sheepish. Abbey gestured to them to go back outside, and she followed and led them to an outdoor shower. She showed them the towel cupboard and the back way to their rooms. She then smirked, "Where's the fish that goes with those outfits? Should I get my camera for your parishioners?"

The men chortled and laughed, said there weren't any fish and thanked Abbey. She thought that they seemed to be having an awfully good time for three men who obviously had had no success today. As she walked away, she couldn't help but giggle as the men experienced the cold well water. Peels of laughter and squeals could surely be heard, even inside. Abbey just had to get the back story. How did they come to be covered in mud and behaving like a bunch of silly frat boys. The ranch seemed to bring out the little kid in all. Abbey remembered Frieda explaining in the past that often for Pastors, their lives were not their own. The outside world was always watching, always waiting for them to mess up. She said they even had to curb their emotions at ball games. Frieda thought it was an impossible task to be watched like that, and never to waiver, like being set up to fail.

Abbey returned to the kitchen and explained to Leah about all the commotion. Leah didn't seem at all surprised. Together they got dinner put out and began serving. With the men it was more about keeping the chafing dishes full and hot. Abbey thought they all looked hungry enough to eat her, so she got the food out and moved away quickly. The guys went through a lot of bread and later pie. Leah told Abbey conspiratorily, that as soon as the wives arrived the men would be reined in a bit!

The three men stopped by to thank Abbey for saving them from their mud issues. They introduced themselves and John, Dave, and Nate. John, the bald one and the obvious leader of the group told the tale with a few interruptions. He began, "Well we were very excited to fish, but we never made it all the way to the pond. We took one of those golf cart things and thought we could get there a bit faster if we crossed the stream. So, Nate says, there's a nice shallow point to the East..."

Nathan interrupted, "You were the one who wanted to cross the stream, I was just looking for the best place," he elbowed John good naturedly.

John continued, "Anyway, long and short of it, it wasn't shallow, and the bottom was really soft mud. They call it Georgia red clay for a reason. So we tried to lift it and push it and shove rocks under the wheels, nothing worked. We all fell in a few times, hence the way you found us. Finally, realizing that we were beaten we went to the equipment barn and found Jonathan."

Philip came up alongside John at that moment, "Gave me a nice laugh! You guys know that your picture may go viral! "

John, Dave, and Nate all shared a look.

John grimaced and said just under his breath, "I will never hear the end of this when my wife sees it! She is gonna have a field day."

Philip, "Well just know that Jonathan got the thing out in two seconds flat with the tractor, but you guys need to know that if you're going forward and you get stuck, do not, under any circumstances, put it in reverse," shaking his head and then the men's hands.

The men were slapping each other on the back, and thanking Abbey for the wonderful meal. They said good night and headed off to their rooms. Abbey figured they better confess, before Philip's picture did indeed go viral!

Abbey and Leah got the pans cleaned out, and the table clothes refreshed, and closed down the kitchen. It had been a pretty easy night. Abbey told Leah, she'd better come up with those names for the kittens before she saw the kids to bed.

Geves and Bug helped collect the chicks and told stories to them. Abbey found them in the chicken coop and learned that they were to help Jess collect eggs in the morning and they were under strict orders not to run, or skip with eggs in tow. Abbey took the exhausted kids up to shower and get ready for bed, and shared the last of the

Dwarves names with them. They fell asleep reciting: "Sneezy, Sleepy, Dopey, Doc, Happy, Bashful, and Grumpy."

Abbey thought she should go find Mark, but it was just dark enough that she was afraid to go down there. She decided to check on Frieda, instead.

Frieda was sleeping and appeared to have everything she needed. Abbey tiptoed out and went to her room to shower and read.

Chapter 36

Abbey woke up bright and early feeling like she could use some exercise. She decided to do some calisthenics in her room. Then, if the day allowed, she might swim. After a bit of exercise, she and the kids went to collect eggs.

Geves had decided that she would let the kittens know their names this morning, and was excited to share the info with all the 'adults' in the barn, too. It took them about twenty-five minutes to collect all the eggs. Bug and Geves ran around collecting feathers and all sorts of other things that slowed the process substantially.

Geves and Bug knew a great deal about the types of chickens and their qualities' Geves began explaining that the rust colored to almost black chickens are Rhode Island Reds and they are some of the best egg layers. The Java chickens were mostly white and black and had smaller combs on their heads, they were sweet. But according to the kids the nicest of all of them were the Barred Plymouth Rock chickens that were 'polka-dotted' according to Geves. Abbey asked about the chickens that had feathers that went all the way down their legs, and Bug explained that they were the Brahmas but that they didn't like children.

Abbey was suitably impressed, her kids had gotten quite an education about chickens. She would have to remember to tell Jess later, thank her and commend her.

Once the eggs were delivered to the kitchen they were washed off and placed in trays in the cooler. Abbey could see why they needed so many; having herself, put more than a gross of eggs in the Hobart mixer over the last week. She marveled at the difference in taste between the fresh eggs and the normal store bought ones, even Bug had mentioned that he like the eggs here better.

Lori spent time explained how much better the fresh warm eggs were for baking and creating.

Abbey took over after breakfast, sending Leah on a break. She got everything prepped for lunch and took a look at the dinner and snack menus. She completed as many of the tasks as she could confidently, she still had thirty minutes before the next session began. Abbey decided to enjoy a huge mug of coffee, then grabbed her note pad and hit the conference room.

Spotting Mark the older one, she decided to ask him about the handouts. "Good morning Mark, how are you?"

Mark reached over took her hand and kissed her cheek, "Good Morning, honey, what can I do for you?"

"Oh, well, I was wondering if I could get a copy of any of your handouts or notes that you use?"

"Of course, I think I have them on my computer, you know I have some of my son-in-law's old notes and my grandson's too. Do you want those, as well?"

Abbey was thrilled, "Yes, that'd be great."

Mark just smiled and winked. "Thank you fro attempting to compose all of tis. I don't do very well sticking to my outlines, but they will show where I intended to go," he grinned. "My grandson is a little more straight forward, of course, so is his material."

The men started to gather at the back of the room. Abbey found a corner towards them as Mark welcomed them. His talk went a great deal like it had the day before, but the pastors were a little more prepared to pepper him with questions. They had gotten together in breakout and composed questions to try to stump Mark. They didn't stand a chance but Mark loved the challenge of it. They pitched outlandish ideas for marketing, challenges, and crazy set ups for Mark. He loved it!

Abbey found if she worked in an outline form, fill in the blanks as best she could and then ask Mark later if she was missing anything. She really wanted to absorb the lecture.

It was time to break for lunch. Abbey decided not to attend the last session because it would be human resource law again, and unlike his grandpa, the younger Mark had wonderful notes and rarely went off message. But being a writer, she found his handouts to be comprehensive and highly readable. She also noticed the copyright, so she would avoid any potential for plagiarism by working from the notes.

She figured she would go for a swim with the kiddos-for some reason she was still feeling restless. After working on her feet for more than a week nonstop, suddenly she was sitting and writing. You'd think it would have been a nice break, but it just made her feel like she wanted to jump out of her skin. So she found her kids, back in the barn, complete with straw poking out of their clothes and hair. Abbey was given an introduction to the kittens, a duck and was shown where the opossum slept. Philip and Jonathan were installing a hay system and repairing some floor boards in a loft of the barn. Presumabley, to move hay up top. They, too were stuck like porcupines, straw sticking out of their clothes, hair, and shoes. The group in the barn had all dined on hamburger and there was the residual ketchup blobs on their clothes, for proof. Abbey asked them if they wanted to swim and thanked Philip. She planned on keeping them until dinner time.

After swimming and playing Marco Polo and sharks and minnows, for over an hour, the kids were exhausted and Abbey felt much better. She was amazed at how long she could swim now. She could never afford the gym or yoga, but her clothes were looser after just a week and a few days at the ranch. Best diet/physical fitness plan ever.

Abbey and the kids ran from the pool to inspect the 'special treat' being prepared for the breakout. Leah had baked some chocolate/chocolate chip cookies, and some macadamia brittle and she watched as the kids ate almost all the broken cookies. They all helped Leah quietly refresh the snack service at the back of the conference room. It was fascinating to see her kids being quiet and serious. Right at that moment she was grateful for all the experiences and the way it was teaching her kids to be responsible.

As the pastors broke for the cookies and the day, Mark invited Abbey and the kids back to his home. He suggested they grab two of the golf carts, and that way the Abbey and the kids could follow and leave when they were ready.

The followed Mark, Abbey knew she never would have found it on her own. You really couldn't see it from the road. The whole path was so overgrown with flowers, hostas, evergreens, and berries. There was even a small orchard. Abbey was shocked that it was all back there. Mark showed them the blackberries and how to pick the ones that were ripe. The kids were repulsed by the tartness of them, especially after all those cookies. The pears and apples were pretty on the trees, but no where near ready to eat, according to Mark. He showed the kids straight in to a magnificient fish tank. It was at least seventy-five gallons and had pretty little schools of fish in it. Black mollies, Orange swordtails, pretty striped neon tetras, flowing angel fish, and some of those ugly fish on the bottom. While the kids were absorbed by the tank, Mark wondered over to a desk that was stacked and covered by all kinds of materials. It was chaotic and messy, which sortof fit the old guy.

Abbey laughed to herself, imagining Bug turning out a bit like him. The boy loved to collect stuff. While Mark printed page after page after page of documents for her, she found herself wondering about the housekeeping staff and if they made it out here very often. It might be overdue.

Mark gathered all the documents placed them in three separate file folders and brought them to Abbey. "The orange folder is my material, the blue one is my son-in-law Dan's, and the green one is my grandson's. Thank you again for doing this. We really appreciate it. I think I am going to take a nap, do you think you can find your way back?"

"Yes, we can. Thank you so much."

With a quick good bye to the kids, Mark again took Abbey's hand and kissed her cheek.

They rode back on the golf cart, the kids singing and smiling the whole way. Both kids wanted a bigger fish tank now, naturally. Abbey thought she worked hard enough cleaning their little one, no way. She hoped the desire would wear off, soon!!!

Geves and Bug agreed that they might change their clothes and rest before dinner. Abbey made them promise to try to read a book. After getting the dinner out for the pastors and staff, Abbey fed the kids, then they all helped clean and prep for breakfast. The kids were surprisingly helpful and thankfully, exhausted. By the time they were showered and in pjs, they were yawning and barely awake. Abbey barely got them into their own beds, and then she was asleep in no time flat.

Chapter 37

Abbey woke to Geraldine calling to let her know she would be in by early afternoon. She sounded really good. In fact, it was probably the happiest Abbey had ever heard her. She asked about the kids, Frieda and even the cat, then said that grandma was more lucid than normal. She couldn't wait to get back.

Abbey hung up smiling and glad that her mother was coming back. Abbey got ready, woke the kids, checked the kitchen and headed out to collect eggs. The kids were quick and really enjoyable. She got them fed and then settled in to help Janna Kay and Philip.

Meanwhile, still serving breakfast, Leah and Jess worked on lunch and dinner. They were doing all the prep work and creating wonderful aromas. They made extra bacon for club sandwiches for lunch. Only a couple of women could make this work. Leah explained to Abbey, later, that Frieda had come up with this working system when she'd been the only one cooking. She used to get breakfast out, and be working on dinner the whole time. Apparently, the ranch had begun with no staff. Of course, all things started small, but Abbey hadn't really stopped to consider it. What a huge and seemingly impossible task. She knew that she would have been overwhelmed, she doubted she could have done it.

She headed back to her room to grab her notebook, and couldn't resist popping in to Frieda's room. Rounding the corner she said,

"Goodmorning Frieda, I'm…." she didn't see her anywhere. She checked the bathroom, her sitting room, and stood in her bedroom scratching her head. No Frieda. She headed out to the hall, but caught movement through the window. There, outside by the fence was Frieda picking the dead flowers off. Abbey skipped down the stairs and out to Frieda.

Frieda was rosy and bright quite the opposite of the dead flowers she pulled. Abbey leaned on the fence smiling, "I see someone is feeling well!"

Freida beamed, "Well good morning dear, yes I am feeling great, Doctor says I am looking good too. We will do an EKG at the end of the week and some other silly tests and then see where we are." She put the dead flowers in her pocket, which was getting really full and glanced at her watch, "you should be about ready to sip from that fire hydrant that I call dad, right?"

"Yes, I am heading into another session, why are you putting the dead flowers in your pocket? Do you want me to throw those out or get you a bag?"

"No, although a small bag or container would have been a good idea. I didn't actually intend to do this now." She reached in her pocket and showed her the flower head and crushed it in her hand, little black and white seeds popped out. "I am collecting the seeds for my care packages. These are giant zinnia and once the seeds start dropping, it's really hard to collect. For some reason, they always bloom so early over here and they tend to go to seed before I catch it. The butterflies and hummingbirds just love them, though."

"Well that's neat. I would be happy to grab you a container or bag."

"No honey, I think I've got about all there is right now."

"Well, I wanted to tell you that my mom is headed back, she had a great visit with grandma and she's looking forward to being back. She said that she loves your car and that she has some sort of surprise for you."

Frieda clapped her hands and grinned, "Oh I cannot wait to see her…hey, let's really welcome her back, flowers in her room, an amazing pie, what do you think she would like?"

"Okay that's a great idea." Abbey hugged Frieda and told her she'd better get inside, and headed to the seminar.

Abbey wasn't sure if Freida meant for her to do the flowers and pie, she probably should check. Sometimes she thought Frieda was getting into her brain, often finding herself thinking about what Frieda had said regarding her mother. It was something that she did recognize. It just wasn't that easy. There were years of hurt, years of poor communication and years of feeling like Abbey had let her mother down. They loved each other sure, but it was like the love you felt for an old pair of shoes. They really weren't that great for your fee, with the support shot and worn tread nor were they pretty at all, but they were comfortable and familiar. Abbey pondered these thoughts all the way to the seminar.

This one began with Mark explaining the distinction of a brand. He asked the pastors if they had mission statements for their churches. One of the younger pastors volunteered his: "Influencing our World for Christ," Mark, impressed, put it on a white board, then went through an exercise where he defined each word independent of the other words. Once they came to an agreement as to the definition then they examined how the statement worked and whether or not they were staying true to their brand. Questions like; 'Are you influencing?' 'What is "our" world in this context?', etc… It was an interesting exercise and Mark showed them how without a clear understanding of your brand, there is no way to manage it, or check it. If so and so's church wants to be influential, they first have to be together and perceptively so. After going through the exercises,

Abbey realized how hard it must be to get a whole church of attitudes and egos to work as a unit. Being a pastor used to look so powerful but listening to these men, it was about as hard as anything could be. For the first time Abbey really got the whole point of this ranch.

Far from the mega church guys that were mostly featured in magazines like hers, most pastors were just trying to meet expectations and needs; trying to turn a group of strangers into brothers and sisters who would genuinely care for each other and anyone outside of the church. No wonder most churches were falling apart at the seams. Abbey, for her part, had read a lot about the decline in the church, she knew that pastors were up against a lot, success was tough. She figured the men here must be doing okay; that or really badly; maybe they had to be here. Either way she expected that Mark was a great encouragement.

The session ended with Mark emphasizing the fact that the pastors could always go back and change mission statements, or redefine. They could use their brand and tweak it or just redefine. Nothing was closed, nothing was finite. He encouraged the men to be creative and to think about it, they would have another more creative session on branding towards the end of the conference. He closed in prayer for the congregations. Abbey was aware of men sniffling during the prayer and was shocked by some tears and all the hugging afterwards. She doodled on her pad and started to flip pages, so she didn't have to look up.

Abbey got up, after she thought most of the men had stepped out, knowing session two was starting in a few minutes, she went to the back of the room and began restocking and checking the drinks and snacks.

Mark came up behind her, "What did you think of this session? Did you see any application for your magazine?"

Mr. Debonair looking for a compliment? He seems sincere, "Yes, of course, I think that your brand application is applicable to almost every character trait, and every job, isn't there? I was thinking I could do a brand extension of 'motherhood'. Might be a fun series. What do you think?"

"You are absolutely right, you can consider any name or title a brand. Although, you would have to restrict it to a particular. I think the broader and more common terms become intertwined with your personal view, in other words if you took Mom from a Judeo-Christian worldview it might look one way, but if you took it from a local or cultural perspective it might mean something else entirely. It's tough, You know you have probably defined motherhood for your kids very differently from your own mother or grandmother. And, just wait till they are teens, it'll change again… I certainly don't want to discourage you in any way, you could do a series of articles on Mom alone. There are some old movies like <u>Mommie Dearest</u>, for the overbearing and abusive mom, <u>Father Knows Best</u> gives you the ideal mom of the 50's, and go to the Bible for some strong moms like Hannah who promised and did give up her son to be a priest. I think you could have a ball with the dichotomy. You should do it Abbey, if you like I'd be happy to give you input, but I don't think you'll need it."

Abbey was astonished, Holy Cow, that is fun, yeah, I could really do that. It was astonishing how the fire hydrant was fun when it really interested you. "Thank you, I really like that idea."

"Well, it was your idea… by the way, I wanted to know if you would like to speak at the next session. Perhaps some of your publishing knowledge would be very helpful. I am suggesting in the next session that getting interviews with local papers and city magazines can be a real boost. How would you like to speak about how to get their attention?"

"Oh no, thank you, …I am not a speaker," Abbey stammered. The idea of speaking in front of all those people made her stomach flip.

Mark knew that Frieda had taken a liking to Abbey and wanted to fold her in to the ranch family. He really wanted her to feel more like part of the family and less like a record keeper. "Abbey you really captured the essence of things. Your article on our little place spoke volumes of the way that you are able to dig out the heart. You're a very good writer, but I am most appreciative of your thoughts. You are a professional writer, you get published all the time. Besides, I think these gentleman would enjoy looking at a lovely girl rather than an old man. Nevertheless, if you don't want to speak, that's fine, can I have your permission to use your ideas?"

"Certainly, so is the next session focusing on publishing?"

"Yes, in part, I think you'll get a kick out of it, we discuss hiring practices and then fold in basic use of the media first with finding staff and second with announcing the church's presence. You've gotten to know some of the folks who make our place run, I think you will get a good sense of how to employ people… but right now, I've got to hit the little boy's room; I'll be back." And with that he was darting out of the room.

Abbey smiled, 'the little boy's room' what a strange expression. She guessed it was something of a throwback to when Mark was raising his own daughter, and Abbey realized she didn't know if Frieda had any siblings, she thought it was really curious; it hadn't come up. Whether she had siblings or not, they might not even still be around. Abbey had a reporter's mind and wondered at the absence of any mention. Could it be that they weren't Christians, perhaps they were estranged. Hmmmm. Something to casually ask about.

The session started and Mark was joined by his grandson. They made a good team. Abbey got some good points: human resource law was constantly changing, applications needed to be revamped from time to time, and the pastors had to put some real effort into complying with the law. Mark the younger, listed several websites that made the information quite clear and suggested two bloggers that he followed for the latest on issues for compliance. Abbey was pleased she felt like she had gotten some good comprehensive notes.

As the session was wrapping up, Abbey saw her chance to escape, she had forgotten all about the flowers for her mother. She dashed out the back and ran to check her mother's room. Seeing that nothing was there; she ran outside and cut a bouquest, taking them to the kitchen she placed the flowers in a vase. There was some pink and yellow tulle that she wrapped around the vase with a soft bow. Pleased witht eh small arrangement, she went looking for the kids.

She ran first to the chickens, then to the pool, when she didn't discover the kids or Janna Kay, Jess or Philip, she went up to the rooms. Discovering a note on her door, the kids were off rafting at the pond and would be back by two. She grinned happily imagining that her kiddos were gonna get wet and potentially covered in mud. A cold outdoor shower may be in their future. She envisioned the peals of laughter...smiling, it occurred to her that her kids had never had this many people that they trusted so completely. Or maybe it was more that she had never so trusted so many with her kiddos. Figuring she had a bit of time, she showered and redressed and waiting for the kids and her mom.

Geraldine practically waltzed into the lodge, she was wearing a bowler hat. It didn't look like her at all, but she loved it. She went to her room first to pull out the hat she had gotten for Frieda and the amazing posters, she hoped to model for the kids and Abbey. Seeing the flowers, she was surprised and thrilled: she began singing quietly and thanking her Jesus—it occurred to her that she may have changed pretty dramatically for Abbey and the kids. They didn't know her when she was little and loved the Lord. For Gerladine, it felt like a homecoming, but it would be a striking change for her family. She needed to be careful—she said out loud to herself in the mirror, "Ger, BE the Bible, don't preach it!" With a jaunty tilt of her hat, she went down to Frieda's room.

Announcing herself, she entered Frieda's room saying "Good afternoon," and posing in her hat.

Frieda grinned, "Welcome back! Have you seen Abbey, how'd it go?"

The women hugged and Geraldine thanked Frieda for the gorgeous flowers.

Frieda gave a huge grin, "Oh that must have been Abbey."

Just then Geraldine's grandkids came racing downt he hall and hugged their grandma. Abbey was immediately behind them.

"Hi guys," and to Abbey, "thank you so much for the lovely bouquet. That was so thoughtful and I must say you are all a sight for sore eyes. I really missed you all," she kept her eye contact with her daughter the whole time.

Abbey was surprised, but something about her mother seemed really strange. First of all, the ridiculous hat, and then her eye contact. Her mother had never been one to hug or be demonstrative, she wondered if her something had happened with her grandma. She couldn't wait to hear. She finally responded, "I'm thrilled that you are back here safely. Did everything go okay on the drive?"

"Oh yes, but I may develop a lead foot, if I get to drive that car again! That thing has so much power and too few bumps. It's the perfect car, but I kept catching myself speeding..." she winked and grinned at Frieda.

Frieda explained, "Abbey, you've not seen my hot rod."

Abbey cracked up and the kids giggled, "You have a hot rod?"

Frieda went on pretending to be offended, "Why yes, it is my... little... vice, I love that wonderful old car. It's a thirty plus year old powerhouse, and I'm afraid I've earned a few speeding tickets throughout the years. I do repent and ask forgiveness, both of the police officers and God."

Surprised, and shaking her head, Abbey regarded the two women, "So Frieda are you gonna corrupt my mother?"

They all laughed and had to explain the word corrupt to Bug.

Abbey still waiting to hear about the hat, et al, asked her mother, "So are you hungry, do you want me to get you something to eat? Dinner smells like heaven and it'll be done about five, if you can wait. Otherwise, Leah has been making great cookies for the afternoon breaks. I'd be happy to get you a couple."

The kids were immediately entranced by the word cookies, they were on their mother tugging at her to go get some.

"You know, a cookie sounds delicious, I think that Bug and Geves look really hungry, too." Geraldine was winking at her grandchildren. "Thank you sweetheart."

Sweetheart? Abbey hadn't been called that very often by her mom. Turning to take the kids to grab the cookies, she noted that her mother had a matching hat she was handing to Frieda. The two of them were an odd pair.

They found Leah in the kitchen pulling out a hot batch of peanut butter chocolate chip—mmm, getting the nod from Leah, Abbey grabbed all the broken ones with a spatula, two whole ones, a couple of bottles of water, two small milk cartons, and headed back to Frieda's sitting room. When they got back, the two ladies were excitedly looking at an old movie poster. Abbey walked around to see it, and recognized <u>Casa Blanca</u> with Humphrey Bogart. She noticed they were both wearing the hats.

Frieda and Geraldine attempted to explain their Casa Blanca themed night, complete with appetizers. It sounded like fun although it might go over some of the guests' heads. Abbey had no doubt that they would make it wonderful.

Abbey had an idea about creating a small dinner for the five of them, and she would help Leah get the dinner out for the guys. She suggested and everyone agreed. So she left the kids with their grandma and Frieda and headed down to the kitchen.

After prepping the individual pans and creating the perfect chicken pot pies, Abbey finished up with the salad. She was dicing and slicing and chopping when Leah arrived in the kitchen.

Shocked Leah hugged Abbey, "Thank you, you did it all, didn't you?"

"Yes, I think I have all the chicken pot pies ready to go, I have the ovens heating up, so…the recipe you left out showed that they should all be done in roughly forty minutes, so looks like we'll have time to spare…how do we serve these?"

"Actually, it's easy as pie," Leah said chirpily with a cheesy grin on her face. When Abbey just grimaced, she continued, "we'll just slide them on the tables, we have these great covers, they actually need to rest for about 15 minutes, so right before the guys are due, we'll put them all on the tables. The salads will be there, too. Although, I bet you only ten percent of them will touch em."

They got dinner out and watched through the door as none of the men even glanced at their salads. Leah gave Abbey a high five and they both cracked up.

The cheesecakes slices were on the tables, drinks were going slowly and all in all it was fairly easy dinner service.

Leah helped Abbey create the meal for her family, and then shoved Abbey out of the kitchen, "You did all the prep, I'll do all the clean up! Thanks Abbey, go be with your family."

Abbey happily headed upstairs with dinner and a whole cheesecake. Seemed decadent but wonderful. Frieda, Geraldine, and the kids loved the meal and the cheesecake was cold and rich with just a hint of lemon. Perfectly delicious. They laughed about the hats, and even the kids had some on.

Their mealtime chatter was fairly benign, nothing earth shattering or personal, mostly the children talking about animals, and rafts and all the fun things they were doing.

Geraldine began the end, "Well, I'm exhausted, I know Frieda and a certain cowboy and cowgirl could use some shut-eye. Let's head to bed, tomorrow will be full of it's own."

Abbey agreed, and they all gave Frieda a hug and headed to bed.

Chapter 38

Frieda woke with a start, but she wasn't sure what woke her up. She began praying with fervor for everyone, for the ranch, for her boys, her grandchildren, her dad and all the people who worked with her, for those who were far off and for those who would be returning. When she began praying for Sharon, she became consumed and really prayed for her well-being, her health, her safety, and her family. After about an hour of prayer, mostly focused on Sharon, she felt much better. As the roosters began crowing, she left her dearest Sharon in God's hands and fell asleep.

Hearing the crowing of roosters, Abbey smiled and hit off on her alarm clock. Who knew, she might come to appreciate those dumb birds. Abbey got up, did some quick stretches, and got herself ready for the day. Collecting eggs with her kids had become a really sweet time. They loved talking to the hens and telling them how well they were doing. Geves would tell the hens that they were feeding lots and lots of people. Abbey went to get the kids to head out.

Seeing Geves up and at em, Abbey went in to tackle her youngest.

Bug was always slow in the mornings, but he seemed a little less difficult now that his task included kittens, chickens, and the barn. He was getting ready with prodding.

While waiting for Bug, Geves darted towards her mom looking concerned... "What's the matter honey?"

"Are we eating baby chickens, when we eat the eggs?"

Abbey had anticipated the question. "No honey, you know how some families have lots of children, and some have only one," seeing Geves nod, she continued, "mamas and hens have lots of chances to have children but not all become children. More of them don't. The eggs that we collect, won't become chicks, they don't have everything that they need to be babies. That's why the hens don't care that we take the eggs. They know that the ones that we take won't be babies, just eggs."

Geves pondered that for a moment and Bug was listening now, "how come these don't have what they need to be baby chickens?"

"Well the eggs aren't fertilized by a rooster." Abbey was really hoping that would be sufficient.

She hated getting into discussions with the kids about anything having to do with fatherhood and dads. Geves and Bug hadn't seen their dad since they were infants. He was a sperm donor more than a father. He walked out when Bug was two months old. Well, that wasn't completely true; he was pushed out when Abbey discovered his penchant for other women, while she was caring for the kids by herself. She gave him an ultimatum and he said he'd like to have both, blaming her for being so tired all the time. Abbey showed him the door. He never cared much for the kids and they were so little, he just never wanted anything to do with them. He eventually moved, or at least that's what Abbey understood, the state couldn't seem to locate him for purposes of child support, water under the bridge.

Thankfully, Geves seemed content as the threesome made their way to the barn. They collected the eggs as they did their good morning routine with the hens. After carefully delivering the eggs to the kitchen, Geves and Bug wanted to rush back out to the barn to help put the chicks and hens out in the yard. Abbey assured Leah, on the way out, that she'd be right back. Geraldine met Abbey and the kids and volunteered to take the kids back to the barn.

Surprised, all Abbey could say was, "thanks, I'll get back to the kitchen."

Making her way to the kitchen, Abbey got curious about the chickens, it seemed like they only had hens on the ranch, where were all the males? She knew she had heard roosters every morning, but she hadn't seen them. Strange, she'd have to ask. She should probably just wait and ask Jess.

After cleaning the eggs and placing them in the cooler, Leah showed up and the two women got the breakfast quickly. Leah shooed her out of the kitchen, so she headed up to grab her notebooks and pens. There were two seminars to attend today with Mark. Abbey felt confident that her notes were good. Mark's handouts and the rough outline she had started with were really coming together. So far, it looked like a great marketing piece for the seminars, and a nice thousand word article that she would title, <u>The Business of the Church</u>. Arriving in the conference room, she was greeted by a huge welcoming grin from Mark.

With the seminars finished for the day, lunch over, and some of the dinner prep out of the way, she decided to hit the computer for an hour before tracking down her kids and mom. Being a lone made it easy to get a bunch done. Halfway through, it occurred to her that she was avoiding the *conversation* with her mother. She had promised Frieda, and knew she was right …but she did have to work and her mom had only been back or twenty-four hours…time to pay the piper, Abbey set out to find her family.

Finding everyone in the barn was not a surprise. The kids had shown their grandma all sorts of tricks and critters. Geves and Bug had to explain it all over again to their mom as they climbed very high up into the loft to swing down into the hay. Abbey was terrified at first but her mother put her hand on her arm, nodded, and smiled. The kids were giggling so much that it became infectious. They all decided to go for a quick swim but Abbey still wanted to know about the hens.

Catching up with Jess, she asked, "Hey Jess, how come I never see any roosters, I know that I hear them in the morning, do they hide out all day?"

Jess laughed, "Oh, well, we are under explicit orders not to keep the males. It's a crazy Frieda story."

Abbey smiled, "Do tell!"

"First of all, to be fair, Frieda could never stand to see any of her 'pets' get butchered, so that was probably where it originated, but we all think it had to do with a certain rooster named Floyd. He lived here for a long time and loved to pester Frieda. He followed her everywhere and got into constant trouble. Floyd was forever trying to go wherever she went, so he was trying to get into the kitchen, the lodge, her car, everywhere. Frieda said that Floyd thought he was a person. Birds, and roosters in particular can be really smelly creatures, as you've seen in the hen house. They are not the cleanest, Frieda says that's why we call them fowl." Jess grinned and continued, " One of Floyd's biggest issues was that he was just obsessed with his own reflection, he would stop at any shiny object, take one look and become mesmorized by his own image, he would turn this way and that," she was demonstrating now, "he would turn and notice his fine plumage—it was funny, and Frieda would always say, 'mirror, mirror,' whenever she caught him. This became a particular problem with her bumper, Floyd would follow Frieda and as he was rounding the back of the car, he would suddenly stop and notice himself, he wouldn't move from that spot. She was terrified that she'd hit her little narcissist. Anyway, one day she had left her sunroof open and Floyd had discovered a wealth of amazing mirrors, the entire windshield and the rearview mirrors made him most happy. Problem was, he would not get out. It took us weeks to get the odor out from Floyd's two-day encampment. She was livid." Jess paused.

Abbey was hanging on every word, "please go on."

"One day there was a delivery vehicle with a new driver who didn't check the bumper, Floyd finally got hit. Frieda cried herself silly. She always claimed to hate that dumb bird, especially after he trashed her car, but she was devastated by his loss. She immediately bought a book on sexing chicks and since, then no roosters, we bring them all down to the Amish folks and then they raise, butcher, and sell the meat back to us. Perfect in many ways and a great deal for them and us. We don't really have the manpower to do all the butchering, anyway."

"Wow, that is a crazy Frieda story. How long ago was all of this? And tell me about the sexing of the chickens?"

"Gosh, I think it was bout three years ago, it was one of the things that I happened to be very good at. Right up under the tail feathers there is what is called a vent, and if there is a pimple like form on the vent, it is most likely a male. By about four to six weeks the combs are distinctive enough. I'm pretty good at spotting the males and I just run them down to the Amish."

Abbey was about to say something but Jess rushed on.

"Oh and you probably hear roosters from nearby farms in the morning, some are free range, so I would imagine they may even migrate over here from time to time. They aren't great flyers but they can fly. Sometimes we tease Frieda that Floyd is still with us."

Satisfied, Abbey thanked Jess for all the info and the wonderful 'crazy Frieda' story. She thought it would make a cute quip for Reader's Digest. Too bad she didn't work for them.

She rejoined the kids and her mom and asked if they wouldn't all like to go for a swim, she took the opportunity to try to keep her promise to Frieda as they walked.

"Mom, I want you to know that I am so glad that you are here with us, …I have to say that I really hated seeing you go and I'm genuinely glad that you're back…"

Assuming, that Abbey meant for the kids, Geraldine was about to brush her off, but when she really looked at her-she sensed that it really was meant for her. She was delighted and her first instinct was to thank God. She wished she knew what Abbey wanted from her but until she figured it out, she intended to move cautiously, "Abbey, I missed you all. This place is really amazing I can see why you and the kids love it so and I am really thrilled that you wanted me to join you. I am also so proud and tickled at what you are doing here. You have always been a wonderful writer, but I had no idea you could run a kitchen. I wished I had had your confidence at your age."

"Thanks mom-I love it here, too. Though I'm not running the kitchen, I am just a cog in this wheel. The thing practically runs itself and I am still learning. It does feel good and I love the whole food service thing. Of course, I cannot imagine this business operates the same way anywhere else in the world."

"I am proud of you, though…that's what I wanted you to know." Geradine reached over and gave her a one armed hug as they followed the kids through the lodge. They were making their way up to their rooms when they noticed someone walking into Frieda's room.

Curious, they followed the stranger.

"Zsa Zsa! You look amazing!"

"Princess???" Frieda hopped out of bed and rushed to the woman, "You look like a kid! Where did you come from and why didn't' you tell me you were coming?!"

Geraldine and Abbey smiled and figured this was another story…the woman was lovely and was busy piling presents on top of Frieda and her bed. Seeing them, a beaming Frieda gestured them in. "This is my very best friend, Jeanette, otherwise known as Princess Dory."

Jeanette turned towards the ladies and grinned, "Howdy! – I think Frieda calls everyone her 'very best friend.'"

"Not true! Although, I have a couple. This is Abbey and Gerladine. Oh and they will love how you got your name." Without taking a breath Frieda told the story, "Years and years ago, our boys were in a science competition in Kansas City and we took the boys to the Crown Center Plaza in Kansas City and naturally they have a *Wizard of Oz* shop, you know from the movie. Well Jeanette was recently divorced from a real jerk and we saw a small sign. It was Dorothy asking how come all the men she met had: 'no heart, no brains, and no courage' we laughed ourselves silly and Jeanette became Princess Dory!"

Jeanette chimed in, "she always treated me like a princess, too. And you wouldn't know it today but Ms. Frieda here is Zsa Zsa… when Dan moved Frieda out to the sticks, she was not a happy camper. She had hay fever, and was allergic to everything growing, she had hives constantly and was always with an epi pen or an inhaler. Abbey, you're too young to remember but Geraldine, the show <u>Green Acres</u>, 'New York is where I'd rather stay…'" Geraldine nodded and chimed in with both Jeanette and Frieda singing, "I get allergic smelling hay, I just adore a penthouse view, darling I love you but give me Park Avenue."

They laughed and Jeanette continued, "The actress in the show was Ava Gabor but neither of us were up on trivia, so I called her Zsa Zsa from then on. At least it was a Gabor." They dissolved into laughter.

Abbey had heard a little about Frieda's initial dislike of country living. Perhaps she was the embodiment of taking lemons and making lemonade.

Abbey and Geraldine could see that Frieda was in good hands they excused themselves, got their swimsuits on and headed to the pool with the kids. While they splashed and enjoyed the cool water with the kids they spoke about Frieda and Jeanette and what a nice friendship. After getting water logged, they made their way back inside to get ready for dinner. Abbey made herself useful in the kitchen until they joined Jeanette and Frieda for dinner. Jeanette or rather, Princess was so much fun. She told stories of Frieda corrupting her two boys and spoke endlessly of fun times. Frieda showed them a curio cabinet filled entirely of gifts from Princess. Jeanette was just passing through because she had to be in Atlanta for a presentation. She was getting an award for single handedly getting D.E.C.A., a marketing training program, into seventy-seven percent of the inner city schools across the United States. Frieda had every intention of attending the event and was behaving herself so that the doctor would give his blessing.

They were having such a dynamite time, that the hours got away from them. When Abbey looked up and realized that it was pretty late, she excused herself and the children for bed. Chickens would be waiting in the morning and there were two sessions to cover tomorrow. Abbey was pooped, but feeling very happy about the earlier conversation with her mother.

Chapter 39

The egg gathering went without a hitch, although Abbey felt like they had collected more today than usual. The kids assisted with the washing and packing of the eggs. Abbey and Leah got breakfast out, with Leah stopping briefly to teach bug how to light the sternos. He was actually really careful and Abbey was pleased to see him behaving so beautifully. Geves got started with the juicing machine, and really got a kick out of it. Maybe food service was in their blood. Abbey checked in with Mark about the session schedule for the day and after she made her plans, she dropped the kids off with her mom. Geraldine had stayed up into the wee hours with Jeanette and Frieda- apparently those two didn't miss a beat, but both slept in this morning.

After covering the sessions, Abbey checked the dinner planning and assumed her role. Leah and Jess had gotten quite a bit done yesterday and there was only one more day of the conference that Abbey would be concerned about. The families would be arriving late morning and throughout the afternoon on Satruday, so she knew it'd be a busy week again.

Lori and Sharon were due in tonight and Abbey thought it'd be fun to get them something. Abbey looked into the menu schedule and particulars for the upsoming week and got some ideas. She then went in search of the cleaning women to see what she could do to welcome those two back. She found Shirley leaving Mark's place. She hadn't yet cleaned Lori or Sharon's homes, but she planned to put some fresh juices in the refrigerators and some wonderful bread that had just been delivered. Abbey asked if it would be alright if she made some floral arrangements for them. Shirley loved the idea and said that she would take them over with her when she went to clean. Abbey gathered the same flowers that she had for her mother, two vases, and some beautiful yellow tulle. She got them done quickly and caught up with Shirley, to let her know they were in the kitchen. Pleased with herself, Abbey did a mental check mark.

Abbey then made her way into the computer to finish up some of her notes from the session work; on her door was a note with Frieda's handwriting. Abbey looked inside and found a note and a check. It was for eight thousand dollars, made out to Abbey and drawn off of the Miller Marketing Group. What was that about? The note read;

> *Abbey dear, we have received a substantial gift from my dear friend, Princess. She has elected to give a separate gift to you to fund what she believes is your great gift for service and stewardship. I did not request this, nor did I know what amount she intended. I simply discussed salaries with her and, you know, this is her thing. Please accept her gift graciously, Abbey. She wouldn't give it if she really didn't want you to have it. We are all so proud of you. I hope this money will help alleviate any concerns that you might have about being here. I still intend ot give you a salary of sorts, we will discuss later. Love, Frieda.*

Abbey was shocked, but very appreciative. She knew that his money would come in very handy, but she just didn't know what to expect. She wasn't sure about Jeanette or anything else. She read the note through several times and came to no real conclusion. She supposed that Frieda was worried that she wouldn't receive this well and yet it wasn't asking abbey for anything extra. She would wait to cash it but she could sure use the money and before she knew it she was mentally spending it. Abbey realized that she should stop, put it away before she could focus on nothing else. She tucked the note and check into her suitcase and tried to finish some thing son the computer. When her work didn't go as planned, she gave up and went down to the kitchen.

Geraldine came in with the kids that evening and they all ate with the staff. It was a pleasant evening with no sign of Jeanette and Frieda. Abbey didn't know how she would react, but she would definitely try to be obtuse, yet gracious. At the end of the evening Geraldine explained that Frieda had gone back to Atlanta with Jeanette, they were going to 'do the town' and then go to Jeanette's ceremony on Sunday, which explained the note. Abbey waited to see if her mother knew of the check, but there was no mention. She had no idea what the others were paid, or what they would think. It bothered her that she and her family were getting so much attention and reward.

The kids decide that they wanted to see a movie, from the ranch's little library of DVD's. Jonathan told the kids that he would be happy to set them up. He led them to a screen and a projector hooked up in a small room off the main lobby. The kids picked an old animated movie that they liked and Abbey grabbed her laptop. They passed a pleasant evening and Abbey even got some work done. She intended to complete another article on the ranch, the hand-outs for Mark, and other book review and she wanted to frame out an article on The Business of the Church. She had some good ideas about how people might see that the church is ill equipped to deal with the vast sweeping changes in human resource law, or the tax code. She hoped that all the input she heard at the conference would give her all the info that she might need. Some of the material, though, still confused her, she wondered if she should consult an attorney just in case. She'd ask Ed after she got the article done, he'd know and maybe run it through the magazine's legal desk.

While Abbey got a lot done, she had given herself an impossible amount of work. The handouts were close to finished, but that was about it. She gave up and ate some popcorn with the kids, and finally put herself and them to bed.

Chapter 40

Abbey woke knowing that today would be fun. The families came back today, and she'd be working with Lori and Sharon again. Things would feel normal, at least by ranch standards. Plus there would be kids for Geves and Bug. She was excited while waking the children for egg duty. Loulabelle the cat had gotten really strong and had become their escort in the mornings. She was quite the little cat, Abbey couldn't believe how attached they all were to this little spitfire. While small, she would stand up to the biggest dogs and nuzzle against the horses, she was fearless and funny. The cat accompanied them to the barn, to the kitchen and back to their rooms. She spent her days with Shasta and the two- dog and cat went on long walks.

Gathering the eggs quickly, Abbey fed the kids a big breakfast right in the kitchen. She was checking the kitchen computer for tonight's schedule, and something caught her eye out the window. Moses was standing just outside the kitchen. She hadn't seen him all week, she grabbed a bunch of carrots and some sugar cubes for him.

She motioned to the kids, "Hey look who's outside?"

The kids jumped up and took the treats out of her hands and raced out to visit the giant horse.

Abbey was glad that her day started this way; she was looking forward to a fabulous weekend and upcoming week. Leah helped put out a simple continental breakfast and they got the lunches prepared.

The break station was set up with coffee, water, soft drinks, and some whole fruits. Abbey and Leah got together all the ingredients for tonight's <u>Greek Fest</u>. Abbey went to the storage room to look for the Greek cart but couldn't find it anywhere. She came back to the kitchen to ask Leah. Leah, for her part; had forgotten, that Abbey hadn't been there for a Greek night yet. "I am so sorry, the Greek Night is done outside, and so the cart is in the end hall closet. Come on." Leah showed her where everything was and they began setting up the lights, colored tablecloths, hanging lanterns, garlic strings, olive oil, and olive jars on every table. There were canvas awnings that erected like a pup tent and flowing curtains for around the buffet, which was set up like tables in a market stall. You could wind throughout the 'market' and fill your plate with giant Greek olives, feta and cucumber dressings and salads; there was a stall with every kind of pita and toppings; gyros, baklava, Greek spaghetti, and spicy lamb. They draped flowering bougainvillea in pinks, reds and purples throughout the stalls and dining tables. All of the tables had colorful draping, olive branches, grapes, and candles. Apparently some dancers were coming that evening, a local dance troop that was practicing for the annual Greek Festival in Atlanta would get their first opportunity to perform for the pastors and their families. They were also willing to teach some of the kids the dances. Abbey knew that Geves would love it.

Abbey was nervously wondering if they were going to be wearing togas or something, but Leah assured her that there were colorful flowing dresses fro the women and linen shirts with billowing sleeves for the men. The Grecian influence of today was more about color and comfort. The traditional blue design would adorn the men's shirts. Abbey wondered what it was called, she thought it always looked like interlocking J's. Leah went on to say, "Togas seemed to fraternity like for Frieda, and besides how would you ever get anything done in a toga?"

Leah had returned to the kitchen, while Abbey finished up placing the candles on the tables. After Abbey finished outside, she raced back to the kitchen and ran into a joyous reunion with Sharon and Lori. Both were smiling and hugging Abbey like a long lost cousin. Abbey was so pleased to see them, and it surprised her how much she cared about them. Lori was all about showing pictures of the grandkids, while Sharon was quietly smiling and saying how much she enjoyed her trip. Lori couldn't wait to squeal about her daughter being pregnant, AGAIN! It was number four for her. Sharon didn't speak much but when she spoke she told them tales of her son's obsession with the perfect lawn and his knowledge and explanations of every conceivable variety of weed or 'wrong grass'. They were rolling on the floor in laughter with Sharon's tale.

Lori announced that she had spoken with Jeanette, and that Frieda and she were getting pedicures. Apparently, this was very unusual but also a blast. Knowing that Jeanette was taking care of Frieda made them all happy. Abbey realized that what Frieda may have meant in her note, was that Jeanette liked to take care of others. Maybe the fact that she had been a single mom, too...for now she was grateful to know that Frieda was in such good hands.

They began carting the food to the "Greek Market" and noticed some of the other staff coming around to get their attire and stations . Plates were carried out, silverware added to the tables, and the drink machines made ready to go. Waters, teas, and juices along with frozen juice smoothing, made up the drinks while the final touch were the luminaries. Philip, Jana Kay, and Jess had an assembly line going with brown paper sacks, Philip was scooping sand into the sacks and lining them along the walkway. Into each sack Jana Kay placed a candle, and Jess came behind them to light the candle.

As the sun set, the lights became more brilliant. Everything was completely ready to go, so Abbey went ot her room to freshen up and change into her dress, it was a white flowing dress with ribbons streaming from the shoulders down past the hem. The ribbons were in every conceivable color and the dress billowed and moved as Abbey did. It was flattering and actually a little heavy due to all the ribbons. Abbey loved it and couldn't wait to see the kids.

Arriving at Geraldine's room she found Geves and Bug all dressed and very excited to see the festival. They had heard everything from Jess and Philip while they followed them around that day. Abbey was delighted to lead the down the path. The food was fantastic, Bug even tried squid. The dancing was particularly wonderful – Abbey thought to herself, it's no wonder the Greeks were so thin—such a complicated and hectic dance. There was a belly dancing segment and it was done in a very modest way, it was quite lovely. The luminaries created a subtle back light and a romantic path.

By the time the evening came to a conclusion, most of the food tables and market area had already been cleared. The only stuff left were some of the décor and the odd glass or silverware. The luminaries were each going out as the candle burned down into the sand, it was just a matter of blowing them out and dumping the candles in the trash and sand into a bucket and returning it all back to the Greek Cart. Abbey loved how effortlessly everything came together and went back. She actually felt a sense of mastery in some of this.

Chapter 41

That morning Abbey returned to the kitchen to help with the giant breakfast. She resumed her post at the Hobart with over fifty eggs. It was great to be working with the giant mixer again, she couldn't believe how much she had missed the smell fo warming syrup and sizzling bacon.

Hearing squeals from the dining room, she went to investigate. She found and met Pastor Don and his wife Debbie. They were seated on the floor in a circle witht heir four kids, three precocious little ones and a sullen teen. They were playing Duck, Duck, Goose, but their young son, who appeared to be all of three, just wouldn't pick a goose. He went round and round and round saying Duck each time. It was really tedious and the teen looked about ready to scream. No wonder he was sullen. Abbey snickered, and Don smiled at her. She was a bit shocked when she realized who he looked like, he could have been Billy Graham forty years ago. He had a gentle slow smile that spoke to you. Abbey said that although breakfast would be another fifteen minutes or so, she would be delighted to get some juices and milks out immediately. He grinned from ear to ear while Debbie spouted thanks with the most beautiful southern accent. After getting their drink orders, seating them at a table, and engaging the family, Abbey learned that they were from North Carolina.

Abbey rushed back to the kitchen, informing the others that there were some very hungry little ones waiting for breakfast, she grabbed cartons of chocolate milk, regular milk, and prepared three lidded cups of orange juice. She added three adult orange juices and three mugs for coffee, too.

The little boy was still not calling for a goose, so his good natured father, made himself the goose and tackled the little boy into his lap. He proceeded to tickle the child while the rest of his family got up and went to the table for their drinks. Debbie got the one little girl settled in and helped the other young boy open his carton of chocolate milk. The older boy was a the typical teenager, wanting to be grown just not quite there. Abbey remembered how that felt. He had a bit of an attitude, but nothing unusual. In many ways he seemed unhappy, but his dad and mom obviously adored him. He was a prize to them, and you could tell. Abbey spent most of the breakfast period assisting this family. There weren't that many guests in this week, and something about this family just seemed very special. She enjoyed telling them a bit about the ranch and even offered to show them the baby chicks and kittens after breakfast. Geves and Bug showed up so Abbey introduced them.

Geves immediately took over, "I can introduce you to snow white and the seven dwarfs, they are in the barn…and I can teach you how to handle the baby chickens, but," she was pointing her finger at the boys, "you have to be very delicate with them."

Abbey was tickled with her daughter but thought she needed to slow down, placing her hand on Geves' shoulder, she said, "My daughter has named a whole bunch of kittens that were born in the barn, they are so little and she's right the baby chicks are very delicate but are used to being handled at this point," she rolled her eyes at the other two adults.

Don and Debbie chuckled and glanced at their teen, Don piped up, "Stephen, what do you think?" The young man shrugged, his dad looked at Abbey apologetically and said, "Our Stephen is very artistic, he's a bit less taken with nature for nature's sake and more about the beauty. He can take the most amazing photographs and has an innate ability for film."

Abbey had an idea… "You know Stephen, I could use your help, I'm working on some articles for a magazine- I work for the Christianity Today and I could use some of your expertise with the photos. This month I am volunteering in the kitchen so I don't have a lot of extra time to take shots. Would you be interested in taking some photos for me? Ms. Frieda provides digital cameras for guests to use while they are here, whatchya think?"

He looked a bit unsure, "Well I dunno, what kind of pictures do you want?"

Abbey thought for a moment, "How about whatever you perceive to be right. I keep trying to capture the ranch, but maybe if your artist's eye gets out there, you will get what I can't. You never know, you might just get published, and I will give you credit!"

He shrugged again and said, "okay."

Abbey pointed him towards the office and Philip, where Stephen could get a camera. After he left, Debbie pulled Abbey aside. She hugged Abbey, "I cannot thank you enough, Stephen is so special to us, his artist's brain is a challenge though, and with all the younger ones, ….well, sometimes, it's just tough to meet everyone's needs. I dearly love that boy, but my husband and I are just more methodical and mechanical in our thinking and we seem to always fall short when it comes to engaging our artistic boy. Thank you, so should we meet you guys down at that first barn?" She hugged Abbey again and turned to her husband who was grinning.

Abbey said, "Sure, just let me finish up in the kitchen, it shouldn't take me more than about fifteen minutes. You guys can head on down without me, Geves and Bug can lead the way."

Abbey, Geves, and Bug spent the morning with the young family, they showed them all the wonders of the barn. Debbie had commented specifically about Abbey's help with Stephen. She was surprised that a young mom would be so good with a sulky teen.

Abbey explained, "Being a teen was so hard, I just remember feeling like everything I did was hyper critical and would determine the entire rest of my life, and yet not having any control or decision making power of my own. I was so frustrated. I was also very awkward and unsure of myself. I never fit into a particular group. I was sort of popular with the unpopulars."

Debbie seemed pensive, "That's an interesting concept, I think I was also popular with the unpopulars. I was smart, so that was never a clique, yeah, I think I understand what you are saying. It is so hard being a parent to a teen. Nothing I say is right, but I think he knows how much we love him."

"Oh, I'm sure that he does, it's just a rough time of life. I love teenagers as a rule, but about the time my kids are teens, I may not feel that way..." the two women shared a laugh.

Towards lunchtime, Abbey explained how lunches worked and explained that she had to get back to work but that she would see them this evening. She was purposely cryptic about the scheduled evening, and told them pointedly to get some rest before dinner. It was to be "Dinner at the Castle" and Abbey sincerely hoped that Don and Debbie would enjoy some quality time that evening. She couldn't wait to see Debbie in her costume, and she thought the little girl would be a perfect angel. Abbey didn't dare tell Geves and Bug for fear they'd announce it to all.

They said their good byes and see you laters and Abbey brought the kids to her mother. She then made her way down to the dining hall.

Lori and Sharon were decorating the horse and carriage cookie centerpieces. Abbey watched wanting to see how it was done. The cookies had been made and frozen before they left last week. The decorating, they claimed, was the easy part. They were laid out as a set for each table. With so few tables, Lori was having even more fun with the decorations. They had a rolling cart covered with bottles of icing, sprinkles, food coloring pens, frosting piping, and even wax paper covered with drying frosting designs. Abbey noted that each set seemed to have it's own color theme. She asked Sharon, who then explained that they had already figured out the costumes for the various families, and that the colors were coordinated to go with their table décor. She asked Abbey to go set the tables so that they could set the stage coaches and horses up as soon as they were dried. It was a delicate balancing act that they would rather work out on the tables than in the kitchen. She also offered Abbey a set to do herself. Deciding that she would like to do the ones for Don and Debbie's family, she found out that Debbie and her daughter Rebecca would be dressed in a yellow tulle, with Debbie's dark hair, she would look lovely. Jonathan and Philip began stringing the tulle and lights for the dropped ceiling effect. They also put the fake candles on all the tables where there would be small children. Placing them on the mirrors lit the room magically. Abbey couldn't wait to see all the princesses tonight, and was looking forward to being a behind-the-scenes gal tonight. She hoped to watch Don and Debbie dance the night away but thought that she could entertain the little ones with her crew. Lori and Sharon had managed to pull all the steaks and chicken out to thaw and marinade. They had the orders established upon check in (via the computer), it was quite a system that Abbey thought she'd like to learn about, too. The computer was used for an extensive profile with things like allergies, how food was to be prepared, all the way down to the children's sizes. Much of the profile was filled out prior to arrival but any last minute questions were caught at check-in, and everything was able to be changed or updated. When Lori pulled up the kitchen computer she knew exactly how much of each thing she would be preparing. Abbey was glad to know that it was a lot more planned than she originally thought.

With the dining room ready; stagecoaches on the tables, a grand castle entrance, drawbridge, and costumes in the bungalows and cabins, all systems were go!

Abbey wouldn't need to be back in the kitchen until forty-five minutes before dinner. Salads were on rolling carts in the walk-in refrigerator, they would then fill water glasses and light the burners. Desserts would be delivered last. Jonathan had the sound system ready to go and he would wait for the arrival of the band.

Abbey returned to her room, made a few notes to herself and took a long hot shower. It felt good to be working so hard again—her body didn't feel so restless. It was also great that Frieda would be coming back tonight. Somehow it seemed fitting that Frieda would return on this night. Abbey was also excited that Matt would be returning, but tried to keep her mind from staying there.

Her daughter came bounding into the room, "Mama! It's princess night again! Yeah! Rebecca is gonna love it I can't wait to tell her."

"Sweetie, you can't tell her, remember how fun it was when you were surprised with your princess dress and all the pretty lights? Let Rebecca enjoy it as a surprise, okay?"

"Yeah, but it won't ruin it if I show her our dresses and I tell her a little…."

"Honey, no, it needs to be a surprise. But, you can teach her to dance, won't that be fun? You can also show her that we get to eat the decorations on the table. Okay!"

Geves loved the idea of teaching her to dance and squealed as she ran from the room. Abbey heard her squeal again as she spied her gown and matching slippers. Abbey smiled and lay still, what a glorious time, she thought of Debbie's family and was thrilled for her. While she was ruminating, she heard Geves holler, "Ms. Frieda's back!" Then up like a shot, she ran down the hall and stairs. Geraldine was fast on her heels.

The old lady came in beaming; looking like the cat that swallowed the canary.

Frieda said nothing about the bag she held, but hugged everyone and said, "Oh my trip was just what the doctor ordered. Jeanette got a nice bit of credit for all of her work and we were just our silly old selves. We did all the ridiculous things that we did in our youth. We had a grand time. I am tired, but I feel really good." Taking note of Abbey's and Geraldine's looks of concern, she continued, "No worries girls, I am on top of my game." She turned to Geraldine, "We have so much work to do before we roll out Casa Blanca." There was a gleam in her eye.

She excused herself and went to her room. Everyone split up to get ready for dinner; Abbey to the kitchen, and the rest to their respective rooms. Gerladine had never seen this event and Abbey was sure that she would be astounded. She had carefully selected a shade of green that was a bit muted with a lovely neckline for her mother. Most everything was sort of a one -size –fits- all for the women with some much larger sizes available. The materials were fit with ties, and hooks and loops so that each piece could fit well. Frieda had acquired this design fro a costume shop in Atlanta and she haunted the local thrift stores finding as many prom dresses, bridesmaid, and wedding dresses as possible. She had also found a seamstress to help make more. There was literally a wardrobe room for several of the events. Selection was only limited by the numbers of folks in attendance. Abbey checked with Sharon and took care of the water glasses, candles, and snapped on the twinkle lights. She placed salads and wished she had time to help Debbie get ready, but since she was running tight on time she thought she'd just have to be there to see her face. She got dressed an ran into Matt o her way back to the dining hall. He was heavily engrossed in conversation with one of the priests who had stayed over after the conference—a really handsome man, movie star handsome. Abbey had seen him in one of the seminars and assumed that he was a pastor until Mark had addressed him as 'Father'. She remembered thinking it a shame that such a handsome man would be a priest. He was extrememly polite and good natured, but that was as much as she could say. It appeared that Matt, however, was completely enamored with him, but then he saw Abbey and motioned her over.

"Abbey, hi, I'd like for you to meet the man who talked me into seminary, and dragged me right on through it. This is Father John Carlson."

"It's a pleasure to formally meet you, I saw you in our seminars taking notes and appreciated all your help. You were kind enough to get me all my strange requests, and I so appreciate that you did that each and every day. I thank you."

Abbey was pleased, "That's right Father, you like hot water with lemon after meals. It was my pleasure to make it available." She then turned to Matt, "This man cannot be the 'old priest' you told me about!"

Matt blushed, "Well I don't think I called him old, but he was a priest while I was still a confused teen, so I may have made him sound like the wise old sage that he is. By-the-way Abbey you look fantastic."

Abbey twirled around, "Why thank you sir, it's pretty hard not to when dressed as a princess. I had better get into the dining hall. There is a wonderful family here, Oh you probably know Pastor Don, he was in the seminars with you…anyway, I cannot wait to see their faces as they come in."

Father John responded, "Our pastor Don is one of the finest ment I have ever known, he and I go way back, so I am looking forward to seeing Debbie and those kids. Quite a brood. They make an 'old priest,' " said with a wink and a nod, "cheery! Allow me to escort you in my dear." The priest elbowed Matt out of the way.

Matt feigning pain, said he needed to get to work.

Blushing slightly, Abbey turned to Father John and took his arm, she had to practically skip to keep up with him. They wound their way into the ballroom and he found a great spot to watch the door. Abbey excused herself to get back to work.

Abbey checked in with Lori and Sharon, they were still chatting about their families and told her that they wouldn't begin the main course until people started with their salads. They told her that she could signal them by table color. They had the various meals laid out by color code. The chicken and steaks were all partially cooked; it was simply a matter of finishing to the people's tastes and making warm.

The vegetable medley, rice pilaf, pasta with vinaigrette, and plain rice were all prepared and ready to plate up.

Abbey positioned herself near the drawbridge but behind the door, with a camera ready planning to catch several people, but really dying to capture this for Debbie.

She saw several families come in one at a time and took lots of photos but also welcomed them. Stephen, the young teen showed up and had the same idea that Abbey did, he stationed himself next to Abbey. When his family showed up, Abbey and he began snapping away. Debbie joked that, not only did she feel like a princess, now she had to deal with paparazzi. Don was beaming with pride the whole way. The boys were so cute with their little tux shirts, and they were very entertained by the drawbridge, they ran up and over it at least a dozen times. But, Rebecca, she was just adorable, her yellow dress was so long that it made her look to be floating, she had a huge yellow bow in her hair and she was so surprised that her little lips made the perfect 'o' shape. She was clearly thrilled and just as cute as could be.

Father John made his way to Debbie; who then insisted that he sit with them, the little ones determined that he needed to be between the littlest boys. Their parents giggled. After the meal, she danced three times with Father John. He was just so dapper that Abbey couldn't understand why he would be a priest. It felt like such a waste, to her. Someone like him, never marrying, seemed bizarre. To Abbey it seemed like all the best guys were married, gay, or priests. Of course, she'd revise her thinking a little when she saw Matt later; he was a pretty good guy too.

The priest was quite the dancer, however and danced with Geraldine and Frieda most of the night. He even danced with Geves. The band played as Abbey worked; clearing tables and refreshing drinks, she was astounded at the serenity of it all. There was peacefulness even in this party atmosphere. People working up a sweat cleaning, clearing, or dancing, it was still calming. She, again, had to recognize that there was something about these people and this place.

As soon as all the families had retired for the evening, she changed out of her gown and back to more workable clothing. After helping Lori and Sharon finish a few tasks in the kitchen, she began on the dining hall. Matt was there too, and they bantered about the evening and some of the cute things the children had done. Matt had noticed Loulabelle in the lodge and was tickled that she looked almost one hudred percent better. Remarking that it was wonderful for him to see his mentor, and how he hoped to spend a lot of time with Father John, Matt seemed more than a good guy. Father John had stayed on after the conference just so that he could visit with Matt. Abbey quizzed him about the priesthood and why someone like Father John would want ot be a priest when he so obviously enjoyed the company of women.

Matt thought about it for a while, then "How much do you understand about the Catholic church?"

"Not too much, I know they don't eat meat on some Fridays, that they observe lent, their priests don't marry and that some take a vow of poverty. I've interviewed a few nuns, and to me it seemed obvious why they were nuns. Beyond that I guess I don't know too much. I have seen some beautiful churches and artwork, though."

"You probably know more than most. The fact is Paul in the New Testament spoke of being unmarried, and how it gave you a benefit. You could truly be dedicated to God only if you were unmarried. He claimed that to be a better choice. I think the Catholics decided that only those who are unmarried can truly be unencumbered enough to be a priest, and I do actually think there is a lot of merit there. Paul also said, though, that if you couldn't resist the temptation, that is the desire for a woman, then you should be married because it was better to marry than to burn in sin. He spoke of the pulls of this world when you are married; you have to concern yourself with home and hearth when you have a spouse. Again, this is true. I personally, felt hat for me it would be unnatural not to have a family and I look forward to having a wife and children. Being an only child, I have always dreamt of a house filled with kids—I want to have a home that is warm and filled with noise. Having this desire is only a sin if I act on it without the holiness of matrimony. So, again, as I believe, there is nothing wrong with not being married.

Father John is delighted with his life and he genuinely loves scholarly pursuits and not having anyone ot whom he is responsible. He loves the church, the mass, and dealing with everyone, but he also loves his freedom. Besides, I think he has more family than anyone I know. That guy has fresh baked goods in his parsonage every week and a variety that you cannot even imagine. The ladies of his church take good care of him- he is welcome everywhere. I once spent a week with him and I can assure you he didn't lack for company. He was busy from dawn to dusk. He has this open door policy, and he likes it that way. I can no more imagine a wife in that picture than I can see mine without. Does that answer your question?"

"Yes, I suppose you did, but I still cannot help but think that some poor woman's heart broke the day he signed on."

"I'm sure you're right, but I don't intend to ask." Looking around them, everything was done and ready for the morning, so Matt said, "Well, looks like we're through, sweet dreams Abbey, see you tomorrow."

"Night Matt!"

Chapter 42

The day dawned with rain but it didn't stop the egg collection, Geves and Bug were armed with buckets and ready to go. Abbey knew that they didn't need to do this any longer but the kids were really enjoying it and the responsibility was good for them.

As they went about their duties, Abbey noticed how much better the kids were getting along. No longer did Geves have to correct Bug's every statement and Bug didn't seem to need to compete with Geves to the degree that he usually did. Abbey figured she'd better enjoy it while it lasted. She delivered the eggs to the kitchen, the kids to her mother, and caught sight of Matt and Father John walking with Frieda. Both Father John and Frieda were what Matt referred to as 'state side parents; and Matt could've easily been their son. It was funny how people who needed one another often found each other.

The day progressed normally with visits from Don, Debbie and the kids and they were thrilled with the assignment Abbey had given Stephen. Stephen had taken an interest in photographing the scenery and some of the people, it seemed that his favorite subjects were pictures of people that weren't necessarily at their best. Abbey figured it was a teen being a teen and she would simply delete the pics, because Stephen had no accesss to the computers, there would be no harm.

Abbey tried to channel him towards the more attractive aspects. The little ones were enchanted by everything and the family took

Abbey's suggestion to grab some rafts and set out for the pond. She mentioned to Stephen that some nice shots of his family would be helpful.

Father John stopped in to see her when she was finishing up breakfast and prepping a few picnics. He actually thanked her for helping Frieda.

"Abbey you are a breath of fresh air, and I don't know how you did it," he was wagging his finger and smiling at her, "getting Frieda to ask for help. Whatever did you do? You must be a little miracle worker....she never asks for help." He shook his head in bewilderment, "Well whatever you did, it was a very good thing and so god of you to come and lend a hand."

Abbey enjoyed the praise, but didn't feel it was deserved. It did make her want to go see Frieda, though. After he left, Abbey double checked everything in the kitchen and made her way up to Frieda's rooms.

"Knock knock," Abbey breezed in to see Frieda doing a devotional, she stopped short, but Frieda smiled and waved her on in.

The first topic of discussion was Jeanette's check, and Frieda made it clear that it was something Jeanette needed to do. "Remember dear, she too was once a single mom... Jeanette really prayed about it and decided who and how much. It's a good thing and she has more than enough money, don't worry. Be blessed, say thank you and enjoy it."

Abbey didn't think that Jeanette seemed all that religious but Frieda assured her that while Jeanette was a go getter and a force she was also sold out for Jesus Christ and did nothing without consulting Him. Abbey relaxed about the money, feeling relieved. Frieda told her that she planned to pay her seven hundred dollars per week, and while it wasn't as extravagant as Jeanette's gift, it was what the ranch could swing. She also told Abbey that the doctor was very pleased with her recover. She did not tell Abbey that the doctor told her that if she would just follow all of his orders that she might not have another episode. She planned to behave now and also letting Abbey get back to her life. She knew that God's purpose had been accomplished, if not immediately, then at least for now. Geraldine was proof that Frieda's illness was for good. Abbey and the kids might take more time, but seeds were definitely planted and watered and fertilized. With Abbey making friends like Don, Debbie, and Matt; she knew of no more that she could do. So she got ready to go over the rest of the week with Abbey.

"Abbey, you have been a gift from God—I have been so thrilled having you, your mother, and the kids here and it has been so soothing knowing that you were standing in for me while I couldn't work…you've done a marvelous job. There have been constant positive comments from guests and staff, for which I am so thankful. Now that you have given me all the time that I needed to heal, I can finally send you back next week to your life. Thank you for giving this to me. I cannot tell you, there will never be words to explain the balm that you've been for this old woman." Frieda was starting to tear up, "But Abbey, I just love you honey, I hope that you will feel like the ranch is a place where you belong, because I promise to call you again fro work and I ask that you consider us for a visit." She finished sniffling.

Abbey wasn't really surprised, but deflated somehow. She had hoped this was a Charlie moment from Willie Wonka, where Charlie is told that he is needed to take over the chocolate factory and the little Umpa Loompas. She really did feel a part of the ranch, it was ridiculous to think that Frieda was ever going to hand the reigns over to her but it was a dream. Abbey actually hated the idea of even leaving the ranch, the people, and worse taking her mother and kids from here. She should have realized that this was coming but, well she really should have…..she realized it was time to stop pretending and be a grown up.

"Frieda, it has been wonderful being here and I have loved every bit of it. I actually don't need your pay because of what your friend did. It is more than enough. I also hope to get a few articles written out of it. As a matter of fact, I've got about two almost done. I will hate leaving here and all the people that work here. Over the course of my three visits here, and the last three weeks I have fallen in love with so many things – I will miss you most of all and I worry that my mother will be crushed to leave you. The kids will be very sad, of course, and would be devastated if we didn't have any plans to see you again soon." Abbey was blubbering but she was trying to say that she really loved the ranch.

Frieda's eyes lit up, "I know! We'll make plans before you go, we have our annual end of summer staff gathering and then thanksgiving….promise me -you'll be here for both!" Frieda was clapping her hands and Abbey got caught up in her enthusiasm.

Cheering up immediately, "Absolutely, that sounds fantastic!"

"And Abbey, you will take that pay, I cannot ever trust you if you don't. I asked for your help and I promised you a pay check, okay." It was not a question.

Abbey nodded her agreement. She also decided she needed to get back to work, so she hugged Frieda and said, "Off with me to the kitchen, I've work to do!"

Fortunately, tonight was <u>Country Night</u>, so she could get busy setting up outside, the rain had left everything sparkling clean . She knew just how to set everything up—the long buffet with the fry tale in the middle- the ice cream sundae bar at the end, and the popular sweet tea- she could do it fast-she also rolled the table décor cart out. The square dancing and all the hooting and hollering were bound to make her feel happy, so she worked hard and tried to stay clear headed about the whole thing. She couldn't believe how disappointed she felt, that she was going home, she dreaded telling the kids. Having made up her mind to focus and wait a day or two to prepare the kids, she hoped that Geraldine would be prepared by Frieda. Heck she probably knew first. Abbey derailed her mind, she turned her thoughts to Don and Debbie and how much they would love tonight. She assumed that with their southern heritage, this would be a very comfortable and enjoyable evening for them. Plus, it was always good for parents of young children to eat outside…a whole lot less stress. Abbey grinned at the sudden image of three little kids plastered in ice cream.

Abbey worked very quickly outside, getting done before long. She then headed to the kitchen to help with food prep, where once again Lori and Sharon were slicing and dicing. They had trays upon trays of fryer chicken, all battered and rolled and ready for the fryer. Abbey remembered from last time that Philip liked to man the fryer. Sharon liked to bake it for half and hour to forty-five minutes and then Philip would toss it into the fryer basket and pull it out all crispy and southern. Sharon believed that it was healthier because the oils didn't actually cook the meat for too long and she only used the best canola oils anyway.

Abbey took out the huge sacks of fresh corn, she knew how to prepare it. She peeled the corn husks, and pulled all the little strings. Taking the aluminum foil sheets and brushing the butter brush to cover the foil, she then sprinkled with salt and rolled and sealed the foil around the cob. The corn would also go into the ovens for a short time and finish on the grill. Meanwhile, Lori was working on three kinds of slaw; she made the conventional mayo base with cabbage, a broccoli and carrot with a vinegar and sugar dressing, then some kind of crunchy cabbage, oriental noodles, and bok choy with a honey-ginger dressing. Sharon was onto the potato salads; one german style and one creamy mustard potato salad. Abbey laughed at all the jello concoctions, the pickles, and other colorful things for the buffet. Putting it all out on the buffet was colorful and wild for the senses, the heavy vinegars, cabbages, pickles, and the sweet smells and then all the smokey flavors made Abbey's mouth water.

She got out as much as she dared for the ice cream bar, it didn't feel cold enough for any of the whip creams or soft chocolates or the ice cream. She got the unit turned down more so that it would cool in time to bring the ice cream out.

Matt came out in time to help while Father John poked in to attempt to tast test for the women Lori allowed him to, but Sharon swatted the air with her wooden spoon. Apparently, they all went way back, and it was delightful that Father John was such a terrible tease. Good news, he was also a highly revered priest. As Abbey understood it, Father John was truly a beacon for other men of the cloth. Silly man—but genuine in his life.

Abbey and Matt spoke a bit about him leaving on Friday and her leaving on Sunday. They spoke briefly about the end of summer staff celebration and Thanksgiving. Matt made her promise that they would correspond and call every so often. He not only valued her friendship but figured a writer had no excuse for not keeping in touch. He thanked her for listening to him when he was talking through the sadness in his church, it was especially helpful having someone on the outside. It occurred to Abbey that she hadn't asked about Julie and her session with Matt, she wasn't even sure if he could tell her anything. She figured it didn't hurt to show interest, so she asked.

"Oh, thank you for asking, Julie did speak at church and she did a wonderful job. Of course, she choked up a bit but once she got going her heart came through…you know when she discussed picking out the 13 inch coffin, everyone cried. She made it clear that it was horrible and yet she described the cool smooth white shell and the soft puffy cloud like lining. She felt like it was okay to lay her little baby in it… it was something… I think she really helped some women, though, who were struggling with fertility issues and fears in their own lives."

"And what about her husband, did he speak, was he able to support her?"

Matt winced, it was still a sore spot… "No not really, he just couldn't handle it. He didn't have a great excuse but just didn't seem to be able to that for her. It honestly made me mad, I really wanted him to be a man and show up for his wife. I was truly disappointed, but it is my job to love him and support them both. Tough being the pastor sometimes. –Anyway, good news, Julie is a trooper and the women of the church continue to surround her. She is being very understanding of her husband, I hope she can stay strong."

Abbey thought about it for a few moments and realized that she could actually offer some insight there. "Years ago, I was working on an article. I was trying to ferret out why people avoid loved ones in times of their greatest need. Essentially, I was trying to determine what about hospitals or divorce court or funeral homes were so daunting.

My premise was that the facilities we find ourselves in at our lowest moments are part of the problem. There is just nothing more daunting that a hospital or a court room they are uninviting, cold and sterile environments…I don't want to go in there for happy events… you know, …anyway, I have to tell you Matt, I was wrong. People avoid others in pain because they simply do not know what to do or say. It is easier to do or say nothing than to stick your neck out and potentially cause further harm or make yourself feel stupid.

It is a rotten thing because it self-perpetuates; once you have done or said nothing for any period of time, it becomes easier to avoid the other person because you are embarrassed for not having done or said anything. It's a stupid and terrible trap to get into."

Matt considered what she was saying, he nodded and asked Abbey if she could get him a copy of her article. "I think you may be on to something, I'd like to read it and maybe, with your permission, use it to reach some people, perhaps through some of my sermon notes. You are a wise woman, and I'm not shocked at all."

"Oh sure," Abbey was flattered, she looked down, afraid for Matt to see,"I'll send it to you next week with my permission to do with it as you please."

Matt noticed Abbey's embarrassment and wondered what it would be like to have his words written and picked apart. He made a living with words, although spoken. In all honesty most people were pretty kind to pastors, they allowed them their idosycrysies and foibles… but he thought, it must be harder for her.

While Matt was thinking, Abbey became uncomfortable with the silence. She blurted out, "It's really hard sometimes, when you write something that feels like a fresh insight and then wait for others to get it. I remember being in class in college, I had a professor, Dr. Brightman who would ask, 'Let me see what you see.' I couldn't wait to blurt out what I was thinking, and I loved it when a few of the others would suddenly come along side me. When they didn't though, ugh, it was rough. My professor was always great, he would stroke his bearded chin and smile. But not having the 'Aha' moments shared was grating. I think it is why writing is where I landed. I can get excited about the discoveries and assume that others will get it, too. Is that strange?"

Matt looked at Abbey grinning, "Are you kidding, you just summed up my entire pastoral career…I stand in front of groups of people sometimes big, mostly small, and I am constantly laying my 'Aha' moments bare for all to see. I search out a nod, a bright eye, a smile, anything that will convey that someone gets it…. Abbey, I get it!" He gave her a sideways hug and then continued to set up the buffet.

Heading into the kitchen, they stopped short at the door when they realized there was another woman with Lori and Sharon, she was holding hands with the others and they were praying. They were praying and Abbey studied the woman, she had very dark hair and porcelain skin, she was a study in contrasts. But she also had a softness about her—a melodic, gentle voice, she was average height but seemed to fill the whole room with her exuberance and joy. After a gentle amen, Abbey was introduced to Angelique.

This was the woman who ran the huge para church organization that equipped and counseled teens and their families. Angelique Dalt was know throughout the world as a fighter for families and a fried of God. Abbey was pleased to meet her and hoped that she would make an impression on her. She would definitely mention this to Ed at the magazine, it'd be awesome to do a story on this lady.

Angelique was just what you would expect from someone who healed broken people. She was gentle but authoritative without being over-bearing, intensely interested in everyone, and seemed to remember the most mundane facts about everyone. Abbey was pretty much star struck and hadn't said two smart things tot the woman when Matt began talking to Angelique about Abbey's intuitive writing.

Angelique shocked Abbey further by saying, "I know, I read her amazing piece on the ranch I am hoping that someday she'll do an article on us!"

Abbey was blown away and stammered something that she hoped was definitive. (Not too brilliant or intuitive, she was mentally kicking herself.)

They all separated to get ready for dinner, and Angelique hugged Abbey and told her that she was certain that they would be chatting later. For now, Angelique needed to go 'surprise the snot' out of her friend, Frieda.

Abbey was still kicking herself for sounding so uninspired when she spoke with Angelique. Matt was whistling and oblivious to her frustration. Oh well, she thought to herself, follow his lead: Blissful ignorance...

With everything ready to go, Abbey went to her room to get ready for the *Hoe Down* she checked in with her mom and the kids and heard Angelique and Frieda were laughing and carrying on in Frieda's room. Apparently, everyone was rearing to go and in great spirits...

Heading back down for dinner service, she still battled internally, she was sad about leaving, she didn't know why but she thought she'd be there a lot longer. She was glad that Frieda was so much better, but she was torn about taking the kids back to the city. This place was a haven for her and her kids, even her mom was better. Fortunately, the work load got heavy and she stopped dwelling...

With everyone running back and forth to the buffet with the hot food and all the cold salads, Abbey was the only one in the kitchen when a man showed up, "How can I help?"

Abbey smiled, but rather than introducing herself, she just handed him a large tray with two pans full of serving forks, spoons, knives, tongs, and spatulas. She asked him if he knew the way, he smiled and nodded. Abbey stayed in the kitchen gathering some more bowls filled with ice and ice water. Seemed the only thing that they couldn't have too much of, ice.

The man showed back up and Abbey handed him the ice bowls. Abbey was feeling sad, and she was being selfish, she just didn't want to know one more person that she was going to have to say good-bye too. Ridiculous! She chided herself.

Philip came in for the beginning portions of chicken, he told Abbey the fryers were hot enough and people were starting to make their way down to the lodge. Thus began the steady stream from kitchen to buffet for Abbey and Sharon. Lori, Matt, and Philip stayed at the buffet, explaining ingredients and choices, as families arrived and scoped out the buffet.

The same band that had been their before, was all set up and had run through a series of nice sounding tests. They announced over the speakers that the 'Soup is on!' Abbey was on the run but did hear everything quiet and someone praying.

As things slowed, and the ravenous families, were filled, Abbey had a chance to stand and watch. She caught sight of her kids who were ensconced with Don and Debbie and their kids. They all seemed to be having a good time. Abbey caught Debbie's eye, making sure that it was okay that her kids were there, Debbie smiled and waved her off. She kept looking around and spotted Frieda with Angelique and the strange man who had helped. Her mom was with them and they were laughing and raising their glasses to each other. The man kept trying to get Frieda up on her feet, it looked like he was trying to get her to dance, but he clearly was crazy in love with Angelique. Each look and touch and was really about her.

It suddenly dawned on her, that guy had to be Angelique's husband, David. How embarrassing, and she hadn't even introduced herself. Oh no! Abbey was mortified. She suddenly wanted to bolt for the kitchen, when she saw him moving up into the bandstand. She stood rooted to the ground, waiting to see what was happening. The band wound down their song and David announced that he had a joke, groans were heard from the staff, and Frieda's table, this could be good…

"There was an old ranch owner who farmed a small ranch in Missouri. The Missouri Department of Human Resources and Land Management claimed he was not paying proper wages to his workers and sent an marshall out to interview him.

'I need a list of your employees and how much you pay them,' demanded the marshall.

'Well,' he replied, 'There's my ranch hand who's been with me for 5 years. I pay him $600 a week plus free room and board. The cook has been here for 16 months, and I pay her $500 a week plus free room and board. Then there's the half-wit who works about 18 hours every day and does about 90% of all the work around here. He makes about $10 per week, pays his own room and board and I buy him a whole pie every Saturday night.'

'That's the guy I want to talk to, the half-wit,' says the agent.

'That would be me,' replied the old rancher."

David's delivery was really good, with great timing. When the laughter died down, David turned towards his table and looked directly at Frieda and said, "Our resident half-wit and host Frieda needs a round of applause and our prayers. She has been battling through an unknown illness and has rallied, but we mustn't give up on praying. So here's to Frieda, and keep praying!" David raised his hands clapping and stepped down from the stage. People clapped loudly and everyone was on their feet. It was cute, Frieda obviously hated the attention but it also looked like David was someone she could never be mad at. Hugging her man as he got to the table Angelique was smiling and David, well, he beamed.

The band announced the Sundae bar and David ran over to man it. He was a pistol putting as much of everything as he could fit into each cup or cone, (and quite a bit that didn't). Matt dragged Abbey to the sundae bar claiming that he had to see this, he clapped David on the shoulder and said, "This is old Dave Dalt, and this is Abbey."

David gave Abbey a big bear hug and said, " I am thrilled to meet you, and I look forward to having you out to headquarters."

Abbey looked confused but David just laughed, "Obviously you don't know my wife, but you have been summoned. My wife gets an idea and it will happen, no point questioning or trying to figure it out, she'll get it done."

"Um, okay but I mean that's a terrific idea, but I just work for a small magazine, I'm not at all certain...."

David cut her off and said, "Don't sweat it, my Ang will take care of everything, heck she'll probably get you flown in by some big shot, no worries...do you sing Abbey?"

"What, no I don't sing?" She was feeling shell shocked and very uncertain. This could be a wonderful opportunity but singing, what in the world?

David grabbed Matt, and wiggled his eyebrows, "Karaoke time!"

Matt laughed and the two made their way to the stage, they sang several tunes, very badly and ended the night with 'Goodnight Ladies'. It was fun and light hearted, Abbey found herself giggling and enjoying the mood. Once the kids and all the guests were done for the evening, she helped finish up in the kitchen.

Saying goodnight to everyone herself, she made her way to bed, and found that the emotional ups and downs of the day had really exhausted her. She fell asleep immediately.

Chapter 43

Geraldine and Frieda began sharing morning devotions. At first Geraldine was uncomfortable praying out loud, but then listening to Frieda heard how conversational she was, she really got into it. She gave it a try, with words and tears flowing freely. They prayed for Abbey and the kids. Frieda really pressed Geraldine about them.

Frieda was determined, "Ger, you still haven't really talked to Abbey about what has happened for you. You haven't shared your history or what just happened with your own mother. It is past time. You two are going to be going home soon, don't you think you should prepare her?"

"I know there just never seems to be the right time, I am praying but I don't know how to just confess all my failings and ...I just don't know. I will, I have to, I know that, but maybe when we are in the car on the way home. Oh Frieda, pray for me. With my mother, I had a captive audience, it was easy, I don't have to try to live it out in front of her. With Abbey, I'm going to have to get it right. I am afraid."

"Of course you are, and that's fine. Just remember who goes before you and who stays with you. You are both in his hands and those precious children and your wonderful daughter need you to be just who HE made you to be. You can do this. You will be great. Of course you will blow it from time to time, the thing is that now you know to ask for forgiveness and grace from both God and your daughter."

Frieda told Geraldine that there were many who were praying diligently for Abbey and she gave her some scriptures to look up and left her with a new Bible which was monogrammed. Naturally, because it was from Frieda, it simply said, 'Ger'.

Geraldine looked up the two verses; Matthew 18:20 "For where two or three come together in my name, there am I with them," and Ecclesiastes 4:12b "A cord of three strands is not quickly broken." Geraldine knew from her long talks with Frieda that Abbey was truly in God's hands, but she just felt huge regret, Geraldine had been away from God for so long and had denied her daughter the knowledge and opportunity. She sought the Lord's forgiveness, and knowing that she'd gotten it, she prayed out loud, "God, please lead Abbey, as I have failed too, she is in your hands. I have missed you and I have been away for so long, please bring Abbey to you quickly. Amen." Geraldine tried to relax and knew that with all the others praying that Abbey was in good hands.

The kids were planning to go fishing with Don, Debbie, their kiddos and Philip, so Abbey brought coffee, and some pastries up to her mother and Frieda. They were going to brainstorm the Casa Blanca event. They gathered in Frieda's sitting room and after pouring coffee and grabbing her notebook, Abbey was trying to be patient, but they were just meandering and looking at the bowler hats, and the three life size cutouts of Humphrey Bogart. They kept looking at the movie posters, and they just gabbed. Abbey was tapping her feet and her pen against her leg while waiting for the ladies to settle in and start the planning. She was getting frustrated and not really listening.

Frieda noticed Abbey just sitting there, "Dear what do you see when you look at this poster?"

"Um, well, I see a plane, a runway and the two stars, all the advertising and names."

"Yes, okay, that's all there, but do you get a feel for the era. For the time? Does anything hit you in terms of your senses? What we are after is creating an event where you feel like you are a part of it…anything?"

Abbey saw where she was going, "Well everything feels old, but very crisp. Their outfits were very polished looking and while they are not in color, I imagine them to be wool and maybe colored but somewhat dull." She tilted her head and really looked, "I suppose it would have been noisy on the airfield and in a bar… it feels a little hectic, I think…"

"Yes, yes, that's what I was thinking. We need to watch the movie or at least have it going as we meet, things will hit us as we do."

They turned on the movie and spent two hours discussing theme and how to get the feel of it. Ger came up with some amazing backdrop ideas and Abbey suggested a huge model plane would be great. Frieda produced a prom catalogue and showed Abbey some amazing props that weren't terribly expensive. They created what should be a fantastic event.

"Well girls, I think we've got the bulk of it. One of the keys to a successful event is making sure there are components for adults and children alike. The plane is a masterful element and I think the inflatable one that could be suspended from the ceiling will enthrall the little boys for sure. All we have left is to solidify the appetizer theme." Frieda was beaming.

Abbey learned that Jess loved to make fruit and cheese into animals using cookie and paring knives. Abbey remembered a kiwi 'mouse' at one of the functions. Looking through the list and the wild array of foods, Abbey knew it would be hugely popular.

They devised a complete menu, and with several copies of the video, figured they could even show it on several of the screens in the background. The Moroccan skyline was a bit trickier, but Frieda knew that the crafts lady would love to try her hand at it. They would use gatorfoam and look for some designs on line. She went on to explain that they would take the skyline and copy it on to a transparency and then they would use an overhead projector, shoot it onto the 'gatorfoam wall' and trace the outline. Then it was just a matter of painting it. She made it sound so simple. They determined that the booths from Italian night and simply putting lampshades over the hurricane globes, then adding fringed placemats and a pianist.

Abbey querried, "Who's the pianist?"

"Father John, of course." Frieda answered, Abbey was already nodding. "I would like for you and Matt to locate the lampshades for the globes and help Father John download some piano music."

Abbey agreed, Frieda put together the food order and excused herself to go further discuss with Lori and Sharon. Abbey headed down to find Matt and to speak with Jonathan about the video for Casa Blanca night.

Abbey headed towards the storeroom thinking that Matt might be down there already hauling stuff out for tonight's theme, Oriental Night, she didn't find Matt but started poking around in the storeroom for boxes marked lampshades, or globes. She rolled out the Oriental Carts to make more room, and grabbing an empty cart, she started stacking things that seemed like they might work for Casa Blanca Night.

She found some placemats that could do in a pinch and she located the globe box towards the back, she couldn't reach it though, so went looking for a ladder. She found Jonathan instead, who was already playing around with one of the videos. He explained that he had heard Frieda talking in the kitchen and knew he had a job to do...

Abbey laughed and they spoke about the videos. She also got Jonathan's help with a ladder and Matt showed up in time to climb the thing. It occurred to Abbey that she really didn't want to overstep her mother, she was so excited and it had been her idea, so she decided not to make any decisions or any further declarative statements.

With Matt's help they got the dusty boxes down and opened, the lamp shades inside were dark maroon with little tassels and puff balls, and kind of silly looking. Each had a metal apparatus that held it suspended about the candle. She thought they would be ideal but would hold her tongue until her mother and Frieda could take a look. She and Matt set everything aside on the new cart, it seemed to be coming together.

Abbey commented, "Well Matt, we better get to work for tonight…we have a gong to assemble as well as a dining hall. Are you ready to get to work?"

Matt responded, "Not quite, I will be right back, I know I saw something in the old barn, some kind of plane stuff… I'm going to run out and check. You go ahead and get started, I'll be along soon and save the gong for me, it's heavy!" With that he was off.

Abbey kind of laughed, shrugged her shoulders at Jonathan and said, "I guess I have my marching orders. I best get to busy!"

Jonathan smiled, told her to holler if she needed anything.

Rolling the carts toward the dining hall, Abbey started working on the tables first. She loved all the delicate tea sets and brilliant colors, it was bright and beautiful and yet so dainty. Such a strange combination of delicate things and powerful colors. Abbey had gotten quite a bit accomplished when Geves came tearing in to the hall.

"Mama, Mama," as she slammed into Abbey hugging her legs, she knocked her into a chair, "I got Jesus Christ and Stephen said I should baptist and so I did, I did! Bug wanted to as soon as he saw me and so he did too!"

Just then a very wet Bug landed in her lap, too. Abbey realized that both the kids were soaking wet, and she was now too. They were both excited and happy, it was something that she should have expected, but somehow, she hadn't.

"Slow down guys, you are both all wet, do you mean that you got baptized? You said that Stephen baptized you, what do you mean?"

Genevieve tried to slow down but was so full fo excitement that she practically stuttered. "I wanted to ask Jesus in to my heart, like everyone here, so I was talking to Patrick and Stephen and Debbie and Stephen said that I needed to just tell Jesus that I needed Him, that I believed that he did everything to cover all my sins and he died on a cross, and then went up to heaven and will take care of us. Stephen said you have to be Baptist. Can we go to church now, which church will we go to Mama? Debbie says it doesn't matter about denomins...as long as they are Bible based."

Abbey interrupted her with a clarification, "Baptized, you mean going into the water. Church denominations, I suppose we can find a church we will have to look and ask around."

"Yeah, Yeah Baptized, and I did it and Bug just had to do it too! You know he always has to do whatever I do..."

"I do not, I wanted to because I'm the man." Bug interjected.

"Anyway, we gotta go tell grandma," and they were off like a shot, before she could even process all of it.

She sat there for a few seconds litting it all register; not really sure what to do with it all. Realizing that her mother might not respond very well, she dragged herself up, and went after the kids. By the time she got there, she was recognizing how wet she was and that she'd need to change. She stopped at her room and grabbed a dry t-shirt and when she got to her mother's rooms she found them hugging and kissing their grandma, who was in tears. Abbey, perplexed, wondered why er mother appeared to be so pleased? It didn't make any sense to her.

She interrupted them by telling the kids to go get changed and wash off the mud. She approached her mother, cautiously, "Mom why are you crying?"

Geraldine paced herself, praying silently. (Father give me words). "Abbey, I'm thrilled, because I too, have renewed my faith since being here." At her daughter's look fo shock, Geraldine held up her hand, "Abbey we have a whole lot to talk about. Let me say quickly that I was saved as a child and then hurt very badly by a religious leader It crushed me, and I blamed God. I walked away Abbey, I left, but HE never left me. I finally saw it here. Frieda has been a big help and that was why I simply had to go to Atlanta to see my mom. It is a relief to be connected again to God.

So, yes I am ecstatic that Genevieve and Winston have found this peace, this hope, and this joy. I have changed and I hope you will see that over time."

Abbey shook her head and continued to look confused, "Mom, I don't really know what to do with all of this. You have been so negative about Christians my whole life. Grandma was this crazy overbearing zealot and I guess I thought that was all there was. I have been working inside the Christina community for several years now, until the ranch,.... I don't' know, I have always felt like an outsider. Here, there is something very special. I am very unsure, of course, I don't mind the kids accepting Jesus or what have you, heck they still both expect the toothfairy. But, you, that is gonna take some getting used to. I am happy that you are happy and I hope that it lasts for you forever. I just don't know what I think yet. Can we just let it lay for a while? I have a ton to do for tonight's dinner, lets table our conversation for a bit." She turned to go, but stopped and looked at her mom again, "I really am so happy to see you happy, if

God is the reason for that, then great!" She gave her mom a quick kiss on the cheek.

Geraldine was thrilled, she couldn't remember the last time that Abbey had really looked at her. She was so pleased. It would take time, she had been the one to ingrain in Abbey that God was not all there was to life. She had been so wrong. She prayed, and determined to celebrate her grandbabies faith! She headed out to find Frieda and Angelique. Celebrating, they were all giddy, Geraldine couldn't help but be disappointed that Abbey wasn't sharing in this particular joy.

Assembling the last of the tables, she was placing the miniature parasols; thinking about her mom and the kids. On the one hand, she was somewhat upset that Debbie and her son had taken it upon themselves to talk the kids into religion and baptism- she also thought it rather bold that they would go ahead and baptize without even asking her- then she thought that it had probably never occurred to Debbie that Abbey wouldn't be overjoyed. She was muddling this all over in her brain, when Debbie walked in with Matt.

Debbie walked over to Abbey and embraced her, she asked her to forgive her. Abbey was shocked but Debbie continued, "I had no idea Stephen was planning on baptizing your children, or I would have come to get you. I just didn't know what they were doing.

Geves and Bug kept asking all these questions, and I supposed that you had left their decision to them, so I tried to keep my answers clear and aligned with all that this ranch stands for. I am sorry you missed it, but it was very sweet. And I have to tell you that watching our son baptize was a gift for us. He has been this antagonistic, sullen teenager, and suddenly he is this loving big brother, who genuinely wanted to be certain that Geves and Bug were heaven bound. So I am so sorry but I also thank you Abbey for sharing your children and giving us a reminder of our wonderful son."

Abbey was torn in two, she was mad, how dare Debbie, but she saw Debbie's genuine appreciation and was sure that she didn't intend to take anything away from Abbey. She just nodded and mumbled about getting back to work.

Matt, sensing her distress, took over, "Debbie, this is a ll really surprising, I'm sure Abbey has a lot to process."

Debbie seemed to understand, but she recognized that Abbey wasn't as thrilled as Debbie had assumed. She wondered if it was the disappointment of missing the event and not something else. Debbie asked God to show Abbey the joys of being his child, to lead Abbey in her walk, thanked Him for allowing her to be a part of things. She also pleaded for forgiveness, that Abbey would be filled with grace and mercy for Stephen, as well.

Abbey got to work on hauling out the large oriental screens, the rugs, and the fringed table runners. The sauces were placed on the tables and the gong finally brought in and assembled. It made her think of Bug, how he enjoyed being here. She processed through the belonging that she felt and assumed that the kids were experiencing the same. They had never had a big family, and being children of divorce with an uninvolved father, maybe they were just looking for acceptance…or maybe God could fill the void for them. Examining her own heart, she had to admit that they were all happier here surrounded by loving and genuine folks. 'Well,' she said to herself, 'If my mom can be changed, we shall see, the truth will be when we get home, then I'll know.'

With a last check over the effect of the hall, Abbey knew her end was ready. Matt and Jonathan were busy chatting over something so, she popped into the kitchen and told Lori and Sharon that if they had everything under control she was going to go check with Frieda. They waved her off.

Frieda was still with Angelique and Abbey wasn't all that comfortable with interrupting them, so she waved and headed out to the barn. She found Philip and Jess working on the hay bales again, singing along with music, they had a nice harmony, she stopped and listened for a moment…

"Still a man in need of a Savior, I want to be in the light, as you are in the light, I want to shine like the stars in the heavens.'

It was a funky, fun song about Jesus and had a terrific beat. As soon as they saw Abbey, Jess reached over and cut off the music. They explained that some critter, other than the usual occuppants of this particular barn, were burrowing and making a mess of the hay. They were trying to figure out where the scoundrel was getting in.

Jess, always educating, "Raccoon feces could be really bad stuff and it wasn't good for the horses, there were several diseases that they caused all by themselves- it could also cause a fire if the animals were wetting the hay down." They had dug down far enough to find the hole under the barn wall, now they had to seal it up properly and deter anything from coming in.

Abbey explained that she was looking for her kids, Philip responded that they had caught some fish earlier that pastor Don was probably showing them how to clean them. Abbey thanked them, and wondered how she would react to pastor Don.

She was trying to get over her agitation, she started walking towards the fish shed, but the more she thought about the mud and the pond, the more it she decided that she wanted no part of those mud flavored fish. She reversed course, and headed to the lodge to change her clothes. She would be one of the Oriental Princesses delivering egg rolls and fabulous dishes. She had chosen a lavender dress for herself and it suited her mood. She loved the look of the ballerina slippers and thanks to Sharon and her compression socks, she actually had support and comfort, too.

Once everyone was ready and it was time for dinner, Abbey stood near the back of the hall. She heard the gong sound and watched as a wave flooded into the room; women in long gorgeous dresses with high mandarin collars and tiny little prints all over the dresses, the little girls wore similar dresses but shorter. The colors were outstanding; bold brights and soft pastels. The young men and adult males were all in Kimonos and the little boys looked like little ninjas. It was incredible. They arrived, with huge grins, something about dressing in costume made them more a part of the scene. They settled at tables and served themselves tea, the little ones getting cute little plastic tea cups filled with sweet cold tea. Abbey and the rest of the staff made their way to the tables with the crispy huge egg rolls and soft warm wonton appetizers. The colorful fried rice mixed with eggs, peas, and carrots would be next. Everywhere you looked it was an explosion of colors.

Abbey kept inhaling through her nose, she found the scents intoxicating: ginger, cinnamon, mint, terryaki, and orange. She delivered plate after plate from the kitchen and floated on the smells. The writer in her wanted to name the her experience, <u>A Symphony of Scents</u>. Silly, she knew, but it was powerful. Each time she went to the kitchen Lori would direct her- which order went where. Abbey couldn't help herself and taste tested anything that Lori would allow her to.

Lori pinched her when she saw her eating moo shu in the corner… she was laughing and delighted. Abbey told her around a bite of food, "This is the most incredible food. Delicious, everything is absolutely delicious."

The lady beamed, "I picked up my little oriental flare from a woman who used to work with Frieda. She was a missionary from the Cantonese province- I never could pronounce the name- anyway, she worked here for two years while she and her husband were trying to get back home. Seems the Chinese government had arrested her husband for his Christian leanings and they had beaten him severly before exiling them. Frieda didn't even have an Oriental night until, Ms. Lie. Frieda is a free spirit, even in her cooking, she just never had a chance to perfect the oriental cuisine, afterall," Lori winked conspiratorily, "It requires the use of a measuring cup.

It just so happens that I was going through some upheaval in my life, and wasn't sure where I wanted to be. Timing was right, Frieda begged me to come and I've been here ever since. I love being here-love the work-and I know that God has placed me here for now."

Abbey took it all in, smiled at Lori and headed out to deliver the last of the dinners and the beginning of the fortune cookies. She, too, loved working here, everyone seemed to just fit here. She recalled a conversation she had had with Marilyn, the first missionary she met here...she had said something to the effect that Frieda really didn't get how...how...what was the word she used? FABULOUS, that's it, Frieda didn't get how fabulous it all was. She so wanted to show everyone a wonderful time, and she just kept doing more and more until she couldn't think of one more thing.

Abbey was still ruminating, when she catches Debbie waving at her. She approached their table. "Abbey, did you have something to do with the fortunes we got?"

Having no idea what she was talking about, "Um, no I'm sorry, what was your fortune?"

Debbie looked at Don, then Abbey, she attempted a silly Asian accent: "*Your great joy, your great surprise, your children will delight.*"

"I would love to take credit, I think Frieda just orders special boxes, I don't believe there is any grand scheme, probably just a coincidence."

Debbie did one of her mom looks, "Tsk, tsk, Abbey, you should no by now, we don't believe in coincidences. It is not accident or chance that we met you! We thank God for you Abbey, you are a gift and now a friend. No way will I count that as coincidence."

"Oh Debbie, I love you guys too," Abbey leaned down and hugged her. "We need to exchange addresses, I think that our boys could use a little practice with being pen pals. Anything, to get that boy of mine to sit and write, that'd be great."

Debbie and Don both nodded, clearly liking the idea. They were about to say something when the Samurai team made their elaborate entrance. Every eye in the room followed the team, to watch and see. The lights were lowered as they made their way to the stage. Spotlights were caught in the spinning swirling swords and the light show was fantastic.

Knowing that the time was short, Abbey ran around collecting what she could quietly and discreetly. She made multiple trips back and forth to the kitchen running along side several others. Sharon, Matt, Philip, and Janna Kay were all clearing the room quickly. The evening flew by and as the guests made their way out of the dining hall Abbey and the others flipped the room and readied it for breakfast.

Abbey was pleased that the night was over, it was late and she made her way wearily to her room. Walking in, she saw it anew… the bed with the old fashioned quilt in a pattern of pinks and mint greens, and the brass head and footboard was to her right. She walked over and stroked the hard dark wood of the old secretary style desk and glanced around the sitting area straight ahead. She looked at the rag rug, all the colors had dulled over the years, but it made the room soft and cheerful. Even the curtains were soft paisley pinks so light that you almost couldn't make out the pattern. The overstuffed chairs were light green and white striped. Funny, Abbey thought, initially it had all looked old and dull but seeing it tonight, it was soft, inviting, and warm. Knowing she was leaving, made it so much more lovely.

Abbey sighed, and got ready for bed.

Chapter 44

Wednesday, Abbey awoke with a start, "How can it already be Wednesday?" She thought through the rest of the week. Tonight was <u>Italian night</u> and Thursday would be <u>Mexican Fiesta</u> and there was just a bit more time to work on <u>Casa Blanca</u> for Friday. Abbey was thrilled but knew how busy this week would be. She gathered her kids; they delivered the eggs and Abbey set to work in the kitchen.

After breakfast, Geves and Bug told Abbey that Ms. Frieda was going to let them help make the pizza dough. Abbey decided to join them. She knew it involved another kitchen appliance and that appealed to her.

Frieda showed up to give direction, "Okay, so the trick is to get the ingredients into the giant Hobart mixer a bit at a time but keeping your fingers away from the blade." She was great with Bug, watching him like a hawk and treating him like a little adult.

"Now Winston, I am going to give you the job of the flour, you are going to put a scoop in right here, everytime I say *Add*. Genevieve, I want you to add the water in on this side and I have a mix of the other ingredients that I will just dump in now."

When the kids nodded and got themselves ready, Frieda started the Hobart. She stopped it every so often so that one or the other of the kids could catch up.

At one point, and Abbey swore it was intentional, Frieda started the Hobart up really fast when the flour was in before the water, a dusting commenced and Bug was covered, "Oops, you look like Casper." Frieda laughed.

They worked together making over fifty crusts for the pizzas that evening. It was a lot of fun, everyone was covered in flour and the kids had some nifty new terms. The proofer was a big warming unit that allowed the dough to rise in pans. No one seemed to know the name of the dough flattening contraption. Before putting the dough in pans, it was weighed and cut, rolled into a ball, and dropped down a chute and it came out flatter, you could put it through several times, to get the basic round flat shape. Then you'd spin it in the air to get rid of air bubbles. After proofing, the dough could be made thinner or allowed to stay thick, the dough went into the refrigerator to stifle the 'proofing' process. The kids were completely enamored with the whole process; they thought we could all be professionals. After their morning, Abbey was pretty sure that they were correct.

Dropping the kids with her mom, Abbey wrapped up her hand-outs and decided to deliver them to Mark. She called over to his house and grabbed a golf cart to run over. Mark was jovial as always, he was such a neat guy. He planned to look at the hand-outs later, as he had a 'hot date.' Abbey was really taken back, how does a ninety-eight year old man have a hot date? Never mind, she really didn't want that much information. Chuckling, as she left, she thought: one good thing, he'd be in a good mood when he read her handouts. Ha.

She found Lori and Sharon making the lasagnas and garlic bread. They had left salad prep for Abbey. So she got to work chopping Romaine lettuce and some freh basil. The smells were heavenly and Abbey relished standing in the kitchen. She did think that she might turn into a clove of garlic. She smelled to high heaven. There was something so intrusive about garlic, but secretly she loved it. Salads done, it was time to set up the dining hall. There were some local opera students coming in tonight for a practice run. Abbey realized that the ranch being situated between a large college and Atlanta, they could probably find no end of entertainment and talent.

She began pulling the cart out of the storage room, but it was already pulled. Most all the booths were already out, too. Abbey made her way to the hall and saw Matt, Father John, Philip, and Jonathan all pulling the whole room together. They had even put the checkered tablecloths out.

Abbey was feeling silly, so she announced her presence, "Hey you guys, what are you trying to do? Put me outta work? What's the big idea?" She said it with a smile but she did stop the in their tracks. It was funny, she wound up laughing at them.

They were obviously relieved that she was playing with them. Abbey grabbed the rest of the tablecloths and placed them on the remaining tables, she added the candles and checked the guys' work. After adding the silverware, she checked her watch and decided she had time to go grab a mule and the kids so that she could see Moses. Abbey took off, waving to the guys that she'd see them later.

Abbey tracked down the kids and grabbed the mule. They had a sack of carrots and some sugar cubes. They drove down following the fences and spotted Moses just over the crest of the hill. He looked so beautiful standing in the distance. Abbey knew that they had driven out further than she had planned but expected that she had enough time. Moses had heard the vehicle and perked up, he walked towards them, as they got out of the vehicle to move the gate. They spoke to Moses, and he whinnied at them, recognizing the rustle of the plastic bag that contained the carrots, he made his way more quickly. He was huge, but he looked off. Abbey felt ill equipped to judge the condition of the horse...but she was pretty sure something was wrong. It looked like something was out with his hip or something.

Abbey recalled the story of Mikala and Christian and Moses having an abcess, she wondered if this was the same type of thing, but knowing nothing about horses, she didn't quite know what she was looking at. They fed him the treats and then raced back to the lodge to tell Philip and Matt.

Arriving at the lodge, they found the guys, but Matt said he'd be useless. Philip grabbed his cell phone and called Caleb. Abbey would show them where Moses was. She checked in the kitchen and told Lori and Sharon what she was up to . They had it all covered. Abbey shooed the kids in with her mom and told them what was going on. Frieda thought she should help, but Abbey assured her that Caleb was on his way.

Abbey led the way and Caleb joined them within one half hour. Everyone could hear Caleb coming for several miles, he had the biggest navy blue pick-up truck that Abbey had ever seen. It sounded very powerful. When he arrived, Abbey was struck by the man's size, he obviously belonged in the over-sized truck He was a very handsome man, and he resembled Frieda greatly. He was at least six foot six, maybe taller and had shoulders that made Abbey wonder if he could lift Moses. Now here was a guy that went with Moses. They exchanged pleasantries as they were introduced. Caleb looked over Moses with the confidence that you'd expect from a professional large animal vet. He took Moses' temperature and checked all of his feet, he noted swelling one of his legs and determined that Moses had probably stepped in a hole or something and had strained what would be our knee. Caleb was kind and explained what he was seeing as he went.

Caleb gave Moses a shot to reduce swelling and pain, he haltered Moses to bring him back to the barn. Abbey was worried about this horse being put into a stall but Caleb assured her that Moses would have a lot of company. Philip ran back to the barn with the mule and brought a horse trailer back to attach to Caleb's much larger truck. They put Moses in the trailer very slowly and Caleb drove him back to the barn. Once Moses was at the barn they unloaded him, put hi in a stall and saw to his every comfort. True to form, Moses had even the young fillies entranced. All of them wandered in and out of the barn to see Moses. He whinnied and and about five mares answered him. He actually seemed happy. It was a bit humorous seeing this giant of a man with a giant horse. They were both so gentle. Caleb assured them that Moses would be fine and went in to see his mom. When Philip mentioned that the Dalts were in town, he practically ran.

Checking her watch, Abbey did a bit of a run herself, to the kitchen, she hadn't been paying much attention to the time. Lori, Sharon, Jess, and Janna Kay had everything under control. Pizza's were bubbling in the oven, the cheese turning golden, it smelled like an herb garden with onion, garlic, oregano, and pepper. Abbey realized that she was starving. Sharon told Abbey to take some time, shower and enjoy dinner with her family. The other women practically pushed her out of the kitchen, saying that they had it under control, although they would lover her help with clearing later. Abbey thanked them, took a shower and surprised her family for dinner at the table. The operatic team performed flawlessly, it was wonderful exposure for her kids and all the other guests. They sang the usual Ave Maria and several more. They ate till they were full, and after kissing her family good night, Abbey got to work clearing tables. It was all quick and painless with the guys moving all the booths, and tables. They set things back up for the breakfast buffet and Abbey helped get everything finished in the kitchen. She was laughing in the kitchen with Sharon, when it occurred to her that she could easily run out to the barn and say good night to Moses.

Abbey made her way to the barn with a flash light and a sweet good night to Moses. He looked very content and Abbey was really glad that she and the kids had gone to visit him today. She was also delighted with Caleb, she noticed him in the dining hall with Frieda and the Dalts. They were having a great time laughing and David and Caleb had an obvious affinity for one another. He was also obviously watching his mother for any sign of illness. A good son, Abbey thought.

Smiling and yawning, Abbey made her way to bed.

Chapter 45

Abbey woke up early, the kids were exhausted and apparently they had discussed leaving with Frieda and Geraldine. Abbey had hoped to put it off, so they wouldn't ruin the last few days, but the cat was out of the bag. The kids begged to stay and were super cranky. Abbey determined they needed a bit more sleep, so she collected the eggs herself. She was able to get everything cleaned and put away and breakfast started before the kids had even risen. She went in to wake them and spoke gently fo returning home and some of their normal activities. They would need to go back to school shopping and Genevieve would have to tell Suzanna all about everything. Abbey reminded the kids that they would be making piñatas again and that maybe they would like to make one to keep and take home. Maybe even one for a party at home sometime. It seemed to give them some comfort that they would be leaving with everyone else this week, it seemed to make more sense to them. Abbey marched them to the craft shed and they started discussing what was a 'dumb pinata'.

Abbey went to see her mother and found her with Frieda in the sitting room. They were actually doing some sort of Bible Study together. Abbey was somewhat amazed and more than a little bit curious. "What are you two studying?"

"We are considering God's holiness, and how God's justice is recorded in scripture, our conviction of sin and to appreciate his amazing mercy and grace...in other words we are racing down bunny trails." Frieda grinned from ear to ear. She placed her hand on top of Geraldines and said, "If that doesn't sound too heady"

They cracked up, Abbey knew she was missing the joke but just said, "That, ah, should take some time, huh?"

"We are only scratching the surface, but I asked Frieda about the 'angry God of the old Testament' and the 'compassionate God of the new', I had no idea what I was getting into. I might even be a little bit sorry that I asked," Gerladine was teasing Frieda now.

Abbey wasn't sure that she understood the chain of though but she could see that they were actually enjoying themselves and it was a question that Abbey had heard a few times. She gathered her courage, "Okay, so how do you reconcile the two?"

"I heard an old theologian say that the real mystery is not that a holy perfect God exercises justice, but that he puts up with selfish rebellious creatures, at all. We forget that mercy is given by someone, not earned, not even requested." Frieda stopped to ponder her own answer and finished with, "A loving parent will punish his child because he wants them to be their best, the same loving parent will give mercy and forgive that same child."

"I understand that, why can't all Pastors just talk like you do Frieda, half the world would get it, like that." Abbey snapped her fingers for emphasis and hugged Frieda and her mom. Abbey considered what Frieda had said, who wouldn't want to be forgiven for everything they had ever done wrong. It was a wonderful concept. Abbey didn't see the benefit for someone like her, who tried so hard to do everything right. IT wasn't like she set out to harm or even cheat anyone. And yet, it was her husband who was abusive and walked away. Geves and Bug didn't deserve it and just what had they ever done to be forgiven of? It was all kind of off-putting. Matt had tried to make it a Ten Commandments issue, but even that didn't seem to fit her particular situation. While Abbey did not think that she was perfect, she also didn't think that she was some depraved being who was deserving of misery and death. Abbey excused herself and wound her way to the crafts area for the making of the piñatas. Abbey wanted to see how it was done.

Abbey met Becky in the Crafts barn and found she really enjoyed it. All the families sent at least one representative. They started with a balloon base, which provided the cavity for the candy. They covered it with some quick drying flour and water mixed and some old strips of newspaper. They then used colored tissue to 'paint' the creatures. Becky was good at keeping the mixture just wet enough. Becky used blow dryers and fans, and good ole sunshine to get the things dry in time for the evening festivities. While drying, the kids were wrapping wooden dowels with colorful papers to be the "bat", the balloons were popped after the creature or shaped dried completely. Abbey decided to make one for Father John. She decide to make one that looked like a Grand Piano, since he would be their Sam on Friday night. She got excited about it, and couldn't' wait to present him with it. She even wrote Sam on the lid of the piano. She thought he would appreciate it, since he had no children of his own.

Abbey made her way to the kitchen, saw that everything was under control and decided she could begin the set up for the evening. She ran into Philip, he was with Diane, the gal from the other night. They were reintroduced. Diane explained that she worked here but had recently had surgery on her ankle. Thanks to prayers, she was back on her feet and couldn't wait to get back to the ranch. She missed everyone so much. "Six weeks at home was just too much."

Abbey couldn't imagine but told her to take it easy. Diane went on to tell Abbey what a God send she was. She told her about a couple of local young ladies who had had babies; Cathy and Bonnie, both had been due in May but one of the little buggers didn't show up until June. Bonnie was coming back next week but Cathy wouldn't be back until the end of August. "Both love it here and we are so flexible with hours. We're hoping that they will enjoy working just dinners for a couple of months."

Abbey thought is sounded about perfect. She would have loved to have done this when her babies were little.

Hanging the jalapeno lights and decorating the tables gave Abbey a chance to get to know Diane. She was funny and very energetic. They got the buffet tables ready for food and determined that it was time to go get the piñatas. They took the golf cart and Becky was waiting with six boxes. Abbey couldn't resist opening one and looking at the creatures. Many remained a mystery but most resembled cats, dogs, elephants, and there were the requisite guns and tanks done by the boys. Abbey and Diane got them put out on the tables and were pleased with the results. They had a little bit before dinner, so they agreed to meet in the kitchen in an hour.

Abbey decided to go visit Moses again, she just thought he was special. When she got there she saw that Philip was rubbing something all over the walls in the stall. He explained that Moses was 'cribbing' which meant that he was chewing his way around the stall. Since Moses hated to take his vitamins, they were rubbing them all over the stall to see if he would quit. There was such a thing as a cribbing collar that wouldn't allow him to chew unless he stretched his neck. It was terribly uncomfortable and they actually didn't have one large enough for Moses. Philip went on to explain. "Caleb is bringing out some toys for Moses tomorrow. He had to go back to Atlanta to pick some more up."

Abbey asked, "Horse toys?"

Philip said, "Just something to entertain him, something he can move, or chew or notice. He's used to being out free, this stall is boring and confining. Think prison for him."

"Oh, well, what if you just strung ropes up over the rafters and had them dangle down, at least there'd be some movement."

Philip nodded liking the idea, "Now that's great, we could put a medicine ball on one, or maybe a small bale of hay....yeah, I like it, do you wanna help?"

Abbey grinned, "Of course!" They grabbed some ropes and worked together setting up some things that might keep him entertained. Moses wasn't sure what to make of it all at first, but Abbey played with some of it and Moses at least noticed it. Abbey also thought he was looking better. She was relieved.

Abbey got back to the kitchen and Diane was icing down glasses to run to the tables. It was time to get everything heated, cooled, and running. They got the Mexican Fiesta off to a great start, Debbie and Don and their kids were delighted by the piñatas and the Mariachi band was fantastic. Everyone had a wonderful evening and Father John laughed and laughed about his piñata. He asked if he could keep it and not break it open. Abbey told him that was fine, but it had candy in it. He demonstrated that he could get candy without breaking it, and Abbey laughed thinking he was a smart alek.

Once the kitchen was clean, and the last stragglers left the dining area, Abbey wandered out to start putting things away. Philip, Matt, and Jonathan told her to go to bed, that they had it all under control. They told her that Friday night they would be utterly dependent on her, none of them were particularly creative and they had no idea what a Casa Blanca night should be.

Abbey responded, "Hey, I'm in the same boat, we'll all have to rely on the amazing Frieda!" She followed with, "Good night, thanks guys."

Chapter 46

Friday, Abbey realized, it was their last full day at the ranch. They would be going home; she looked forward to some down time. This was an exhausting life. It has been super for the whole family, but it was going to be good to get back tot normal life. She tried to get herself excited about leaving. She made mental plans to write and thought because of Jeanette's gift, she'd really be able to get the kids completely ready for the new school year. She also needed to think through Bug's birthday coming up. She got herself out of bed and went to see if the kids wanted to collect some eggs.

After collecting the eggs, Abbey checked into the kitchen. Frieda, Lori, and Sharon were playing around and having fun. Frieda told Abbey to go enjoy her day with the kids and see some of Moses' new toys. She said that she would meet Abbey and Gerladine back in the dining hall at about two. Abbey agreed and grabbed her kids and ran to the barn. Moses had a whole bunch of toys and more admirers. He seemed happy, and then they saw Caleb, they asked about Moses' healing. Caleb felt like he was doing really well, just needed a little down time. Horses did stupid things and when they got hurt, it took them a bit longer to heal because they couldn't' just put their feet up. Caleb was very patient with Abbey, the kids, and others who were curious. TI was great to know that Moses would be okay. Abbey told the kids that they should be proud that they spotted the problem. She then asked the kids what they wanted to do, Geves and Bug had different ideas, Geves wanted to go get a paddle boat, and Bug wanted to find the Clemmons and go fishing. Abbey explained that Don and Debbie might have some plans since it was their last day, so they finally agreed to go for a swim and then get a canoe, everyone was somewhat pacified.

After swimming and canoeing they were exhausted and the kids were hungry, so Abbey ran over to the kitchen and saw some of the appetizers that the ladies had been working on. She asked if she could taste test. Lori was delighted, but explained that they had ordered a lot of it in, they would have to determine the most cost effective way to do the appetizers, some were just cheaper to buy prepared. The kids enjoyed eating the nachos and chicken wings for lunch. They thought it was cool. Abbey tried to explain that dinner would be similar. Everything was delicious. The kids full, Abbey found Jess and Philip and asked if anyone was up for fishing with Bug and paddle boating with Geves. She got two thumbs up and left to help create an evening to remember.

Frieda, Geraldine and Abbey got started pulling the room together. They were pleased with the colors, the globes and the small lamp shades. They put the posters up and Jonathan tried a couple fo different screens with the movie. The men had moved the Grand piano into the hall and Father John came in to rehearse while they were putting together the buffet. Becky came in with Matt carrying the skyline of Morroco. It was fantastic, she had a really great eye for color and contrast. There were small white Christmas lights taped to the back of the skyline and poking out of the various buildings and streetlights on the main street of the skyline. She waved off the oohs and ahs of Geraldine and Frieda. They added the bowler style hats to the buffet. There were model airplanes suspended over almost every window. The room was darkly lit, but romantic and very barlike. The foods were varied from buffalo wings, and potato skins, to orzo salad with artichokes and black olives. There were salads, and chocolates, chips, and peanuts, and tiny quiches. Father John was really getting jazzy with his playing, he was clearly enjoying all of it.

Becky carried in the final piece, the welcome sign, it read, 'Casa Blanca, stage left'. Abbey was a little worried that people wouldn't get it, it was such an old movie.

It turned out that abbey was wrong, most all of the parents got it, and the kids could've cared less. The food was a smash hit and Father John was delightful as Sam. He timed everything beautifully and must have watched the movie or found a website with all the music. At one point, David Dalt walked over and put a glass on top of the piano, he placed a five dollar bill in it and everyone cracked up.

Watching her mother, Abbey was so glad, Geraldine couldn't have been more thrilled. For her this was an amazing treat. She had never done anything like this in her life. To see so many people so delighted with it was the best. Geraldine was on cloud nine and Frieda had made a point of telling everyone that it had all been Ger's idea. They laughed and really enjoyed themselves. Abbey recognized that to leave the ranch was sad, but she had a really wonderful feeling of accomplishment. She had been part of finding things that worked and putting it all together. It was a great experience and one she shared with her mom.

Abbey and the crew cleared up the dining hall and clapped themselves on the back. Frieda and Geraldine were in rare form. It was a great nigh of laughter and fun, but it got late in a hurry and they were all dragging by the time they were finished.

Chapter 47

Abbey and Geraldine hadn't taken the time to really discuss when they would depart. Abbey got up as soon as she could and started to pack, she figured she'd have a nightmare with packing the kids. She also didn't know how she would say good-bye to Loulabelle. The little cat had been in and out of her room and seem to find her everytime she visited Moses or got eggs. She would miss the silly little cat. Abbey had to keep moving her out of the luggage as the cat seemed to know what was happening. She picked up the cat and hugged her. She knew the cat was way better off here, but she really had gotten quite attached. As soon as she opened her door, Lou ran out to see Shasta. It was a forgone conclusion, the cat stayed here.

Abbey noticed that Frieda and Gerladine were in the sitting area doing their study and she ventured in. Frieda beckoned Abbey to sit near her. They finished with prayer and Frieda looked at Abbey, "You are just in time, we have something for you to see," nodding for Geraldine it was time, Frieda got up and said, "Lead the way!"

Geraldine led the way down the stairs and towards the entrance hall, everyone was gathered there yelling, "Surprise!" There was a huge banner which read Bon Voyage Abbey, even the kids were there. Abbey was genuinely touched. Lori told Abey that she never got up this early for anyone! Everyone hugged Abbey and told her how much they would miss her. They had all signed cards and listed their addresses and emails to keep in touch. Sharon had gotten Abbey a large travel mug which read; *Kitchen princess*. Matt presented Abbey with a small porcelain horse resembling Moses with thank you written across the saddle, he also gave her a big hug. Abbey loved it. Even Debbie and Don were there. Father John, Mark, Jonathan, Philip, Jess, Leah, Janna Kay, Diane, Becky, everyone was there to tell Abbey that they loved and appreciated her.

Abbey was completely overwhelmed but delighted. Never before had she had so many people gathered to praise and thank her. She was truly touched. It was great for the kids too. Abbey was actually feeling so many things but she was genuinely happy. Leah and Jess left, without Abbey noticing and managed to get the kids and the car packed up. Jonathan and Philip had gotten Abbey's car in great condition for the drive. They put air in her tires, changed her oil, and filled the car with gas. The ladies had them all set up with a picnic, too.

By the time the group broke up, all the guests were packing to go, too, Abbey was left in the front hall with her mother, the kids and Frieda. Frieda hugged Abbey and said, "I am not going to cry. I am very grateful and I love you." She handed her an envelope and asked her to wait until she got home to open it. Frieda turned to Geraldine and hugged her. They looked at each other like old friends. Abbey realized that maybe they were in their hearts.

Frieda struggled, "You two, I will miss you but I know," she stopped to sniffle and hugged the kids to her, "you will all be back for our end of summer party and Thanksgiving. I'm going to see you before I know it." Abbey wasn't sure if she was saying it to make the kids feel better or herself. She was near tears, they all hugged and made their way to the car.

Abbey asked the kids once more about bathroom needs. The hamsters were already in the car and they left Sweet Silver Ranch. It was a quiet exit. Abbey sniffling, the kids crying and even Geraldine slumped. They didn't talk for quite some time. It took about three hours to get home, the whole of the trip was either making small talk or trying not to cry.

Arriving home, Abbey lit up the house, put the hamsters in their place and tried to get everyone settled. Gerladine told Abbey to go have a bath, she wanted her to read the note from Frieda.

Sinking into the warm water, Abbey opened Frieda's envelope, she was delighted to see a long note. There was the check, too. She read the wonderful note, full of accolades and genuine love. It made her feel very calm and safe. She began reading through some of the other notes, she was surprised; they were genuine. The friendships were real, the care and well wishes were true. In this superficial world, she felt like she had found something special and unusual.

She took note that every single note mentioned someone praying for her. She believed that maybe just maybe those prayers were working. She tossed up one of her own, for the first time in her life, she thought of God like a parent. "God, Father, if you are up there, and you orchestrated all of this for me, thanks. Thanks for looking out for me and my kids and thanks for everyone and everything at Sweet Silver Ranch." It wasn't eloquent, it might not mean much, but it was a start.

THE END